Praise for Vanessa Jaye's
Felicity Stripped Bare

"I really enjoyed this book and had a hard time putting it down. Ms. Jaye has not only written a book with several laugh out loud moments but also one that is warm and emotional too. ...I'm looking forward to more of these fun, warm and definitely hard to put down books by Ms. Jaye."

~ *Vanessay Jaye, The Good, The Bad, The Unread*

"FELICITY STRIPPED BARE is my first read of Vanessa Jaye's and certainly won't be my last. ...Felicity is one character who will tug at your heart for a long time after you finish. And if you are a fan of hot and smoldering sex, FELICITY STRIPPED BARE is that perfect book!"

~ *Kate Garrabrant, Romance Reviews Today*

"Felicity Stripped Bare is a very fun read! Felicity is something else and I just loved her, she is so genuine and real. ...Vanessa Jaye did a great job with Felicity Stripped Bare. This is the first story of hers I've read, but it will most definitely not be my last. Reader's looking for a fun, sweet love story that will have them laughing and smiling and rooting for a very deserving couple then Felicity Stripped Bare is a must read."

~ *Ley, Joyfully Reviewed*

Felicity
Stripped Bare

Vanessa Jaye

A SAMHAIN PUBLISHING, LTD. publication.

Samhain Publishing, Ltd.
577 Mulberry Street, Suite 1520
Macon, GA 31201
www.samhainpublishing.com

Felicity Stripped Bare
Copyright © 2009 by Vanessa Jaye
Print ISBN: 978-1-60504-282-4
Digital ISBN: 1-60504-062-2

Editing by Angela James
Cover by Anne Cain

First Samhain Publishing, Ltd. electronic publication: July 2008
First Samhain Publishing, Ltd. print publication: July 2009

Dedication

Thank you to a great bunch of crit partners for their patience, understanding and laughter, sharing their knowledge and just being there—Joyce Holms, Raine Weaver, Julie Cohen, Amie Stuart, Sasha White, Sela Carsen, Kat Glover, and Dee Tenorio. Thank you to Cat Brown, motivator extraordinaire. And to my very best friend, Janice Franklin for being excited and proud of my every accomplishment over the years. And lastly to my wonderful son Dayan, always, for his love and support.

Chapter One

"...*too bootylicious for you babe!*" Felicity belted out the chorus to the old song on the radio for all she was worth. Tonight she and Cheryl were going to hit the town, blow off some steam and celebrate.

So her steps were a bit wobbly as she danced around the room, did she really give a damn she was about to topple from her stillettoed perch? *Hah!*

In the span of one day she'd gained the chance at a new life and lost 175 lbs—kicked him to the curb. *Buh-bye,* Stuart.

As for the other thing, the thing she hadn't even shared with Cheryl... She stopped dancing and hugged herself, recalling the phone message she'd picked up earlier—

"Hello, this is Elise, I'm a tutor with the Metro Toronto Library Adult Literacy Program and I'm calling to let you know your application has been accepted."

The message went on to leave times, dates, contact info and other stuff she'd been too stunned to deal with. This was it. A first step towards a better life, more importantly a better her. Wisps of doubt curled in Felicity's chest, echoes of the old taunts, "*retard*" and "*stupid*", that she'd endured till she dropped out of school—

She inhaled, squeezing her eyes shut. Nothing was going to steal her joy at the moment, and no way was she coming down to earth closer than her four-inch heels. She got back to some serious booty-shaking.

When a series of knocks sounded at her door—Cheryl, *finally!*—she gyrated across the living room and flung the door open with one last shimmy thrown in for the hell of it.

"*I don't think you're ready, for this—*" Her hips stopped in mid-wiggle as two pairs of male eyes focused on her.

"Hey, hey, Felicity, you wanna dance!" Mr. Lombardi raised his arms above his head and moved the bottom half of his roly-poly body in an extremely distressing fashion.

Wincing, she looked away from the landlord's seizure-rhythmic boogie-down to the man who stood behind him. The stranger was dressed in jeans and a black turtleneck that made his shoulder-length hair look impossibly blond; as she watched, his mouth curved in appreciation while his cool green gaze swept her from head to toe, *slowly.* A shiver scrabbled down Felicity's spine and her lungs stalled on the next breath.

Alrighty then. She obviously hadn't thought this tight-jeans, high-heels thing through, hadn't covered all the contingencies. For instance, the way this guy's interest was making her feel like she had on way too much clothing for his liking. And not enough for her own. She took a tottery step back.

"M-Mr. Lombardi, what are you doing here?"

"Yeah, yeah, yesterday I say I gonna come by, for show Daniel around. Don't tell me you forget."

Okay, she wouldn't tell him. Her gaze drifted back to Daniel. *Phew.* Was it hot in here, or was it just him? What did Lombardi just say, something about repairs?

The buzzer sounded, partially snapping her out of her hormone-induced stupor. She gestured the men in, then pushed the intercom button. It was Cheryl.

With her brain still on reconnaissance in Blondland, it took Felicity two tries to hit the open button for the front door downstairs.

"I hope you no mind we come now?" Lombardi asked.

And what if she did mind? What if she didn't want this Daniel, with his hot bod and suggestive stare, leaving hot-bod footprints all over her flat?

"No problem at all." Really what was she gonna say?

Mesmerized by Daniel's rolling gait and compact butt, she watched the two men walk over to the small kitchen area of the main room.

"So, who's Tarzan?" Cheryl, newly arrived, whispered in her ear.

Felicity spun round. "Holy shi—"

Cheryl raised an eyebrow, a reminder of their recent bet that Felicity couldn't flush the potty-mouth routine.

For too many years growing up, swearing had been her first response to the name-calling, and it had worked too, on all but the most sadistic of her tormentors. Now she was determined to clean up her act.

"You scared the daylights out of me," she amended.

"'Daylights'? Girl, you better go back to swearing your damn fool head off."

"Nope, I can do this; 'daylights' works just fine."

Cheryl rolled her eyes just as Lombardi called out, "*Helloo,* Cheryl." He wiggled his fingers at her.

"Hi, Mr. L." Cheryl, one Sweet-'n-Low packet short of nauseating, wiggled her fingers back.

"Yes—ah, Daniel, you come, I show you." A crimson-faced Lombardi bustled towards the bedroom with the Yumminator following close behind.

And speaking of behinds... Felicity once again found herself paying close attention to the way Daniel's butt did that clench and relax thing.

"So who is that?" Cheryl repeated, disrupting Felicity's lust-a-thon.

"Who?"

"The luscious one with Lombardi the lecherous but loveable landlord. Say *that* five times fast."

"That, that, that, that, that."

Cheryl made a face and stuck her tongue out as Felicity herded her over to the second-hand couch that dominated the small living area. "He's some contractor Lombardi hired. They'll be done soon and then we can leave."

The men returned from the bedroom. Felicity caught Daniel's gaze, and all the air got sucked out of the room. At least it felt that way. Why else would she be panting?

"*Yowzah!*" Cheryl said in an undertone.

That was putting it mildly.

"Forget it. *Yowzah* is *howzah* I ended up with Stuart in the first place. Now that he's out of the picture—"

"Uh-huh," Cheryl interrupted and reached for a decorating magazine on the coffee table as the guys walked past, headed for the deck. She slowly licked a finger and absently flipped a page as she checked out Daniel's ass.

Felicity leaned forward, blocking Cheryl's view. "I'm serious this time. Stuart and I are over."

Cheryl pouted, but she straightened up. "You're serious every time. This week you and my boy *Stuuu*-pid break up, next week y'all are back together. Same ole, same ole."

"This time it's for real, I—" Felicity stopped. While Mr. Lombardi locked the deck door, Daniel stood a few feet away, staring at her from beneath half-lowered lids. Heat stole into her face, and other places.

"We're having a personal conversation here, in case it escaped your notice."

"Trust me," his voice was a sexy rumble, "*nothing*...escaped my notice."

"Now, Felicity, even I myself cannot help to hear some of

what you talk about." Mr. Lombardi gestured back and forth. "Daniel here no mean any disrespect. And your boyfriend he no deserve you, anyhow. Nice girl like you, go with nice boy. Get married, make lots of the bambini. Cheryl, you no agree?"

"Oh yeah, get married, make lots and lots of babies. Lots and lots and—hey!"

Felicity didn't think she'd pinched Cheryl all that hard. Then again thinking clearly was out of the question, what with the way Daniel continued to eyeball her.

A sweep of thorny warmth tightened the tips of her breasts and his hooded gaze drifted lower, zoning in on those hardened tips, obviously thinking of the specific "lots and lots" involved in baby-making.

She watched the quick, discreet slide of his tongue across his lips, as if he could taste the pool of hot 'n' bothered she was sitting in.

One thing for sure, Lombardi wasn't referring to Daniel.

He definitely was *not* a nice boy.

At least Stuart's brand of self-confidence masqueraded itself as boyish charm. This one was just too sure of himself. She didn't dwell on whether that confidence was earned or not.

"Okay, Felicity, we go now. Thank you for your time."

"No problem, Mr. Lombardi." She got up and followed them to the door.

Daniel paused as the men filed out, his broad-shouldered body filling the doorway and his citron aftershave teasing at her. Made her want to lick the *delicious* right off him.

If that were even possible.

"See you later, naked and spread-eagle—" Felicity blinked. What he really said was, "See you later."

"Much." She swung the door shut and leaned against it, heart beating like crazy, panties drenched, and nipples so stiff they could fly their own flags. She made a mental note *never* to be home when the repairs started.

Cheryl opened her mouth to say something, most likely outrageous and dirty. Felicity pointed a warning finger and said something that pretty much translated to temporarily losing their bet. Drinks were on her tonight.

Frig.

"I show to you the flat upstairs now." Mr. Lombardi looked over his shoulder.

Daniel nodded, but his thoughts were still on the tenant in 2b, with her large gray eyes and lush mouth.

He almost walked into the little Italian when that man stopped suddenly. "*Ahhh* that Cheryl." He flashed one hand back and forth. "Every time I see her, I feel like a-brand new. She is *bellissima.*"

Daniel smiled in agreement, following as Mr. Lombardi resumed his climb up the stairs. Felicity's friend, with her dark skin, long braids and even longer legs was definitely attractive.

But...his thoughts slid back to the very nice package of Felicity herself, from her silky brown curls done up in a sexy little do, to her painted toes peeking out of those ridiculously high, strappy heels.

Bellissima worked, but, he smiled, *bootylicious* was more apt.

Thoughts of Felicity continued to tease at the edges of his mind as he and the landlord entered the empty third floor flat. He walked around the space as Mr. Lombardi continued to point out various features and gloss over imperfections that Daniel had already pinpointed with an experienced eye.

He opened a closet door, automatically gauging the dimensions and figured that if Felicity grabbed on to the bar overhead and wrapped those lean legs around him while he pumped—

12

What the hell was he doing?

Daniel slammed the door shut, literally and on all his pervy fantasies. He had enough on his plate between winding down his role at the law office and juggling construction projects with Rob, without adding more complications.

He refocused on the point of this visit. The place had good bones, and already he could picture it after the extensive renovations needed to convert it back to a single family home.

He and Rob would make a nice profit on the flip. Daniel turned to the little man and smiled. "I think you have a sale."

ఴ

Something sharp ricocheted off Felicity's ass.

"Oh f—frak!" She jumped back from the spray of water and almost lost her footing. A minute later she identified her butt-missile as a tiny piece of plastic from the showerhead.

That was the last straw. She punched off the water, stomped out of the tub, and stalked into the bedroom.

Nude, dripping and pissed off, she grabbed the phone and punched in the number for her *new* landlord. Did it help that it took her a couple of tries to get the number right?

That she had to remember to calm down and focus on the frickin' buttons so she wouldn't get the freakin' 6 and frickin' 9 mixed up?

That sixty-nine was not a number she wanted to think about just as she was calling her super-hunky landlord?

The phone stopped mid-ring and a low male voice slid into her ear. "Hello."

"Daniel." She put just enough "pseudo" in her pseudo-chirpy tone to make the chirpiness suspect. "It's Felicity. Do you know when you'll be able to fix the shower? I just got hit in the ass."

"In the shower?"

"No, in the ass. I-I mean *yes*, in the shower."

There was a long uncomfortable pause until he cleared his throat. "Do you want to clarify that for me?" The timbre of his voice deepened, sweeping prickly heat over her drying skin.

Felicity became keenly aware of her nakedness. Her knees gave out and she plopped down on the bed, hugging a pillow to her stomach.

"The showerhead is broken; a piece of it just hit me in the— uhm, look I told you it was loose last week. You said you'd be by to fix it and take a look at the roof—which started leaking again when it rained on Monday, by the way."

"So, I did." A loud blast of air came through the phone.

The man actually had the nerve to sigh.

"Look, I'm on a job right now. I'll be over later."

"When later?"

"What time are you home?"

She checked the bedside clock-radio with its extra-large LCD numbers for easy readability. Shit, she was going to be late for work again.

"I won't get home till late. Can you come by tomorrow, between twelve and three? No wait!" She had a tutoring session then. "Make it after four."

"I'll see what I can do. Look, I'm tied up at the moment. I'll come by when I can."

"Gotta go" was her only warning before the dial tone whined in her ear. How did she ever think the man was good-looking?

In the short time it took her to dress and pack her gear, an impressive combination of curses were birthed. Any friggin' ideas she'd had that her friggin' habit wasn't firmly friggin' entrenched were dispelled. *Loathsome man.*

Frig.

Pain-in-the-ass woman. Daniel shook his head, snorting at the unintended pun. Then for several moments he contemplated the exact dimensions and shape of the delectable ass in question.

"So how's the little lady?" Rob cut into his thong-n-baby-oil daydream.

"Annoying." Daniel scowled as he clipped the cell back on his belt. "Are we going to stand here yakking all day?" He bent and got a good hold on the newly delivered cabinet beside him.

Rob smirked, but squatted and grabbed the other end of the unit without further comment. "Ready?"

Daniel nodded. They rose in unison and walked the unit across what would be the recreation area of the basement renovation. Working efficiently with the ease of long practice, they secured the unit to the wall.

When they were through, Rob slapped him on the back. "You can't say I'm just another pretty face." He batted his long lashes, the ones all the ladies went ga-ga over, at Daniel.

Rob was about six-three and topped 230 pounds easy; with his wildly curling black hair and a neatly trimmed goatee, the eye-fuck was the stupidest damn thing Daniel had witnessed in a long while.

"No I can't say that at all, partner." He looked around. "Hey, didn't we get those lights in?"

Rob pointed to a stack of boxes near the stairs, and the both of them headed over.

"So how is your favorite tenant?"

Rob used to pick his scabs as a kid. Now he metaphorically picked other people's.

"It's all your fault she's on my case."

"Whaddaya mean it's my fault?"

"You said you'd take a look at her shower by Wednesday.

15

And someone should've checked out the roof by now."

"I'll try and do it by the end of the week. Promise. Don't know why I haven't made it over yet. She's kinda easy on the eyes."

Daniel pushed aside the unease he felt at Rob's speculative expression and pried open a corrugated box to inspect the fixtures. "She's a looker all right. Too bad all you can look at are her tonsils 'cause her mouth is always flapping."

Rob chuckled. "Sure you don't want to go yourself? I thought I was picking up on something between the two of you."

"Try picking your nose next time. Any heated glances she's throwing my way would fall under the category of burn-in-hell. She acts as if I'm at her beck and call, like some kind of handyman."

"You *are* some kind of handyman."

"Hey, thanks for pointing that out."

"I could also point out that you wouldn't be dealing with tenant complaints if you got moving on the plans for the reno."

"Yeah, well, you can blame my old man for that. He's riding me hard on this last merger. Anything to delay me leaving. And every time I turn around lately, seems like something else is wrong with the Southview property." Daniel shook his head. Of course he'd seen it happen time and again on other renovation projects. He'd just been hoping to hell it wouldn't happen with this one. "I'll get on with the plans for Southview soon. But we might as well keep the tenants for now to cover the mortgage payments."

Rob shrugged and nodded, but Daniel could see his partner wasn't totally convinced. He couldn't blame him. If he were completely honest with himself, he'd admit that his foot dragging might have something to do with the kissable lips that made up the complaining mouth of one pain-in-the-ass tenant.

଼ଠ

Felicity arrived uptown at The Uptown. Late. Again. Moving quickly, she kept her head down, shoulders trussed with tension, eyes averted from the stage.

She braced for Tony's first sarcastic salvo as she scurried past the bar with an apologetic smile. He didn't smile back. Instead she felt his guillotine gaze, multiplied repeatedly in the mirrored walls, track her progress to the Employees Only area in the back.

The tiny change-room cum storage-room was in a state of chaos as usual. Girls in various states of undress; clothes, shoes and jackets strewn around the place. Makeup, curling irons, hairsprays and hairpieces scattered on every available surface. The air was blue with smoke and thick with a miasma of warring perfumes.

Cheryl, wrapped in a silk kimono robe and perched on the space-hogging meat freezer, looked up from checking her face in a hand mirror. "Fil baby, you're late."

Felicity dropped her knapsack, then unzipped her jeans, kicking her shoes off at the same time. "Thanks for the tip," she said, turning sideways as Tasha, a skinny dancer with a silicone addiction, squeezed past her.

"Tony's in a bad mood today," Tasha warned over her shoulder, then started pounding on the bathroom door. "Marie, ya been in there forever. I gotta go!"

"He's liable to rip into ya like toilet paper at a diarrhea convention," Cheryl added.

"So what else is new?" Felicity wiggled out of her jeans.

"That would be one-ply," Cheryl clarified.

They all burst out laughing and Felicity felt some of her tension ease. This feeling was still new to her, being part of the group if not exactly friends. Sharing the camaraderie, if not her deepest secret. Then again, she sensed that they all had their secrets.

17

Felicity pulled on a pair of black satin short-shorts, what passed for a uniform at The Uptown, then tried to work her foot back into a laced-up running shoe before giving up. "Shit."

Cheryl pounced. "What was that I just heard from your born-again mouth?"

"Did you hear anything?" Felicity asked the other girls.

A chorus of negatives responded. She smirked at Cheryl. Their bet was back on.

She braced her foot on the freezer and undid the knot. Retying was trickier.

"What are you doing there, Fil, making them gift-wrapped?" Cheryl teased.

Heat washed over her and her fingers fumbled with the laces. It was grade school all over again, the things other kids found easy-peasy never failed to cost her twice as much effort.

She was always the last to finish the math sheet. Her spelling tests were always half-done. And she absolutely refused to read out loud, preferring detention instead. Feeling stupider and stupider until they finally figured out what was wrong with her. Dyslexia.

"Forget this." She tucked the laces inside her shoes; she'd do them later without the audience.

"So why are you late this time?" Cheryl asked.

Felicity's lip curled. "Daniel."

"Oh?" Cheryl perked up. "What happened?"

She could only guess what gutters her friend's mind currently waded through, Lord knew she'd charted enough of them herself. She bent and tucked the laces in the other shoe.

"It's what didn't happen. He was supposed to have my shower fixed. Sez he's coming tomorrow. Gee, I've only been complaining about it for the last two friggin' weeks— Friggin' is not a swear word!" She rushed to make the save when Cheryl's face lit up again.

"Not much of one anyways." Marie finally exited the bathroom; Tasha scooted in.

Cheryl pointed to the room at large. "Y'all are conspiring against me."

Felicity stashed her knapsack in her locker. "I'm outta here. See you up front."

Before she reached the lounge area, she checked around, then carefully took her time to tie both laces into perfect bows. Feeling absurdly proud of her small accomplishment, she continued down the hall. Every little victory counted. She had never given in to the lure of Velcro, and she never would.

Felicity waved to Keith as she passed the DJ booth, then made a quick note of the stripper on stage. The more popular the girl, the more drinks were served. Which translated to more tips for the waitress. Even after a year, she was still tickled with the extra cash she was making. Not enough to save, but she was eating better and she'd been able to indulge in her one passion, decorating.

Where before she'd stuck with yard sales and Goodwill, lately she'd begun visiting a few secondhand shops. If you didn't mind digging through the dust and haggling a bit, there were some good finds to be had.

Speaking of finds, Felicity found some courage and approached the bar where Tony's massive presence presided like one of those creepy Easter Island statues—ready to topple her ass flat.

He picked at something caught between his teeth with a long pinky nail, while holding the ever-present cigarette between thumb and forefinger. His raisiny eyes peered out at her from the smoky nimbus that wreathed his head.

Felicity tried to slip past him to grab an apron from under the counter, but he seemed disinclined to move his bulk out of her way.

"Look, I'm sorry I'm late. My shower broke and..."

He stopped picking and flicked away his findings. Felicity didn't look where, afraid she'd see the thing scuttling off. The cigarette now clamped in the corner of his mouth, Tony began pulling a draft.

"Dis is for table tree." He jerked his head towards the main seating area. "Den go see what Al's doin' wid the wings for table ten. I already told him I want none of this *gore-may* shit. Just cook the bird till it stops clucking an dish it up."

"Sure, no problem."

He placed the mugs on the tray with the rest of the order.

"And tell Tasha to get her *ta-tas* up here. She's on next."

Felicity nodded and made a move for the aprons again. Tony braced his muscular arms on either side of the narrow aisle, blocking her. *Right.* She'd get one later.

"Oh, and Felicity." He sent two plumes of smoke streaming from each nostril. "Your shift starts at five." He pointed to the beer-can shaped clock behind him on the wall. "That's five my time. *Capisce?*"

"Understood." She grabbed the tray. When she was safely out of Tony's hearing, she said a few more things under her breath that he would *capisce.*

৪০

Felicity shifted in her seat. Her butt hurt from sitting on the hard plastic library chair and her feet still throbbed from last night's shift.

"Let's finish this chapter." Lise tapped the page Felicity had been struggling through. "You're doing so well with your consonant blends today."

"Whoo hoo."

"Felicity," Lise chided.

She hunched her shoulders and stared down at the page.

Attempts at sarcasm aside, a little glow came to life inside her at Lise's praise. She was making progress.

Sometimes it didn't feel that way. More like just one continuous struggle. Felicity renewed her focus, breaking down the syllables of the next words, sounding them out. The glow dimmed. Progress was not only slow, it was boring.

She rubbed damp palms against her jean-clad thighs and keeping her voice low, read on. Even though she and Lise had a fairly isolated table by the windows, Felicity was aware of the people in the stacks who were blithely choosing books that she could barely skim through.

Instead, she was stuck reading *The Grimm Brothers' Fairytales.* Felicity squirmed in her seat again, a coil of despair twisting her gut. She flipped ahead a couple of pages.

"Is there a story in here about a princess who ran away from home, looking for adventure, but ends up working for an evil chain-smoking ogre?"

"Then her Prince Charming arrives on his white steed?"

"With a satchel full of books on tape."

Lise laughed and sat back in her chair. "I guess that means we're done for today?

"Well to answer your question, no. Because the princess didn't run away to have adventures. I'd guess she ran away *from* a lot of unhappiness."

Felicity dropped her gaze.

"But there is a happy ending. The princess realizes her full potential so when Prince Charming does show up, she can read the pre-nup he tries to foist on her." Lise chuckled and added with a tiny grimace, "Sorry, just a little lawyerly humor."

"You're a lawyer, too?"

"Oh dear me, no! I used to teach, as I mentioned before. There're enough lawyers in our family." Lise's expression sobered a bit and she fiddled with a heavy gold knob at her ear.

"Although there'll be one less soon." A frown pleated her brow momentarily, but just as quickly she pasted on a bright smile. "Speaking of careers, how's work?"

"Fine." Felicity wasn't *exactly* ashamed of Tony's, but the less said about it the better. In fact she was a bit bemused over how Lise had managed to get so much personal information out of her already.

"It's a bar uptown, isn't it? You know, I wouldn't mind dropping by for a glass of wine one day."

Lise, with her discreetly expensive clothes and swingy salon hair at The Uptown? Even more laughable, Tony serving a wine that couldn't also be used as a stain remover? "Er, I don't think you'd feel comfortable there, Lise. Really."

"How bad could it be? Yonge Street is quite nice up there."

Agreed. The north Toronto neighborhoods were *very* nice. But every apple had its worm, and Tony had composted his little piece of real estate just fine.

"It's a real guy's place." Felicity kept a straight face.

Lise wrinkled her nose. "Oh, you mean sports. Well, we'll meet for coffee, then. We could even go now."

She bit back a groan. In the months since they'd started the sessions, Lise had made several attempts to take their relationship beyond student/tutor. The friendship thing didn't come easy to Felicity. Not even with Cheryl had she completely let her guard down.

Then again, maybe that was the best argument for having a cup of coffee with Lise—she knew Felicity's little secret.

Yet, Felicity couldn't quite shake off years of conditioning. Lise was poised, educated and well-off. Tick the "not" box for each of those items on Felicity's list of accomplishments.

"Maybe next time?" she offered, thankful she had a real excuse for begging off. "My landlord is finally coming around to do some repairs."

Lise masked her disappointment at being brushed off

again. "Then we're definitely on for next week. Promise?"

She accepted her fate in the face of Lise's steamroller determination. "Promise."

"Besides I wouldn't want to keep you from being home when your pathetic excuse of a landlord shows up. From what you've told me about him, he wouldn't come by again for another month."

Felicity pursed her mouth. And clenched her thighs. Daniel had that effect on her.

Lise patted her hand. "Poor dear."

Chapter Two

Ping!...Plop!...Ping!...Ping! Ping!...Thop!

Felicity stopped stirring her mac n' cheese to study the pots, pans and bowls scattered around the kitchen—searching for the culprit. *Thop!* There it was again.

She moved towards the window overlooking the deck, eyes shifting between the plastic mixing-bowl and the saucepan placed on the floor.

Thop! There, dead ahead, a tiny spray of water misted the air just behind the bowl. She nudged the bowl over with her foot to catch the rogue drip, and thought of another place she'd like to plant her foot: squarely on the firm butt of Dan the not-so-handy man.

It'd been two whole weeks since he'd promised to come by. It was too dangerous to go out on the roof with all the rain they'd been having, he claimed.

Well, she had news for Mr. Moseying Mackenzie, landlording was a dangerous occupation—shocks from fixing faulty wiring, or irate, waterlogged tenants pushing you off leaky roofs. All in a day's work as far as she was concerned.

The vague thumping overhead indicated Daniel the Delayer was out there now, risking life and limb to investigate the leak. The man was a jerk. Yummy chocolate-coated good-looking on the outside, chewy-moron center.

An ominous popping sizzle had her hotfooting it back to the

stove, but not before she caught sight of movement outside the window. The screen door opened a second later and Daniel stepped inside the flat.

"There're a few loose shingles and some damage to the substructure. We'll have to redo that section of the roof." He stepped over a pot, while he scrutinized the ugly brown stains on the ceiling.

As he studied the damage above their heads, she continued to study him. Call it Hunkology.

A faded pair of paint-splashed jeans, ripped at one knee, emphasized the lean muscular length of his legs, while his sweatshirt did little to hide the powerful breadth of his shoulders and chest.

Then there was the hair—he wore it in a topknot, secured by an elastic band with various pencils sticking out of it. He should've looked ridiculous, but the scraped back hair only emphasized the masculinity of his face.

A finger of disturbance pressed into her chest. His looks were too stark to be handsome, but his mouth was beautiful, kissable, *sure*. That beautiful mouth was moving now.

"The damage's pretty bad, but I think you've seen the worst of it." Daniel's gaze suddenly met hers. And held. His expression changed.

Awareness raced over her skin. *Uh-uh. No way, buddy.* Rather than respond to the smoldering speculation in his eyes, she said, "Really? Because I still have a container or two not on leak duty."

"Maybe you're better off collecting water in them, if that's an example of your cooking." He nodded towards the pot she'd stopped stirring minutes ago.

"Oh, shhhhip-diddy." She snatched the saucepan from the stove and placed it on the tiled counter. *Did I just say ship-diddy?* "I like my Kraft dinner well-done."

"*Riiight*," he said, wide-eyed and sounding like he was

25

talking to some lunatic.

Daniel looked around, then reached for the mop propped in the narrow space between the counter and the window wall. She was about to tell him not to bother cleaning up when he raised the mop and tapped the ceiling.

"Heads up!"

She jumped back as Daniel's warning was followed by a loud whoosh and a curse—that wasn't ship-diddy.

Hand pressed to pounding heart, Felicity took in the counter now covered in bits of plaster and dirty water, then looked up at the new hole in the ceiling, dripping water in a more efficient stream than the previous multiple leaks.

"Thanks a lot!" She waved her hand at the now ruined—okay more ruined—meal. "You could've let me get my dinner out of the way first."

Thoroughly irritated, she tried to snatch the mop from Daniel's grasp. He pulled back. She tugged at the handle again, but to no avail. With a final jerk he wrenched it out of her hand. By his expression she thought it prudent to take a backward step. But not to shut up.

"You never get anything done around here."

"And how the hell am I supposed to do that, when you're always complaining about something new?"

"Face it. You're a lousy landlord."

"And you're the tenant from hell."

"W-what? Me? Well you—" she blanked for a second, "—you suck!" She pointed a nail-bitten finger at him. "I bet you're just trying to drive me out of this apartment."

An odd expression crossed his face.

"Oh, yeah. I'm onto you, Mr. Sucky. You want me out so you can jack up the rent."

Daniel's brows raised a notch, then he threw back his head and laughed, baring strong white teeth. "Mr. Sucky?" He laughed some more, but as his chuckles grew softer, his eyes narrowed.

Felicity, sensing the danger, stepped back.

Daniel, sensing a kill, stepped forward. "I am *not* trying to drive you out of this apartment."

He kept coming; she retreated till she hit up against the fridge. With Daniel towering over her, Felicity had to tilt her head back to glare up at him, which really wasn't satisfying. Glaring down was much more effective—like what he was doing right now.

He leaned forward and placed his hands either side of her head on the fridge. His face was inches from hers, his eyes pinning her to the spot. "You, on the other hand are driving me nuts. And it's proving to be A. Very. Short. Ride." Each word was squeezed through clenched teeth. Then Daniel's gaze slid down to her mouth and lingered.

"Absolutely nuts," he repeated huskily as he bent a little closer. His lips parted as they hovered just above the tip of her nose, the curve of her cheek, then whisper-close to her temple, skimming the surface of her skin in a rustle of warm air through fine downy hairs. Then his mouth was a heartbeat, a finite moment in space and time, away from hers.

"Don't."

"Are you sure?" Each word was a little caress.

She stared at the promise of those lips a moment longer, then with a groan ducked under his arm and moved rapidly away on shaky legs, putting the width of the counter between them.

Daniel sighed and shrugged, shoving his hands deep into his pockets. "I'll have a couple of the guys over tomorrow to start repairs on the roof."

Felicity nodded, squashing the flare of disappointment she felt that he wouldn't be returning himself to do the work. They stood there awkwardly for another minute.

"Let me buy you dinner." He was leaning against the fridge now, but somehow his casual stance didn't ring true. His gaze was too watchful. "I didn't set out to ruin your meal, but I haven't had dinner either since I rushed right over here—"

"Rushed? I called you weeks ago." The mute shock his invitation had caused vanished.

"And weeks ago I couldn't get here. I'm here now. The ceiling and the roof will be fixed."

"What about the shower? Are you going to deal with that?"

"Someone will look at it tomorrow." He grabbed the dishrag hanging over the faucet and lobbed it at her. "Let's clean up this mess then grab something to eat." With that he turned away and reached for the mop again.

Felicity bristled at his command, but she came back to the kitchen. Starting on the counter, she surreptitiously watched Daniel's hypnotic mopping technique—swing to the right, right butt-cheek clench, swing to the left, left butt-cheek clench.

The cheesy culinary disaster got dumped into the garbage as she counted all the reasons for not going out with him. She snuck another look at his *clench-clench* prowess. Suddenly there didn't seem nearly enough reasons not to go.

A part of him wished she'd turned him down flat.

His head told him that anything beyond dinner would be more trouble than the temptation was worth. He should evict any other thoughts. *Evict* being the operative word.

His *other head* said, "Back that thang up."

Daniel looked around the restaurant she'd suggested, taking in the rustic wood floors, the vibrant murals on the walls and the few dancers making energetic use of a small cleared section in front of the bar. At first, the place gave an impression of friendly neighborhood warmth.

But twenty minutes later, seated at a tiny candlelit corner table and cocooned by the sultry Latin beats playing, that initial feeling had morphed into hazy intimacy.

He refocused on Felicity—or at least what he could see of her bent head from behind her menu. When she made no move to come up for air, he reached across the table and slowly tilted back the menu she'd been hiding behind for the past five minutes.

He couldn't help smiling at her obvious reluctance to put the thing down. The lady was nervous, and with good reason. Nothing on the menu looked as good to him as she did.

"You eat here often?"

When she bit down on her bottom lip, he shifted in his seat. She had the most kissable mouth.

"I came here once with my ex," she said, some indefinable emotion lightly dusting her words.

"*Ahh.*" He slid his beer bottle back and forth on the table a couple of times between his hands. "Bad memories?"

She shrugged. "Not all of them."

Not the answer he was looking for, but he checked the impulse to investigate his vague sense of dissatisfaction.

"We came here when we were trying to work things out." Her luscious mouth pruned up.

"And did you?" If she was still pissed off at her ex, it meant she still had some pretty strong feelings about the guy.

"Stuart and I are best off as just friends."

Daniel snorted and her eyes became slits.

"What?"

"Men and women can't be just friends."

"Where'd they find you? In a cave somewhere surrounded by the scattered bones from your last meal?"

He chuckled, retreating in his seat. Man, she was touchy. But all that passion would be so interesting in so many other ways.

"If your ex agreed to that, he's only biding his time till he gets you back." As soon as that little truth fell from his lips, his mood soured again.

"Maybe. But it's a wasted effort if he is." Her expression grew somber as she traced a finger round the lip of her glass.

Daniel wanted to grab her hand. Pull her attention back to him and away from memories of the other guy. He was searching for the words to recapture her attention when she asked, "So you really don't think men and women can be just friends?"

"Nope. The sex thing is always there. The curiosity, the need, never goes away." He pushed aside his beer and leaned forward, pitching his voice lower as her cheeks colored in the candlelight. "Once they both admit it, give in to it, everyone's happy."

Daniel straightened. "Unfortunately, usually the woman wants more. Then everyone's unhappy."

"You know not every woman wants to get a man. Some of us have dreams and goals of our own."

"And more power to you and your friend. But my personal experience has been that when a woman wants more, it usually involves carats."

"Gee, it must be a real pain in the neck—"

"It is."

"—carrying around a head that size."

He laughed again. He'd been doing a lot of it this evening. He liked her sharp tongue, when it wasn't complaining about repairs, that is.

He'd like her tongue soft too. Soft and flickering against his. He took big swallow of beer.

"I'm just saying, I don't want a serious relationship, don't want the responsibility. I've got enough demands in my life.

Don't crucify me for being honest."

She stared at him for several seconds, her color even higher than before. "Well, I'm so glad you got that all off your chest."

His gaze fell a few vital inches to where her bright pink top molded *her* chest like a candy coating.

Daniel felt an ache; it wasn't in his sweet tooth.

"They don't do tricks, so you can stop staring." Her menu—and her hackles—went back up.

"Sorry." And he meant it. He was very sorry she was blocking his view with that menu, but he smiled truce, not wanting to argue with her tonight. Which brought up the question: what he did want to do?

All evening he'd wavered between the need to push this thing between them and knowledge he mustn't.

Reminding himself that he'd be a monumental asshole to pursue a fling with Felicity, considering his plans for Southview, cooled his ardor. Somewhat. He signaled the waiter over.

"You guys ready to order?" the server prompted.

Daniel looked across the table, deferring to Felicity, who was frowning at the menu.

One slender finger traced down the laminated page then curled into her palm. "Why don't you order for both of us?"

"If you're not ready—" he squinted at the waiter's nametag, "—Alejandro here can come back."

"No, that's fine; you order."

"Are you sure? You've been studying the menu—"

"I'm sure. Just order."

This date was going south fast. And maybe that was a good thing, what with the ex-boyfriend and all. It was on the tip of Daniel's tongue to tell the waiter to get lost, then give Felicity the option of leaving. Which she obviously wanted to do. But his stomach interjected with a vociferous rumble. Screw it. He was hungry. At least one of his appetites would be satisfied tonight.

As Daniel and the waiter discussed the preparation of a dish, Felicity eased back in her seat. Her relief was so solid she could have reached over and scratched behind its ear. Instead she pressed a hand to her belly, not sure she could stomach any of the food coming.

Daniel made her nervous. And her nervousness made the words on the menu look more jumbled than ever. She'd stared at the menu till her eyes practically crossed. Running her fingers down the list, pretending to consider her choices, when as far as she was concerned, the whole thing could have been written in Sanskrit. Why hadn't she picked some place that served burgers?

She watched Daniel across the table. Something drew her to him. Okay, it wasn't just something—it was lust, pure and simple. When he was near, she wanted him closer. In every way. And he seemed to feel the same, if the episode by the fridge was anything to go by.

They reacted to each other like two characters out of some novel. He threw a series of searing glances her way and she supplied the heaving bosoms. In short, Daniel tempted Felicity to throw caution—and her panties—to the wind.

She sunk a little lower in her chair. Had she been so obvious? All that talk about not wanting a relationship? Translation: *Gee, Felicity, you look like you would not only jump my bones, but suck out the marrow and use it as lubricant.* Is that what he meant?

Right on cue, he chose that exact moment to glance at her. Felicity grabbed her wine glass and gulped half of it down, almost choking in the process.

"You all right?"

She sputtered the affirmative.

"Is there anything else you want?" He tapped the menu.

You.

Yearning spiked between her shoulder blades. Saliva pooled in her mouth. Oh my God: *drool*.

She swallowed. "No, thank you."

When Alejandro left, Felicity watched him walk away like the last plane out of Baghdad. Now what?

She strummed her fingers on the tabletop and smiled at Daniel. He smiled back, the way a lion smiles at an antelope.

Her pool of drool headed south, morphing into wet heat between her thighs. Oh, mama, where was the rest of the herd?

Daniel was a double-barrel threat, both as the landlord who held control of the roof over her head, leaky though that roof may be, and as a man. So what was she doing here?

Tenants shouldn't get involved with lions, and antelope shouldn't have dinner with landlords. She shook her head. It was hard to make sense with Daniel so close.

"Everything all right?"

"No." It slipped out. "I mean, yes." She meant no.

Daniel inhaled deeply. "Forget this," he muttered and pushed his chair away from the table. "I'll see if we can cancel the order or get it to go."

Felicity immediately felt contrite. He was only trying to be nice and here she was being an ungrateful horny toad.

"No. Wait." She grasped his hand, stopping him.

His fingers curled around her own and Felicity's breath did a pop-fly catch in her throat. Her mouth parted but no words came out as her brain weaved through a minefield of thoughts and impulses.

"I want to stay. Really." Two short sentences and she was barely panting—a real accomplishment in light of the way her heart was pounding.

The bass of the music marked the passing time, but Daniel made no move back to his seat. Instead he just stood there staring down at her in a way that was becoming far too familiar.

"Dance with me."

"What?" She almost choked on the word.

He jerked his head towards the dance floor, his gaze challenging.

Her pulse started to mambo. Gyrating, sweaty, hands on bodies—that kind of dancing?

"Sure." She stood and moved past him, her body barely brushing against his. *I can handle this.* They could do gyrating, sweaty, hands-free dancing, right?

That comforting thought was given the heave-ho when Daniel reached for her. *I can't do this!* She panicked as his hand slid around her waist. Her body, however, had ideas of its own—*traitor!*—as it slipped into the rhythm of music and fell in sync with his. She went dizzy with want, weak-kneed with desire.

Daniel rocked back, his hand bearing light pressure on her as she willingly followed, her body wedged tightly against his as they turned several times. One last turn thrust his groin against hers and Felicity's existence came jerkily back into focus. He was hard. She pressed forward and heat flared in his eyes. Daniel came to a standstill.

"We should go back," she said huskily, pushing against his solid chest.

A pulse beat rapidly at the base of his neck, and his breathing came hard and fast. Not for a second did she think any of it was from the dancing. Not with the way he was looking at her.

Chapter Three

How she made it back to their table Felicity wasn't sure; her mind was focused on how she'd get through the rest of the evening. Without jumping his bones and sucking out the marrow.

Finally, their meal was done, and they were out on the sidewalk facing each other.

"So..." she said.

"So..." He shoved his hands into his pockets.

"That was nice." *Oh yeah, bowl him over with your wit why don't you?*

"It was...interesting." He turned in the direction of Southview Drive, a few blocks away. "C'mon, let's get you home."

Interesting? As in "you're not my type after all" interesting? "What do you mean interesting?"

He glanced at her sideways. "Didn't you enjoy yourself?"

"Yes, but I wouldn't have used 'interesting'."

"No, the word you used was 'nice'. You could always just admit I turn you on."

Right.

"And you could always admit you have a big ego," she said sweetly.

As they turned down the street, Daniel's hand settled

lightly on the small of her back, making her hyper-aware of him. They chit-chatted for the rest of the walk to the house and her nervousness grew. Then all too soon they arrived at her front door.

Daniel stared down at her. "Do you still want to hear what I thought of tonight?"

"Yes—"

His mouth locked onto hers.

Felicity grasped his jacket as his fingers twined into her hair and he backed up to the wooden rail where he settled and pulled her between his thighs. The night air touched her with cool sighs, but Daniel's mouth was pure hungry heat.

Then his kiss turned to soft enticement, reeling her in as he nibbled and licked at her in tiny teasing flicks that beckoned her lips to part and her tongue to seek his. Felicity gave in and leaned into him, wrapping her arms around his broad shoulders as little mewling sounds escaped her.

"I know, baby, I know." He soothed and captured her bottom lip gently between his teeth. Then suddenly the hands that swept caresses along her back were crushing her to him as he stroked his tongue deeper, forcing her to open wider for him.

White-hot yearning rolled through Felicity and she shifted eagerly against his arousal then swallowed the agonized groans that he emptied into her throat.

His hands were everywhere—kneading her ass and pressing her hard against the ridge of his erection, then up to cradle her head, fingers spread as he held her immobile for the scorching path of kisses he traced over her jaw and neck.

She was lightheaded, her mind in a fog of sensations from his kisses, his scent, the deep rumble of his pleasure, the hard length of his cock. Things were happening too fast. With a soft moan, she hunched her shoulders and pulled away.

"Felicity?" he rasped.

She pressed her head against his heaving chest and rubbed

her head slowly from side to side. *No.*

After a few moments she felt some of the tension drain from him, and he played his fingertips lightly along her spine. Afraid to move, not sure if she'd made the right decision, Felicity picked at a loose thread on his shirt.

They stayed that way for a while, neither saying a word, until Daniel eased her away. Because she didn't know what else to do, she fumbled for the key in her pocket, turned, and then lurched across the short distance to the door. She managed to push the key in the lock, and a second later felt the heat of him behind her.

"Maybe you should go now," she said.

There was an awkward silence.

"Okay. I'll have someone in here to work on the roof tomorrow. Call me if you need...anything."

Without answering, she eased the door shut in his face.

ℬ

"C'mon, ya pantywaist. Look at this." Rob turned, jogging in reverse to face Daniel. "Backwards, with one hand behind my back."

When Rob inevitably stumbled, Daniel ran around him, burning rubber.

"Hey, no fair."

He kept the brutal pace until Rob caught up to him, panting, "Mercy, mercy, I take it back. I take it back. We still have another three miles to run."

Lungs burning, Daniel slowed his pace. "Sissy."

Rob gave him the finger and they ran for the next minutes with only the caws of seagulls over the lake and the sounds of their own exertions breaking the silence.

"So are you speaking at all this morning?"

"What's there to say?" Daniel countered. "It's a beautiful day." He waved towards Lake Ontario, where the sun gilded the waters in pale gold and tangerine. "I'm just enjoying it."

"You coulda fooled me with that scowl you've been wearing for the past hour."

Daniel wiped away the sweat that gathered at his neck under his ponytail. Yeah, he was in a bad mood this morning. It was a sequel to his foul mood from last night. All because of one particular female who'd gotten under his skin.

He told himself he should be thanking his lucky stars for the close escape last night. He'd almost let his libido override his rational thought. *It was only supposed to be a kiss.* But at the first taste of Felicity beneath his lips and the feel of her response to his touch, "supposed to be" became a thing of the past. He moved aside onto the grass, allowing a couple of in-line skaters to speed by, then fell back in step on the paved walkway.

"You were over at Felicity's place yesterday, weren't you?"

"So?"

"I'm just surprised you found the time, considering your busy schedule."

"Just say it."

"You shouldn't be shitting in your own backyard, pal. You're the one who taught me that." Rob took a couple of deep breaths. "Keeps things on the non-messy side, right? No emotional demands. No nesting."

Daniel suppressed a shudder. *Nesting.* He rarely let anyone stay over two nights in a row. Much less leave any orphaned belongings to be fostered in his condo. In his experience, you gave a woman an inch and she'd hang two suitcases and a toothbrush on it.

"Nothing's messy. I just took her out for dinner to make up for delays. We had an interesting time." Again, Daniel felt a twinge of conscience.

"I just bet you did. 'Interesting time' my ass." Rob shoved him. "Save the crap, please."

Daniel grinned, but he wasn't copping to anything. "As much as I'd like to, I can't sleep with every beautiful woman I meet. Besides, there has to be more..." He frowned. When had he started to want more?

"That's foolish talk, my man."

"You're hopeless."

"But I can be reformed with the love of a good woman."

"Yeah, right. Your track record is worse than mine."

"Those weren't good women. They were bad. Every last one of them. Good luvin'. *Bad* women." Rob waggled his eyebrows.

Daniel chuckled as he made a detour around some early morning canine offering. Rob wasn't so lucky and he let those in the vicinity know it with a string of curses.

Or maybe he was just describing what he'd stepped in.

While Daniel waited for the big guy to clear the evidence from his shoe, his cell rang.

"Have you looked into getting that thing welded to your ear?"

"Operation's scheduled for next week." Daniel checked the caller ID and swore under his breath, but he was contractually obligated to finalizing the Maple deal for the law firm, so he took the call.

"Daniel here."

"Where the hell are you?"

"Hi, Dad, I'm fine, how are you?"

"Never mind being a smart-ass. Fred Klein just called; he wants to meet over dinner. Some place called Lizzie's Sizzlin' Steak n' Shrimp."

Daniel clenched the phone tighter. It was just his luck to get the last living eccentric billionaire in the western hemisphere as a client. "Why does Fred have to conduct business over a plate of chili-fries at some greasy spoon?"

He could practically hear the old man grinding his teeth. "I don't give a damn if Fred wants to eat stewed brains with some near-extinct tribe. You'll accommodate him. Ask your assistant for the directions." Michael Mackenzie hung up.

Daniel flipped the phone shut with a string of curses. "Let's roll." He set off at a hard pace, and thankfully Rob let him blow off the steam without complaint.

The last quarter hour of their run passed in silence. When they got to Yonge Street, Rob headed north towards his loft in an old converted building several streets away, or more than likely to the nearest subway station, Daniel would bet.

Not that he should be pointing fingers, he conceded as he slowed to a walk the last few blocks to his lakefront condo. His lungs were on fire, his ribs hurt and his legs felt like rubber. Yet even after that hard run, he could feel the tension still coursing through his system.

Daniel pushed open the heavy glass doors to his building, nodding to the concierge as he crossed the marble foyer to the elevators. He jabbed at the button with pent-up frustration. The last thing he wanted to do was deal with Fred Klein or Michael Mackenzie. If it were up to him, he'd work from the condo today. He wasn't in the mood for anybody's company.

Even as he thought it, Daniel realized the lie. There was one person's company he wanted. One person he wanted period, flat on her back and naked beneath him. But remembering Felicity's searching look and the way she'd closed herself off after their kiss, he knew that sex wouldn't be enough for her.

Still...in the minutes that had followed, holding her close, feeling their heartbeats slow to one synchronized beat, there had been a quiet fulfillment in that. It was unexpected, and that was warning enough to stay the hell away, but the memory of her little sighs and the way her body fit against his, teased at Daniel and he knew he wouldn't.

Which was how he ended up driving to Home Depot with her two days later. When he'd shown up at her door, her body language had been a billboard of rejection. He'd reexamined the showerhead and looked for signs of water damage in the immediate area then checked the pipes in the other units.

She'd kept her distance and her silence, curled up on that ratty sofa in the main room of the flat, her head buried in a book.

Finally he'd walked up to her, ignoring the hostility that rolled off her as she slapped the book shut and hugged it to her chest.

"Was it so bad?" he'd asked. "When we kissed? Was it so damn bad?"

He watched her blush deepen and his need grew, to hear her say the kiss had affected her also. That the memory, the hunger for more, also kept her up late at night.

She'd stared back at him with those large gray eyes, her thoughts well hidden beneath their silvery depths. He wanted to know those secrets she kept hidden away.

"It was just a kiss."

He shook his head. "It was more than that. Could be more. Sometimes life gives us opportunities, Felicity. Why not take them?" Now if that wasn't the lamest speech he'd ever uttered. A couple nights of tossing and turning, and stroking himself to release, this is what he came up with?

Yet what else he could have said? Certainly not anything that might even hint at the feelings congealed in his throat. Not that there was emotion involved here except attraction.

He watched as she gave his words some thought, then a slow, tentative smile came across her face, and she hugged the book closer. That smile curled up in his chest. Nested there. Daniel had a sudden urge to sprint for the door.

During the drive Felicity was silent, content to stare out the window at the old buildings that lined St. Clair Ave. West. She loved the vibrancy of the neighborhood with its mix of trendy bars, boutiques and old-fashioned fruit stands and butcher shops. It was home. She'd put down roots here. Finally.

Besides, window-shopping gave her something to do, since Daniel didn't seem inclined to make conversation over the music spilling from the radio. Instead he nodded his head and tapped the steering wheel to the selection of songs, while singing snatches off-key. And under his breath, thankfully.

She was supposedly tagging along to pick out a showerhead of preference. But it felt like a date. Felicity started nibbling on her hangnail collection. *"Why not?"* he'd asked. And her belly had slithered down to her ankles and wrapped itself around them, while her next heartbeat played hide and seek.

He was the candy in the jar that had been moved down to eye-level and he was telling her to reach right in and grab a handful...of his licorice.

Felicity had never grabbed for anything in her life. It had always been a struggle just to keep up. Yet things had changed in the last year—she'd finally found the strength to leave Stuart and then the tutoring had come through. *So...*

She glanced sideways at Daniel's profile, softened by the sensuality of his mouth and thick sweep of lashes and thought, *why not,* indeed?

Then she started thinking about his gumballs.

When they arrived at Home Depot, Daniel parked the truck before hopping out and quickly making his way to her side of the cab to see her out. Felicity took his hand and was rewarded with a current of awareness that shot up her spine and smacked her in the back of her head.

After that, she kept some distance between them as they walked towards the store. So much for gumballs. *Jawbreakers* was more like it.

Once inside the store, she looked around the cavernous warehouse with avid curiosity. She was probably the only person on the face of the planet who hadn't set foot in a Home Depot, but there was never any need to before.

She followed Daniel down the aisle, past displays of every gadget, tool and material needed to build, fix, decorate or destroy, and a jumble of ideas raced through her mind.

Excitement slowed her step as she took it all in, then she took a deep breath of the lumber-scented air...and fell in love. Now *this*, this was a candy store.

Felicity hurried to catch up as Daniel disappeared around a corner. Luckily his tall, broad-shouldered physique made him stand out amongst the Saturday-morning crowd milling around.

As she came up beside him, she tugged on his sleeve. "Can we see what they're doing over there?"

Daniel glanced over at the demonstration taking place. "Sure." Indulgence curved his mouth and she felt an answering warmth flutter in her stomach.

Felicity turned away from that look, that smile, but she couldn't get away from his hand that landed lightly on her back, guiding her forward. Heat radiated from his touch, spreading outward along her limbs.

It was almost impossible to concentrate on the expert's instructions with Daniel standing behind her. She moved slightly to the right, his hand moved to her hip. She stepped forward, his hand came to rest on her shoulder.

She kept fidgeting until Daniel leaned forward and spoke low in her ear, "If you're really interested in this, we're doing some tile work at one of the job sites. I could pick you up one day and bring you by."

Felicity swung her head around. This close to him, she noticed the gold-dusted tips of his darker lashes. "Really?"

"Really."

She watched his lips, inches from her own, shape the word and felt his breath like a kiss.

Abruptly, Felicity faced front again and took a deep calming breath. But images of a bare-chested, tool-belted Daniel kept dancing through her head.

Will you get real! Felicity could almost hear Cheryl's no-nonsense voice. She blinked, and the vision of some fat guy with plumber's bum—oily pimples, hairs and all—lumbered into her imagination. Her pulse slowed some.

"That would be great, if it's not too much trouble."

"Do I look like a guy who's looking for trouble?" he asked dryly. To her relief he straightened and moved back to guide her through the crush of bodies. "Let's go find that showerhead."

They came to the selection of bathroom accessories and Daniel picked a box from the shelf.

"Master Stroke 2000, flexible spray nozzle, three-way adjustable head." He paused, looking up with a decidedly wicked glint in his eyes. "How about it, you interested in a three-way?"

"No thank you." Blushing, she pointed to another model. "This one looks fine."

He moved closer and the faint scent of citrus that emanated from him became stronger. "*Hmmm...*adjustable spray prohibits calcium buildup." He shook his head. "Naw," then his interest shifted to a different package. "Maybe...The Invigorator?"

Bending forward he noted the various features. "'You never dreamed water could do this before. *Enjoy the total satisfaction* of phenomenal power at work.'" He glanced at her and her nipples power-constricted into two tingling vortexes of phenomenal pleasure. Felicity mouth-breathed as Daniel continued.

"'Your body will be revitalized by the *warm, sensual, pulsating* spray—'"

"I don't need my body revitalized, thank you. Just clean. Here, I'll take this one." She grabbed another model. It didn't matter which one. Daniel didn't even touch the box.

"'Eco-friendly, low-flow ceramic valving'," he read the specs off in a monotone. "*Borrring.*"

"Look, I like boring, and energy efficient and-and..."

"Liar." His voice dipped. "You don't like boring. Not with that mouth," he said baldly, barbecuing her on the spot with the heat in his gaze.

Before she could catch her breath he switched gears on her again, his mouth curling in mischief. "So you wouldn't—" he looked down at the package he held, "'—*enjoy a deep, throbbing, fully satisfying massage to all the key areas of your body*'?"

"Throbbing?" she sputtered, very aware of the parts of her that fit that description right now.

He raised his eyebrows innocently.

"The head is extra large."

"Okay, fine! I'll take it!" Felicity shoved the package into his arms. He was obviously determined to continue along this vein.

As they went around to pick up a few other items, she found herself smiling. She liked his teasing, almost as much as she liked him intense and bent on seduction.

Although "like" seemed a wishy-washy way to describe what she felt when he focused his molten green gaze on her. Her smile disappeared.

Suddenly she was crazy with awareness of his large presence beside her, brushing against her with every other step and the peek-a-boo whiffs of his cologne that tantalized her. She had to get away.

As they neared the cash registers the rich aroma of coffee wafting through the air offered her perfect excuse.

"I'll be back in a second." She didn't wait for his answer before beating a hasty retreat for the snack bar.

While Daniel paid for the purchases, she bought two coffees, then met up with him at the exit. She offered him one of the cups. "Black?"

"Thanks. How did you know?"

"I didn't." She pulled some sugar packets and creamers from her pocket with an impish grin.

Deep down inside, though, she had a glow of satisfaction. How could she explain the odd times she'd found herself thinking he would like a certain type of food, or music or that his favorite color was— "Blue?"

"Blue?"

"Your favorite color. You look like a blue type of guy."

His smile hitched her heartbeat. "That's my second favorite." He started walking.

Feeling a little disappointed and foolish, she couldn't help asking, "So what is your first?"

"Gray. Silvery, like lake-water on a cloudy day."

She made a face. *Color me shades of depression. Oh please.*

The drive back home was a repeat of the drive over, only this time with Billie Holiday singing variations on his second favorite color all the way.

They turned onto Southview Blvd. As they drove under the leafy canopy of mature trees a sense of security softly cloaked her. That it was all the sweeter because she was with Daniel didn't bear closer inspection.

He pulled into the driveway, parked, then reached into the back seat. Without thinking, she turned also, coffee in hand.

He swung around again with the shopping bag.

"Oh! Oh! Oh!" Pure reflex made her jerk back against the door, extending her arm as far away from her own body as possible.

Which, coincidentally, happened to be in the vicinity of *right-smack-damn* over Daniel's body.

The cup came to life in her hand, bouncing off each finger in mid-air, then coffee——black, two sugars——splashed down in a steaming waterfall.

"Son of a bitch!" Daniel reared back, dropping the bag, hands in the air. "Awh, fuck!"

She watched in horror as the dark brown stains blossomed on his shirt and khakis.

"Daniel, I'm so sorry."

Felicity fumbled in her pocket for some napkins she'd taken from the coffee kiosk. The two crumpled specimens she pulled out were pathetic, but she attempted to sop up some of the damage anyway.

Daniel clamped her wrist in an iron grip. "What the hell do you think you're doing?" he ground out between clenched teeth.

She froze under his glare. "The coffee stain—I was just trying to help."

"Don't. Help." He shifted gingerly in his seat, grimacing. "Jesus," he said in an almost tortured whisper.

Felicity looked down at his lap and comprehension dawned.

"Oh."

Chapter Four

Daniel let go of her and held his hand over his groin in a protective hover.

"Maybe we can put some ice on it?"

That earned her another withering glance.

"Look, let's get you upstairs. I think a cold shower or an ice pack or something would help."

More glowering.

Was that really such a dumb suggestion? As bad as she felt—and yeah, it wasn't bad as he felt—it was an accident. At least she was trying to do something about it. She met his stubborn expression with one of her own.

It was a glare-off.

"Fine," he grumbled.

Felicity climbed out of the cab. She rolled her eyes. *Men. Big babies with shaving kits.* She went ahead a few paces, then turned to see how he was making out.

Head held high, Daniel walked with the stiff gait of a man desperately holding on to the tattered shreds of his dignity. His steps were careful with legs slightly bent and toes pointed outwards. He looked like a drunken ballerina on steroids.

It wasn't funny.

The man was in pain.

She pressed her lips together tightly and turned around.

"Not funny," Daniel yelled.

That did it. She burst out laughing.

"I'm so, so sorry. I know it's not funny." She bit down on her lip to stifle another eruption when he stopped to experimentally shake a leg. She moved quickly to his side.

"Yes, I can tell how *not* funny you think it is."

He draped an arm around her shoulders while Felicity slipped hers around his waist for extra support. She matched her step to his, their hips swinging in rhythm as they crossed from driveway to garden path. With some tricky navigation they made it up the stairs to the porch, then conquered the ones to the second floor. When they got into her flat, Daniel removed his arm from her shoulders, which caused Felicity to self-consciously drop her own arm from around him.

"Can you do me a favor?" He pulled a set of keys from his pocket and held them out to Felicity. "I have a pair of work pants in the back of the truck, could you get them? I need to get these off." He plucked at the material of his trousers, in obvious discomfort.

"Sure." She eyed the wet spot. "Just go into the bedroom and get off—" Felicity cleared her throat.

"A-and as soon as you get those pants off," she stressed the last three words, "I'll be ready. I mean, I'll be ready for your parts. I mean your pants. With them. To pass them to you. From the truck. Once I get them from the truck..."

Daniel's expression went through several changes as the words continued to flop out of her mouth like fish off a hook.

"Okay, I'm going now." She got out of there fast. *Oh God, what an idiot!* But the minute she shut the door behind her, she let out another groan and squeezed her eyes closed.

After a second there was a click, followed by the soft squeak of the door opening. She opened her eyes and met Daniel's amused gaze. He held up the keys.

"Thank you." She took them.

"It's the black pickup. Parked in the driveway. You can't miss it." His mouth twitched.

Felicity gave him a tight-lipped smile.

She walked quickly down the hall, but as soon as she turned the corner and went down a couple of stairs, her steps slowed. Too bad she couldn't say the same for her pulse rate. The man definitely had an effect on her, she couldn't help that. But she would stomp this attraction into the ground with a pair of Doc Martens before she made a fool of herself. Okay, a bigger fool.

The jeans and a pair of work boots were in the rear of the cab on the floor. She grabbed the denims and the shopping bag from the front seat, locked up the truck and returned to the flat.

Dropping the purchases on the sofa first, she approached the partially closed bedroom door with his jeans. They were worn and faded to a pale blue, liberally splattered with paint, and torn at one knee. They also carried the faint scent that was, in her mind, uniquely Daniel's. She resisted the urge to bury her nose in the fabric.

"Okay I got them," she called out in warning. "I'm going to pass them to you now." Arm outstretched, she pushed the pants through the narrow opening and shook them like a treat.

"Daniel? I've got your jeans. Daniel?"

Maybe he was in the bathroom. She'd just leave them on the bed. Entering the room cautiously, she hesitated at the sight of the chocolate-brown leather jacket thrown down carelessly at the edge of the mattress, along with the ruined shirt on top of it.

Felicity swallowed and hugged the jeans to her chest; there was a certain intimacy implied with the presence of his stuff in her bedroom. Then the significance of the heap of dark fabric on the floor registered.

His pants.

Felicity did the math: Daniel, minus his clothes, equaled...

The bathroom door swung open.

...Magnificent. To the nth degree.

His chest was bared, broad shoulders tapering down to a trim, flat stomach that looked as if it were chiseled out of rock. Below that, wrapped low around his hips, he held a towel in a fisted grip.

The edges of terry cloth came together like a carelessly drawn curtain between which her greedy eyes spied a glimpse of well-defined thigh. The whole of Daniel, chest, arms and legs, was dusted, like icing sugar on a cake, with fine golden hairs.

It was only the random splotches of red across his chest and thighs that kept her drool fiesta in check. She stared at the shadowy edges of the towel where the angry markings on his legs disappeared. Was he okay?

"Everything's in working order. But I could use that ice."

Her blatant examination of him came to a halt. Embarrassed, Felicity shoved the jeans at him. "Here."

Daniel stepped forward. She stepped back. He stopped, raising an eyebrow, and held his hand out.

"Sorry, here." She stood her ground as he approached again and took the workpants from her.

What did she think he was going to do, jump her bones? Standing around almost naked in front of her didn't seem to faze him or, her eyes flicked below his waist as he adjusted the towel, affect him in any way.

"Well, what are you waiting for? The ice? Today maybe."

Jerk.

Felicity spun on her heel and strode from the room, heading for the kitchen. *Jerkface, jerknoid, jerkaramus, jerkhole. See?* She could stop friggin' swearing.

She pulled a clean tea towel from a drawer, then opened the freezer and took out a tray of ice. She slammed the tray down on the counter several times causing tiny slivers of ice to jump out spraying her face. When one piece almost flew into her eye, she stopped. Heart racing. What was happening here?

She braced her arms on the counter, head bowed, and the memory of Daniel's body shunted itself behind closed lids, crowding her brain. Felicity realized that it wasn't really him she was angry at, it was herself for allowing him to get to her so badly and for her oh-so-obvious attraction to him. An attraction that he seemed to find amusing.

She couldn't stand the feeling of being the brunt of someone's private joke. A joke she never got. It brought back too many ugly feelings from her childhood. *"Hey Felici-tard."* That had been one of the favored names to torment her with. She swallowed and pushed those memories away. But other, more recent ones flew in to take their place.

She remembered Daniel's kiss, relived being in his arms; and what about those looks and the things he'd said? Her confusion increased. How could he just turn off and on that kind of heat? Was he like that with all women?

Instant denial cramped in her gut, but she forced herself to face up to the truth. What made her think she was special? She'd never been before. Just because they had some chemistry didn't mean a thing.

She reached for a butter knife and stabbed at the ice cubes, wishing she could just as easily chip away at what she feared went deeper than physical attraction.

Daniel blew out a breath. The expression on Felicity's face had been part curiosity, part anticipation. The type of expression that inspired a man to satisfy both.

He knew he'd been rude; the flash of anger in her eyes before she'd marched out of here confirmed it. But if he hadn't been rude, he would have done something real stupid. And probably very satisfying.

He sat down hard on the mattress/box-spring stacked on the floor. His gut clenched at the too easily imagined images that came to him. He ran a hand through his hair, grasped a handful and tugged slightly, trying to think straight for a minute.

Daniel wanted her. Bad.

The continuous din coming from the kitchen finally caused him to smile. Felicity seemed hell bent on pulverizing the ice into slush, no doubt as a poor substitute for his head. After a final loud bang followed by an almost unnatural silence, she appeared at the doorway holding a bundled tea towel.

"Sounds like you were causing some damage out there."

Felicity gave him a three-watt smile. "You can always deduct it from my rent deposit."

"From what I just heard, there'd be precious little of that left."

"Then you can take it out of my—"

"Hey now, let's be civilized."

Daniel took the ice pack from her, placing it on his lap. The cold brought welcome relief to the stinging warmth caused by the coffee. He scooped a few pieces of ice out of the bundle and rubbed the melting chips across his chest.

"*Oh, yeah.* That's the ticket." He sighed, pleasure twisting through him, then inhaled sharply as frigid cold made contact with his nipple.

From beneath lowered lids he studied the curve of Felicity's hip and the delectable expanse of belly exposed by her low-slung pants and the shirt tied just above her waist. Her navel beckoned to him to explore it with his tongue and lips. But that would just be an initial foray. The real treasure lay further south.

Steel threads of desire coiled in his gut, tighter and tighter. He told himself not to look up.

But he did.

She watched the water drip from between Daniel's fingers, trailing beads of moisture over the hairs of his chest, and lower... Felicity couldn't look away. She didn't want to.

He dropped the ice pack to the floor, held out his hand.

"Come here."

She didn't move.

Warm eyes searched her own, then he captured her wrist in a wet, icy grip and pulled her closer.

"Felicity." It feathered out on a current of breath against her stomach, chased by the soft press of his lips and warm slip of his tongue.

Everything happened so quickly it could have been a trick of her tangled senses. She went weak and braced herself on his shoulders, pressing the solid flesh beneath her hands. Daniel tilted his head back, his thick golden hair sweeping off his shoulders.

"Closer," he whispered as strong hands swept from her wrist to elbow, pressing down until she was brought to her knees, her waist pressed between muscular thighs. They were face to face. Mouths so close that temptation carried on the exhale and promise on the breath drawn in.

He trailed slow hypnotic caresses up and down her arms before moving to her neck, stroking all the little hollows there. Felicity drew a shuddering breath. The truth of Daniel's touch was that it burned and soothed at the same time. Made her heart feel as if it were being squeezed till every drop of emotion pooled at the tips of every nerve ending.

With calloused fingers he cradled her face, tracing lips, cheeks, the curve of an eyebrow. A crooked smile tilted his mouth as he leaned forward.

"Come on, close your eyes," he murmured. When she did, he kissed her softly. The touch of their lips was magic, fairy dust, a dance of butterfly wings. Her eyes eased back open of their own accord, seeking the confirmation that this wasn't a dream.

"Uh-uh, no peeking." He pressed a gentle kiss to each lid, closing them under his sweet seal before returning to her mouth.

She opened up under his delicious strokes, a moan escaping her. She needed more. Felicity dug her fingers into the hard muscles of his arms, her tongue sparring with his.

"Felicity." He said her name like a last prayer as her eager hands sought out more flesh to touch, more contours to discover. More of him.

She ran her palms over the ticklish curls on his chest, her fingers performing a Braille reading of his taut stomach muscles, then her roaming touch was stopped. By hot steel draped in soft cotton.

"*Hmmm.*" Her moan dripped with satisfaction as she wrapped her hand around his thickness, sliding down the rigid length. And Daniel's groan vibrated back over her tongue, filling her mouth as his hand clamped down to trap her grip between the hard strength of his own and the pulsing heat of his cock.

Daniel tore his mouth away from hers, cursing under his breath, depriving her of his drugging kisses. He was breathing heavily, his face hard and his gaze brittle, a man on the edge of breaking. Felicity was more than willing to push him over that edge.

She leaned into him, seeking his mouth again, but he tightened his hold on her hair and his grip on her hand. Again their soft moans wove together, this time with the twisting threads of soft pain and sharp excitement.

Dark color flushed Daniel's face and his hips jerked up convulsively as breath hissed through his clenched teeth. He deliberately moved their hands together——slowly up, then down.

And again.

"Do you want this?" Hoarse desire riddled his voice.

Like she'd never wanted anything else before.

This time she initiated the caress.

He stopped her partway, again tightening his hand over hers. A soft growl escaped him. "Are you sure?" he asked in a slow, dark whisper, unwinding her locks from his grasp. His fingertips scraped lightly against her scalp, sliding along her neck, down, until he held the weight of her breast in his palm. A shudder went through her.

Felicity could have cried in frustration. Why was he asking her to think, when all she wanted to do right now was feel? *Yes!* She wanted this.

She breathed in his scent, filling her lungs, pushing her flesh further into his hand. Her nipple pressed his palm, but the pressure wasn't enough. She didn't want to be teased. She wanted to be branded. Felicity stared at the naked need on his face, wanting everything he had to give her, right this minute. She didn't want to think about afterwards.

But, of course...*now she did.*

Daniel watched the yearning in her gaze cloud over. She wanted him. But also she wanted more.

Her hand slackened on his stiff, aching flesh and he grunted, his physical need still very real and unabated. With equal amounts of pain and regret, he let her go, stifling the urge to say words that would smooth the way for his body to be buried deep and hard and completely into hers.

Felicity rocked back on her heels and rose. Daniel, holding her gaze, followed more slowly, the towel forgotten on the bed.

Nothing more than air, a sliver of space, separated them, and his erection brushed lightly against her bare stomach. An exquisite touch of skin to skin that sent desire clawing through him.

He saw her shiver, saw indecision darken her eyes, and his

blood raced at the challenge. He could still change her mind, he could—

"Maybe we should take it a bit slower," she whispered. A trembling hand pushed the tumble of chestnut curls from her face. "Th-this thing between us is going a little too fast. And you're right, I do need to think about—" a quick inhalation before she rushed on, "—you know, other stuff."

What other stuff? Daniel was down to a couple of brain-cells. One was stamped "hard" and another "on".

But he was quickly coming out of his lust-filled fog, and alarm bells were ringing in the back of his mind where one lone in-case-of-emergency cell was still operational. She meant *stuff* as in relationship stuff. Definitely not the stuff he was hoping for.

"Felicity, I..." He started then stopped. Her face was tight and suffused with color.

Daniel couldn't do it. He'd done it more times than he could remember, but he couldn't find the words to set her straight on what he wanted, and more importantly, didn't want, from her.

He looked into her apprehensive eyes, and reached out to stroke her cheek, knowing his gesture would be misconstrued. Knowing he was digging a hole he'd have to get out of later. This was not the way he usually operated.

That single brain cell rang a warning again. "Why is this so different?" It slipped out by mistake. The question wasn't for her, but himself and Daniel was confident he would figure it out in time. Hopefully before horniness drove him insane.

Felicity blushed more fiercely. "It's never been like this with anyone else—"

"*Shhh.*" He pressed a finger against her mouth. He didn't need to hear her say that to him right now. Not when he had so little control over his baser instincts. It was just the sort of thing to make him ignore his conscience because it was exactly what he wanted to hear. He wanted all her little sighs and caresses, all uniquely, all selfishly, all for him alone.

"I'm not...easy."

"I didn't think you were." He forced a slight smile and moved his hands to her shoulder, mechanically massaging the tense muscles there. "Now why don't you let me get dressed, because not only am I very easy, I'm also still pretty hard."

Her eyes dropped to his raging hard-on. "Oh! Okay, I'll just leave you to, er, deal with that." She flashed him an uncertain smile and left the room.

He sat on the bed again, his cock slapped up against his belly with no intention of being dealt with except by the person who'd just exited the room.

Daniel pressed the heels of his palms to his closed eyes, feeling like the biggest asshole. He'd timed his seduction like a shmuck. The burning sensation in his gut grew hot enough for him to understand it for what it was. He wasn't angry, he was disgusted. With himself.

Because even though he recognized her vulnerability, he knew he was perfectly capable of exploiting it.

And he was perfectly willing to do so.

Because he still wanted her.

Daniel swore viciously and grabbed the melting bundle of ice from the floor, then went into the bathroom where he dumped the contents in the sink. Back in the bedroom, he dressed quickly.

He tried again to work out the puzzle that was Felicity. She was passionate and beautiful. She was also mouthy, prickly and annoying. He picked up his stained clothing and as he shrugged into his jacket, Daniel looked around the room—there were no framed photos of friends, boyfriend or family. In fact he couldn't remember seeing any photos in the entire flat.

He walked out to the living room. Felicity wasn't there, but through the kitchen window he spied her, her back to him, out on the balcony. She turned as he pushed the screen door open.

"So..." She smiled brightly and rubbed her hands on her thighs.

He opened his mouth to say what he had to and get it over with, but Daniel swallowed his words. He found her happiness irresistible, her shyness endearing. He wasn't used to these feelings.

"Is something wrong?" Her smile began to melt away.

"No," he lied. "I was just trying to figure out..." What? "When we should visit the jobsite." He grasped at the excuse. "You still want to see the work, right?"

She took a deep breath, nodding, and smiled.

"I'll have to see how my schedule is, but I'll call you, okay?" The words slid stiffly out of his mouth.

"Okay," she repeated softly.

Daniel wanted out of here before he dug himself any deeper, but instead he crossed to her and pressed his mouth briefly to her forehead.

He left then, and it was only when he was safely in the truck that he remembered about the shower. He'd send Rob over to deal with it tomorrow. If his buddy had taken care of it in the first place, he wouldn't be in this mess. At least that's what he told himself.

Chapter Five

Felicity was a block away from the transit stop when her ride came cruising down St. Clair Ave. Panic set in and she started running but the streetcar just motored through a green light and past the empty transit shelter. Another streetcar wouldn't be by for another ten minutes.

She cursed under her breath. Swearing didn't count if it was inaudible. She was debating whether or not she could afford to splurge on a taxi when someone goosed her from behind, scaring the shit—er, crap, out of her. Felicity whipped around, hand clutched to her heart.

"Hey good-looking, looking for me?"

"Stuart." Her ex of six months and counting. "That would involve turning over a rock. So, no."

"Awhh, why're you hating?" He bent his lanky frame to peer into her face. His boyish smile, punctuated by two dimples, caused a too-familiar ticklish feeling in Felicity's chest.

He wore his shirt open and his jeans low, all the better to expose a tanned six pack. Dressed head to toe in black, with his short brown hair highlighted and expertly tousled, and heavy silver hoops in each ear, he looked the part of a successful DJ/promoter.

The type that drew a lot of female attention.

The type that liked to act on that attention.

Come to think of it, add a long tail and some whiskers and

he'd also look like the rat he was. She shook off his arm. "Where's Valerie?"

"How should I know?" A petulant scowl marred his model looks. "I thought that drama was over, Fil."

"It *is* over. And so are we." She poked him, then seeing a thread of his expensive shirt snag on her ragged nail, poked him again.

He grabbed her finger. "Can't keep your hands off of me can you?" The arm landed around her shoulders again. It felt far too at home there. She twisted away.

"Stuart, I don't have time for this. How did you find me anyway?"

"That's where fate stepped in. I was driving by and saw you—'cause you know I'd recognize you anywhere." He gave her a *soulful* look. "So I made a U-ey. And here we are together again."

"*We* are not together. There is no *we,* Stuart."

He wagged his finger at her. "You say that now..."

"I said that last year. Remember? When I walked in on you and Val—"

"And there goes the ancient-history train leaving the station. Are we going to argue over this again? Tell you what, where're you going? I'll drop you off."

She wanted to tell him where he could shove his little *choo-choo,* but she weighed her options. Accept his offer and grind her teeth for the next ten minutes, while he tried to get back in her good graces, and pants, again.

Or turn him down and deal with Tony.

Not such a hard choice after all. Better the devil you knew than the asshole you worked for. She let him guide her down the street towards an SUV parked halfway up on the sidewalk.

"So, where to?" he asked once they were on their way.

Felicity breathed in his cologne. He smelled different. That is, the cologne was the same, but the effect was different. She didn't melt. Didn't secretly want him to beg her to come back again.

The difference was Daniel. *He smells different from Daniel.* Stuart repeated his question and Felicity gathered her wits. "The Uptown."

"Isn't that the dump where your skeezer friend Cheryl works?" He gave her a sharp, appraising look. "You peeling now, too?"

Something inside her went twisty-twist. It wasn't just the comments about Cheryl—who couldn't care less what anyone, especially Stuart, thought of her—but the look he gave her, and the note in his voice. *Judgment.*

Her hands curled into fists. "No. I wait tables."

Then a sliver of anger tinged the shame she felt. Lots of girls worked in strip bars, as dancers, bartenders and waitresses. She did honest work.

At least she wasn't some low-life two-timing slug who deserved to be pinned down in a petri dish, left out in the desert at high-noon. Then salted.

"Know what? I think I'll take the streetcar after all."

"Okay, okay, let's not fight. Please?" He gave her the disarming smile his groupies fell for. The one she had fallen for. Imagine, all this time she'd thought she hadn't deserved him. She was right.

Felicity looked out the window, willing the ride to be over while she thought about wasted years. But by the time they came to the next red light he'd slipped one of his CD mixes into the player and the tension eased under the relentless beat. Soon they were talking about mutual friends—actually, they were Stuart's friends—then the reminiscing started.

When they drew up in front of The Uptown, Felicity was feeling more than a little charitable towards Stuart. So when he took her hand in his, she didn't pull away.

Until he popped the question.

"Wait. Hold-up. My boy *Lose*-art wanted you two to be what?" Cheryl's mouth remained open.

Felicity pursed her lips. Not about to repeat herself.

Cheryl leaned closer and raised her voice over the music. "Bumping booty buddies?"

Felicity took a sip of her coke.

"Panting panty pals?"

She spewed out the cola. Eyeing Tony, who had his back to them while he tended the till, she wiped up the mess. "Will you quit it?"

"The *noive* of him. The unmitigated gall. So what did you say?"

"What do you mean what did I say? I said no."

"Hey it couldn't hurt. You do seem a bit testy lately."

"I do?"

"Yeah, you do. Maybe you should take the anti-stud up on his offer. Could be you need to release some of that sexual frustration instead of taking it out on your friends."

Cheryl didn't know how right she was. Felicity had sex on the brain. And she wouldn't mind having it on the bed, on the floor, the kitchen table, the sofa—

She took a deep breath. *Okay, get a grip.* "Gotta take it slow with Daniel."

"What?"

She froze. "What, what?"

Under the flashing lounge lights, Cheryl's narrowed dark gaze took on an eerily strobed effect. "You said Daniel."

"Nuh-uh."

"Oh yes you did." Cheryl was barely holding in her

excitement.

Cornered, Felicity continued to shake her head as Cheryl scooched closer, rubbing her hands together. The avaricious gleam in her eyes told Felicity there was no way out of this except to 'fess up.

"I know what I heard, girl. Now start talking."

"We kissed."

"I knew it, I knew it!" Cheryl grasped Felicity's arm. "Hot damn, that man, named Dan."

"It was just a kiss."

"Ain't no 'just' about it. From that goofy expression on your face, I'd say my man Dan knows what's what and where to put it." If it was possible, Cheryl's smile widened a few more inches.

"Getting involved with my landlord isn't a great idea." Felicity rubbed small circles on the table with her cloth.

"Shoulda thought about that *before* you did the lip lambada with him."

Good point. She was saved from answering when Tony caught her eye. Squinting through the cigarette smoke that wreathed his head like a personal greenhouse effect, he pointed to the clock.

Tony was a man of few words but many interpretive threats.

"Break time's up." She pushed away from the table.

"Think it over."

"What?"

"Exactly." Cheryl winked as she got up too. "*What's what and where to put it.*"

Felicity watched her sashay towards the stage. Friends weren't supposed to encourage friends to be dumbasses.

☙

Daniel sat in a tufted leather chair placed in front of his father's mammoth mahogany desk and gazed out the corner office's windows. A muscle pulsed in his clenched jaw while his old man leisurely scanned the latest summary report on the Maple/Klein Industries merger.

"Okay let's wrap this up."

Finally. Now they could get on with the command performance.

Michael Mackenzie made some invisible adjustment to monogrammed cufflinks, before removing his rimless bifocals from their perch on the Mackenzie nose. The same nose Daniel had until age fifteen, when an errant hockey puck kissed it.

"How are you for time on the Maple deal?"

"Another three months, maybe."

His father shrugged. "It's Fred's dime."

"The closing would be faster if we got a few more juniors on it." Daniel let some of his frustration creep into his voice.

His father's dark eyes skewered into him. "This is a real job. The big leagues." He tapped the desk with the bifocals, then pointed at Daniel. "Don't mess this up because of your misguided attempts at being some nobody construction worker."

Daniel sprang up. "Then perhaps you should take this deal and give it to someone more qualified to handle the big league stuff."

"I already have my best man on the job." Michael Mackenzie tilted back his chair and studied Daniel like a principal regarding a recalcitrant student.

"Then stop questioning my every step—" a short rap sounded at the door, but he wasn't through venting, "—like I've turned into some kind of a major fuck-up overnight."

"If you don't mind, you can stop your swearing right now."

His mother closed the door she'd just stepped through.

Daniel swept back his unbuttoned jacket, resting hands on his waist and muttered, "Sorry."

"Why can't you two behave?" Elise Mackenzie pinned both men under her bright green scrutiny.

"It's just business, Elle," his father placated. "I don't know why you get yourself worked up."

"I get myself worked up because it's not just business." She dropped her leather bag in the chair Daniel had vacated. "This has been going on for years, except now you've graduated to swearing. I'm sick of it."

So was he. All his life he'd tried to measure up to his father's impossible standards. No more. "Are we through here?" Daniel checked his watch; he'd told Rob he could spare half an hour this afternoon, but that was before his dad called this meeting.

Right on cue there was another rap at the door. His father gave permission to enter and the door eased open wide enough for Michael Mackenzie's executive assistant to stick her head through. "Daniel? Mr. Caira is at reception for you."

He thanked the assistant, kissed his mother on the cheek and headed for the door.

"Don't forget dinner Friday, sweetheart."

Daniel swallowed a groan, *damn,* and managed to mask his displeasure before facing his mother again. "I'll try."

"Do more than try, Daniel. It's important that we have dinner together as a family. With no business talk." She cast a sharp glance at her husband. "Just a nice, quiet evening. Just the three of us." The smile she gave them brooked no argument.

"Fine." He left, taking deliberate care to shut the door softly behind him.

Before he'd taken half-a-dozen steps, a slim arm snaked through his. "Hi, lover."

He looked down at Deirdra. They'd grown up together, and even shared a brief fling once or twice, always parting as friends. She was one of the few people he was completely at ease with. Right now, though, he didn't want company.

"Hey." She released him, her smile disappearing. "Big Mac on the attack again?" She used the childhood nickname they had for his father.

"Again? When did he ever stop?" He nodded to another lawyer as they continued down the hall.

"I know what could make you feel better." Her hand wrapped around his biceps again. "How about you, me, a bottle of Merlot and some videos? Or any other form of entertainment you'd be interested in," she added in a murmur with a sultry smile. "I'd make dinner, too. Keep up our strength."

They were at reception and Daniel stopped when he saw Rob. Waving his buddy over, he returned his attention to Deirdra. Her straight, dark hair was pulled back into a chic knot, her bright blue eyes full of enticement. Daniel was tempted. He'd been in a state of frustration for the past four days.

But the hair he wanted to wrap around his fist, while her slim legs wrapped around his hips, was a thick curling mass of chestnut-brown. The face he wanted to rain kisses on was clean of makeup. And eyes he wanted to drown in as he came were the palest silvery gray, not blue.

"Just a nice, quiet evening. Just the two of us," she whispered, her body swaying almost imperceptibly towards him.

Her invitation echoed his mom's and induced the same trapped feeling. Daniel pulled his arm away, giving her hand a little squeeze before he dropped it. "I've already got plans, sorry."

"The invitation is always open," she said meaningfully, then flashed a bright smile at Rob. "We're going to have to get you your own office, you're here so often."

"I could always share yours." Rob waggled his eyebrows for good measure.

"I don't think it's big enough."

"I'll take that as a compliment." His partner's grin was slow and suggestive.

She laughed softly and chucked him under the chin, then bid them goodbye. The two men watched her shapely sway continue down the hall.

Rob sighed dramatically. "I can't believe you just turned her down. You're losing your touch, man."

Daniel could assure him he wasn't. But over the past four days he'd been slowly losing his mind. Just as he'd feared— insanity brought on by excessive horniness.

Then Daniel felt a ripple of unease, because it wasn't just lust that had him thinking about Felicity's laugh or wondering what she was doing at odds times during the day. It was more than desire that had him looking forward to seeing her this weekend. Oh, yeah. He was certifiably crazy.

"Come on, let's go to my office." He headed towards that sanctuary like the hounds of hell were nipping at his heels.

Chapter Six

"This ain't going to happen, Fil." Cheryl stopped trying to push her end of the sofa into the alcove.

Reluctantly coming to the same conclusion, Felicity glared at the couch that had thwarted all her plans.

"I told you it wouldn't work," Stuart offered.

"You would know all about *not* working." Cheryl gestured at him, seated on the coffee table, elbows resting on spread knees.

"Hey, why should I work up a sweat and ruin my threads? Besides, what's with all the rearranging, anyway?"

"Why not?" Felicity shot back. It was her new motto. "You of all people should understand about change, Stuart," she said pointedly. "Out with the old, in with the new, right?"

"Yeah, out with the old coochie, in with new hoochie," Cheryl clarified.

"Hello? 'Old coochie' standing right here."

"No offense meant, hon. You ain't that old. I was just going for a little solidarity."

Stuart tossed a sneer in Cheryl's direction before focusing on Felicity. "I agree with you one hundred percent, baby. Out with the past, in with a new future. That's why I think you should give us another chance."

She stared at him, speechless, but good old Cheryl came to the rescue.

"Felicity ain't no charity. She don't need to give no punk-assed, two-timing, *you* another chance."

"You calling me a punk?"

"If the shoe fits." Cheryl rotated her neck.

"Stuart, we've had our run. I can't go back there."

"You keep saying that, but I know you don't mean it."

All that hair gel must have shellacked his brain. He just didn't get it.

"I'll mean it for her, butt-scrub," Cheryl pounced. "Stop dropping by, stop calling, stop asking—go harass someone else. If you need a date so badly, try Rejects R Us, I'm sure they'll hook you up."

"Is that where you find your dates?"

Felicity put a hand up to stall Cheryl, who looked like she was ready to go all *Matrix* on Stuart and drop-kick his ass into next week.

"Stuart, I've moved on. Get used to it." Man, if that didn't sound good.

She'd moved on before. From one dead-end job to another. From her parents' house to a brief stint on the streets, then one rented room after another. And her track record with boyfriends wasn't much better. But now "moved on" was linked with "why not?" in her mind.

Felicity looked around the room, seeing beyond the garage sale finds and junk store bargains. She took in the muted yellow plaster walls and the bare wood floors that creaked their secrets with each step, the drafty old-fashioned casement windows and high stucco ceilings that hinted at another era.

She'd made like Martha Stewart too many times in her imagination with this place. But ever since she and Daniel had gone to Home Depot last weekend, her daydreaming had gotten worse. Now she was plagued with ideas for tearing down walls, adding pot lights, stripping and staining the floors.

These dreams were safer than the ones she had about Daniel, though. The ones where she relived the way he'd touched her, kissed her.

And then afterwards, when he hadn't pushed for more, respecting her choice, despite his obvious condition. That had to mean something, didn't it? In about two hours she'd find out.

Cheryl waved a hand in front of her face. "Earth to Felicity."

"Sorry." She hunched her shoulders.

"You know you've been wearing that goofy smile all day."

"That's because I'm here." Stuart got up and swaggered over to her. He snaked his arms around her waist. "You miss me. Just admit it."

"Stuart, cut it out." She frowned over her shoulder, stared into his puppy-dog brown eyes, and felt...well not exactly *nothing*. But something pretty darn close to it. Another smile slowly spread across her face.

"See? Look at that smile." He moved in for a kiss which she angled away from. "You know we go together, babes."

"You mean like an asshole and a hemorrhoid? No, wait a sec." Cheryl flipped several braids over her shoulder. "That would be your relationship with the rest of humanity."

"No, that would be your relationship with your mirror."

"At least I have a relationship with my mirror. Yours filed for protective custody."

"Know what, I'm tired of your big mouth. Why are you always bitching?"

"Because I speak 'bitching' fluently, in several dialects, including sign." Cheryl gave him the middle finger.

"Don't you wish. 'Fraid you're not my type, Chewbacca."

"Guys!" Felicity tried to interject, wiggling for escape from Stuart's arms.

"Stuart, if you were the last man on earth, I would get a sex change just so I could make you my bitch—"

"Wrong again. Being a bitch is your job."

"What are you *even* doing here?" Cheryl demanded.

"First ask yourself what you're doing with that tragic weave."

"Trying to look like your mama." Cheryl stalked to the door and flung it open. "Leave."

"Guys, enough! Okay? Let's just move the sofa back," Felicity pleaded.

Neither moved.

"Now. Please."

Cheryl pouted. Not a pretty sight. "Fine. But next time you want a decorating challenge, Fil, don't invite Skidmark Stu over. Or ask Tony if you can make some changes—"

"Tony? Who's Tony?" Stuart's hold tightened.

"None of your business." Felicity tugged at his wrists.

"Just tell me who this guy is, so I can go kick his ass."

Cheryl burst out laughing. "You couldn't lift your leg that high, Stu-*runt*."

"Am I interrupting?"

Felicity stopped struggling, her attention drawn to the cold voice that came from the hallway.

Cheryl spun round. "Daniel!" she gushed like they were long-lost friends. "Come in, come in." She grabbed his arm and pulled him into the flat.

The smile he gave Cheryl dimmed when he looked back at Felicity, making her aware of the body still pressed up against her. She gave Stuart's arm another shove. He let go, slowly.

"If we're still on. Whenever you're ready," Daniel said in a monotone.

Gee, if he were any less enthusiastic, she'd have to check for a pulse. Only pride stopped her from asking if *he* was sure he still wanted to go.

"Maybe we should get Daniel to help with the sofa." Cheryl interrupted Felicity's troubled thoughts. "A real man." She glanced dismissively at Stuart.

"Maybe you need a real man to—"

"Okay, okay." Felicity waved her hands. She couldn't deal with any more of their bickering. "Just leave it right there. I'll move it myself later."

But Daniel was already walking over to the sofa; he started pushing and Stuart practically elbowed Felicity out of the way to do his part. In no time the sofa was back in its original spot.

"Can we all leave now?"

Cheryl's brows rose at Felicity's sharpness but she gathered her things without a murmur while Stuart got the evil eye when he didn't move fast enough. Felicity saw them out, then stood by the closed door after they left, gathering her courage as she listened to their renewed bickering trail down the hall.

"You don't have to come if you don't want to."

It took a moment to mask her disappointment before she trusted herself to turn and face Daniel. "What makes you think that?"

He shrugged, threw his keys up in the air and caught them. "You weren't exactly happy to see me. You should have seen your face when I interrupted your little happy reunion."

Bewilderment robbed her of words, but indignation found her a thesaurus. "That wasn't a reunion, that was an invasion. I didn't expect Stuart to drop by and I sure as hell didn't invite him over." She held Daniel's stare for several long seconds.

Finally he sighed, his mouth tilting into a smile as he closed the distance between them. "Our first fight?"

"Maybe," she said, all the fight gone out of her. Heck, right now she was wrapped up in a white flag of surrender and not much else. And Daniel had x-ray vision. And triple x-rated superpowers.

This was *so* much better than her Martha Stewart fantasies.

Once they were in the truck, the awkwardness between them returned. Daniel's attempts at chitchat were lame at best. He couldn't help it. His gut was still coiled from seeing Stuart with his arms around Felicity.

Daniel changed the radio station for the third time in as many minutes, jealousy sitting heavy in his gut. Yeah, she'd been telling her ex to let go, but any fool could see her protests were half-hearted.

He experienced another surge of uncertainty but clamped down on it. She hadn't seemed heartbroken to see Stuart go. And most importantly, he glanced at his silent passenger, she was here with him now.

Daniel felt a surge of another type and didn't know what he wanted to do more. Or do first. Or do more of. Kiss her deep and thoroughly while he buried his fingers in her thick silky hair? Or, his gaze trailed down to her breasts, fill his hands and mouth with other enticements?

He turned his attention back to the road, tightly gripping the steering wheel as he became even more aware of her soapy fresh scent. Daniel forced himself to start the conversation rolling again and kept it up for the remainder of the drive downtown to the tree-lined Parkdale area. By the time they arrived at the old Victorian house his crew was working on, he'd gotten over his chest-beating impulses. *Almost.*

They spent a good half hour on the lower floors, with Felicity surprising him with a barrage of questions. Now they were touring the renovated attic space.

"We combined one of the smaller bedrooms with the old oversized linen closet to make this new study for the owner."

He watched as she walked around the space, lightly touching the back of an upholstered chair, then caressing the parchment shade of a table lamp, her expression rapt.

Daniel's mouth twisted in self-deprecation, and here he thought she'd just wanted an excuse to see him again. "You really love this stuff, don't you?"

She shrugged. "I've done some decorating." She looked up at the ceiling and studied the ornate medallion and chandelier. "Had a lot of practice with all the moves I've had to make." Some of her enthusiasm faded.

His stomach plummeted. Because of him, she'd be moving again. He should tell her about his plans now. But, as she crossed the Berber carpet to the custom built-in bookshelf, and he got an eyeful of her luscious ass, Daniel wrestled with the part of him that didn't want to spoil things between them. Not before he could be with her, *just once.*

That thing slithering across the floor? That was his conscience.

Felicity slowly ran her hands over the books, fingers tracing each title. She removed one or two for closer inspection, before putting them back. "I always thought of each new place as a new chance." Her voice carried an odd note he couldn't place. "A new start, just waiting for me to really make it mine. It could be anything I wanted. The only limit was my imagination. My dreams." She gave him a wry look over her shoulder, her smile tipped with longing so sharp it pierced him.

She turned back to the bookshelf, her hands resting along the dark-stained wood. This was one of the few furnished rooms in the house, yet at the moment it felt the emptiest. Filled with the loneliness that seemed to radiate from her stillness.

"I used to walk past houses like this when I was a kid and dreamed I lived there. You know, the big dining room for big happy family meals. And a little girl's room up in the attic with a canopied bed and everything all pink and white and pretty and...perfect."

Felicity walked along the bookshelf, hand trailing across

the books. "I always believed houses had magic. Just a silly kid thing." She gave him another one of those wry smiles over her shoulder that twisted something inside him.

"But I honestly thought that if the house was big and beautiful and filled with nice things, then the people who lived there would be nice. And happy." She inhaled and after a pause added in a low voice, "We had an ugly little house."

Daniel went to her. Couldn't have stayed away if his feet had been nailed to the floorboards. He placed his hands on delicate shoulders that stiffened even more beneath his palms, then slowly her tension eased and he pulled her closer, his arms crisscrossing just above the swell of her breasts. Her scent satiated his senses. The sweet curve of her ass settling against his groin, her hair so soft along his jaw. Holding her like this felt right.

He thought of her little flat at Southview, with its meager selection of second-hand furniture. And yet it was obvious that each piece had been selected with care and with an eye towards charm and comfort. No less than what his own mother had done in his far more affluent childhood home.

Elise Mackenzie hadn't just filled the four-thousand-square-foot house with expensive things, she'd been filling it with love for him and his dad. Felicity was doing the same at Southview, for herself. Some unnamed emotion lumped in Daniel's throat.

We had an ugly little house.

Another stab of guilt hit him, and he buried his face in her sweet-smelling hair, as if he could hide from his conscience there. As if he could just be overwhelmed by Felicity, her scent and the feel of her in his arms. He didn't want to think about evictions. The place was rented, she had to know she would have to move on one day. Fill another space with her belongings, her passion. Her love.

She took a deep breath, and her breasts pushed against his arms. "One day I'm gonna have a beautiful house like this," she said with that curious mix of vulnerability and determination he associated with her. "Silly dream, huh? For a waitress almost impossible. What does this neighborhood run for, half a mill?"

"More or less."

She made a little sound that made Daniel want to give her hope, maybe to assuage his guilt, maybe because of other feelings he didn't want to explore.

"This bookshelf took several weeks to finish," he murmured in her ear as he reached out and rubbed the oak beneath his thumb. Feeling the inherent strength of the hard wood, the smoothness that came with hours of honest sweat.

"I met with the homeowners to discuss what their needs were, what would make this space uniquely theirs. They showed me some pictures of what they wanted and I took it from there." He shrugged. "There were problems; every little change and delay had a price." He stopped, smoothing one hand back and forth on the shelf.

"See how the beauty of the wood is enhanced by the stain? It took several coats to get just right. And how it feels like satin and warms under your palm? You achieve that by hand sanding with a fine grade paper." Finally his hand rested over hers. "This is the end result.

"That's the thing about dreams, you focus on them, work for them and collect a few splinters along the way..." His hand curled over hers as he scanned the shelves again with a deep sense of pride.

"The homeowners love this place, they filled it with their dreams. That's what makes it truly beautiful. That's what makes any place you want to call a home beautiful. Nothing is impossible, Felicity."

Her fingers moved, intertwining with his. "Thank you," she whispered.

Warmth spread through him. He wanted to say thank you in return. When was the last time he had focused, really focused, on what he loved about this calling? Instead of what he hated about working for his dad? Felicity had this effect on him from their first meeting. Making him feel off-balanced and centered at the same time.

He turned her around and stared down into the silvered depths of her gaze. The world became vast with possibilities, while the moment shrank to the space of a shared heartbeat. Intent on showing this woman in his arms, this enigma of prickly vulnerability, his gratitude, Daniel covered her mouth with his.

What started as an innocent gesture turned into a conflagration. Forget about any chaste "thank you, ma'am" kiss. His body was demanding the "wham-bam" part.

He crowded her up against the bookshelf and she twined her arms around his neck, pressing her soft curves to his ravenous body. Driving him crazy with the little sounds she fed him as her tongue sparred with his.

Daniel ground himself against her. *Shit. More.* He grabbed her ass, pulled her tight against his hard-to-bursting erection, then growled in frustration at the barriers of clothing that denied full satisfaction. He hooked his hands under her thighs, spreading them wide as he lifted her to get better access, then he thrust hard, *one, two, three* times, against her open invitation.

A split second later several books tumbled down around them, one large tome beaning him in the head, and Daniel stumbled back, taking Felicity down with him in a tangle of limbs.

He lay there, trying to catch his breath with the plush carpet underneath him and her lush body spread on top of him.

"Are you okay?" She tentatively touched his forehead.

Daniel winced and, gently pushing her hand away, explored for himself.

"Yeah," he said, frowning, then felt beside him on the floor for the most likely culprit. He grasped a thick glossy-covered hardback and read the title. "*Hrrmph.* Figures."

"What's that supposed to mean? A couple of the girls at work were reading this book. They said it's good."

He made a face. "It's a romance."

"So? All books have some merit."

Daniel turned the book over and quickly scanned the back blurb. Her huffy tone wasn't lost on him, though. "You read this stuff?"

"N-no."

At her hesitant answer, he peered over the book's edge. A deep rose shaded her cheeks and he felt her tense on top of him. Daniel slowly put the book aside, a wicked grin shaping his mouth as he admitted, "I have."

Or at least he thought he had, all these trashy novels looked alike to a couple of pimply-faced ninth graders. Rob had egged him on, "Find out what the chicks want, man" and they'd spent several hilarious hours pilfering through his mother's stash. Which had proved *very enlightening* to two horny teenage boys.

Thank God for trashy novels.

"I'll save you some money and reading time." Daniel rolled so she was trapped under his body. "Here's the synopsis." He laid a kiss on her worthy of any romance hero. Hot, ravaging, thorough. And her bosoms? They were heaving, dude. *Awesome.* All said, it was a pretty detailed and in-depth summary.

The opening of the front door had Daniel coming up for air. A male voice called his name and he answered that he'd be right down. "Looks like we're out of time." He rubbed a thumb across her mouth. "The guys are here, and I should be down in the basement already painting."

Felicity felt a sharp pang at Daniel's words. It couldn't be over yet. "I'd like to stay," she said huskily. "Can I help? I'm pretty good at it."

His slow smile curled her toes. "Babes, I'd say you were more than pretty good." He lowered his mouth to hers again.

He wasn't half bad himself, in her humble opinion.

A short while later they went downstairs. When she and Daniel passed the small crew working in the kitchen, silence descended and Felicity felt like a walking CSI specimen with Daniel's mouth and handprints glowing neon all over her.

Thankfully, her embarrassment was soon forgotten once she and Daniel got down to business painting the basement. Though they worked companionably, every now and then she'd look up to find his gaze heavy on her. Each time she gave him a nervous smile. But the tension grew as the minutes went by.

Chapter Seven

Daniel started another section of drywall, applying the primer in long easy glides. The job should have soothed his restlessness, but it wasn't the type of stroking he needed.

Pounding. That's what he needed to do. Buried to the hilt inside of Felicity while her body clenched around him.

And kissing. Lots of it. Tongues entwined, with mouths leaving wet sucking caresses all over each other's bodies. Then losing himself in her body and in her gaze as they came together. God, he could stare into those gray eyes forever— *Forever?*

Daniel jammed the roller into the paint tray, causing paint to spill onto the plastic sheet spread on the floor. He ignored it, just as he'd tried to ignore the undercurrent to this growing attraction he felt for Felicity.

She'd gotten deep under his skin and he was kidding himself in thinking she was just an itch to be scratched. Felicity was a full-body rash.

Daniel slapped paint on the wall with a tad more energy than required, while Felicity painted along the taped-off baseboard, seemingly oblivious to his torment.

It was a few minutes before he realized she'd stopped painting the baseboards and was staring off into space. It was a shock when her attention suddenly snapped onto him.

"What's this place going to be used for?"

He wiped a forearm over his brow. "The owners want a rec room. The entertainment components will go here." He thumbed the wall nearest him. "And the pool table over by where you're standing."

"My parents' whole house could practically fit down here." She shook her head and resumed painting. "We didn't have a rec room; the basement was just a crawlspace. I used to play with my dolls in the kitchen while my ma made dinner."

"You were close to your mom?"

Her laugh was a bitter huff. Close in the sense that sticking near her ma kept her out of range of her da's temper. But was she close to her mom?

Felicity stopped painting, remembering her last visit out to the Scarborough suburbs, six months ago. She cringed at the unfamiliar wheedling note that echoed in her memory. *"Daddy, it would be just for a few weeks at the most."*

"Ten years out in the world and yer skull's just as thick as ever." From his recliner, her da jerked his chin towards the window. The large wall to wall expanse of glass was the one thing that saved the tiny living room—crammed with faded furniture and ambitions—from utter dreariness.

"I've said my piece. Why don't you move back in with that boyfriend of yours? You seem to have a liking for living a dirty life without benefit of the church." He took a long swallow of beer, and then wiped his mouth with the back of a hand.

"Or is it now that he's drunk the milk, he's put the cow out to pasture?"

"Leslie, don't say that." A weak protest at best, from her ma tucked amongst the pillows on the couch. Just another dull accessory. A doormat. A woman Felicity didn't understand.

She came back to the present. "It's hard to feel close to someone who really isn't there." She swallowed. "It was hard to exist around my da. Big personality, you know?" *Big fists, too.*

"Don't." She'd seen the pitying look on his face. "Don't feel sorry for me."

Felicity looked around at the large unfinished space. One day she'd have more and better. One day she could have a place, a home, like this, and all it represented—acceptance, success, belonging. Things she'd learned in so many indefinable ways growing up, at home and school, that she somehow didn't deserve.

But she'd have it, and she'd fill it with love, just like Daniel had said upstairs. She ducked her head, determinedly focused on painting above the baseboards. After awhile, he followed her lead, and she breathed easier, thankful that he didn't press to ask awkward questions about her past.

But thinking about her past made Felicity more curious about his. For instance what fueled his obvious love for his job? He certainly took pride in what he did; it resonated in his voice as he spoke about finishes and materials and the skills required.

She cleared her throat. "Did you always want to be in construction?"

Daniel froze, then nodded; his gaze took the same path hers had earlier around the room and a smile curved his mouth.

"Yeah, from the first set of building blocks my nan—my grandmother—got me for Christmas when I was six."

She could almost picture a tiny version of Daniel wiggling around on the floor, building empires and demolishing them. Felicity's heart contracted, because she wanted to reach out and crush that little boy in her arms, brush his hair aside, kiss his boo-boos. She sucked in air and started coughing.

First she was fantasizing about the man, then dreaming about houses, and now she was imagining little boys who looked like him. Reality check. Emotional road-kill alert. She applied herself to the task at hand, vowing to have no more stray delusional thoughts.

"So, why didn't you go for architecture?" she asked, still hungry for a few more details.

"I like old houses. The stability. The love apparent in the craftsmanship and the mystery in the history of the previous owners. My nan used to live in this great big house—a real storybook Victorian with gingerbread trim, a dumbwaiter, the works..." He shrugged, then dipped his roller into the paint tray and started another coat.

"I spent a lot of happy times in that house. Besides, you're not the only one with an overbearing father." Daniel's mouth quirked to the side and his eyes narrowed.

"My dad spent a great deal of time instilling in me the importance of history and tradition. That's another reason why I went into restorations and renovating."

As he spoke, she used up the last of her paint and walked over to the cans that were stacked close by Daniel.

"Is your dad a contractor too?"

His bark of laughter was short on humor. "No. This is definitely not the family business my father had in mind for his grandiose plans."

Felicity gave his arm a comforting squeeze. She heard the bitterness in his voice, yet she couldn't help but wonder— "Was it really so bad to have someone want so much of you? To expect the best?"

"If it's the best for them and not for me, yeah." His eyes were bright and hard.

"But he loved you enough to want it," she persisted. "I wish I'd had that."

"If *you* want what's best for you, that's all it takes."

Sigh. She could tell him that it took a whole lot more than just wanting what was best. "Yeah, sure." She flicked her paintbrush in half-hearted enthusiasm, and several large splatters of paint landed on Daniel.

He looked down at himself, then looked at her. Felicity's

mouth made a wide "O" before she slapped her hand over it. A gurgle of laughter still escaped.

"Oh, I'm so sorry. It was an accident."

He wiped his left cheek, then drew the heel of his palm over his chin where he felt another wet splotch.

"Here let me get that for you." Before he knew it, she'd brushed the tip of his nose. Her eyes went wide with shock then shone with mirth as she took in her handiwork.

So she wants to play it like that, does she? He rubbed his nose on his forearm, his eyes narrowed.

"Looks like you got some on yourself."

"Where?" Felicity pulled her top away from her body, searching, then she looked up and let out a little squeal. She made a run for it, but the extension handle of the roller made for easy pickings. He caught her backside with a wide swath.

"Oh, no!" She stopped, twisting to view the damage. "These are my favorite jeans. I just bought them too."

They looked kinda worn-in to him—very nicely so—but that was the in look. Pricked by guilt, he dropped the roller and went to her.

"It's latex paint, you can—" She tried to get him again. "Oh no you don't." He grasped her wrist, raising her arm above her head and away from him. Daniel looked down at Felicity, her face alight with mischievous enjoyment and a rush of happiness slid over him. This was good.

Giggling, she investigated the rips in his top with her free hand. "Holey sweatshirts, Batman."

He twisted his body away and surprise dawned on her face. "You're ticklish."

"No. I'm not."

She feinted a time or two, before moving in for the kill. Her fingers fluttered mercilessly against his side.

Their laughter mingled as he tried to escape the delicious

shivers lancing through him. Finally he captured her other wrist and turned her around, crossing her arms in front of her with her hands firmly gripped in his and her back pressed tightly against him.

"Who's your daddy now?"

"Wh-what did you just say?" She doubled over in laughter.

Daniel grimaced. *What a tool.* He let go of her wrists and rested his hands on her waist.

It was as easy as that.

Instantaneous. Combustion.

He slid his hands down to her hips, holding her ass snug against his groin as he felt himself rising to the occasion.

Daniel pressed forward, heard her quick intake of breath, then felt heat surge through him as she rocked back.

He swore and turned her around into his arms. Beneath the desire in her gaze, another emotion glowed in the depths, beckoning him to come closer. He did what any smart man in his situation would do. He kissed her.

Dumb move.

℃

Rob swung a size 14 Kodiak up onto Daniel's desk followed shortly thereafter by a second steel-toed boot, which he crossed at the ankles.

Daniel raised an eyebrow. Rob raised two.

"Didn't your mother tell you to keep your feet off the furniture?"

"*Her* furniture, yeah." Rob grinned unrepentantly.

Daniel shook his head, but said nothing more. The desk came with the office; he hated it, and Rob knew it. It was his dad's choice, an oversize mahogany monument to the affluence of Mackenzie Phillips and Bassett.

Rob used his foot to nudge the rolled up blueprints. "So did you get a look at the changes?"

"Yeah, I did, looks like all systems go." Daniel leaned back in his chair, fingers strumming on the armrest.

"I thought this was what you wanted. Why so glum chum?" Rob reached for his mug of coffee and took a healthy swallow. "What the—?" He gagged and swung his legs down from the desk. "Who the hell makes this crap?"

"Tastes a damn sight better than the shit you brew up."

"That shit'll put hair on your chest."

"That shit'll kill ya. Besides I already have hair on my chest. And I was hoping to have kids one day," Daniel added for some unknown reason.

"Kids? Is one of Toronto's most eligible bachelors thinking about settling down? Inquiring minds want to know." Rob put his cup down on the desk and gave it an extra little push away.

"Oh yeah, I plan to take over the world one day with an army of little Mackenzies."

Rob tsked. "You grow more like your father every day."

"Any more talk like that and you're out of here, buddy."

"Something's bugging you." Rob stroked down both sides of his goatee with finger and thumb. "C'mon, you can tell your Uncle Rob."

Daniel shrugged, then took up a pen and started tapping the side of his mug. He knew better than to come totally clean with Rob—but he could approach the problem from an oblique angle. "We still have the evictions to do...."

"Funny you should mention that." Rob's slumberous gaze turned sharp. "I thought you and Felicity were playing a bit of 'who's your daddy'?"

So much for the oblique approach. Not much got past Rob. Daniel flung down the pen, pushed away from his desk and walked to the bank of windows that ran the length of two walls. From the thirty-second floor of the Canadian Equity Trustco building the view of the city was spectacular and virtually unimpeded. There was nothing to block his sight lines as he scanned to the west, picking out the various landmarks.

Somewhere beyond the distinctive stone gray turrets of Casa Loma, below the dense spread of treetop foliage, was 23 Southview. Idly he wondered if Felicity was home. What was she doing? Should he call? They'd gone out again last night. Another night of torture for him. His mouth went dry. How the hell had he stopped?

Because she wants to take it slow. Because maybe he knew he didn't deserve her, not with what he planned to do afterwards.

Because somewhere along the line Daniel realized he wanted more than her body. He wanted her trust, he wanted....a sliver of fear slid between his ribs, cutting off that train of thought.

He let loose a low mirthless laugh. Once she knew about his plans for her home, Felicity wouldn't give him the time of day, never mind her trust...or anything else.

A low whistle sounded behind him. "I haven't seen you this distracted by a lady in a long time. Not since the blow-up with Sandy."

He winced as the old feeling of guilt stirred. That relationship should have never happened. They'd been too young and out to please everyone but themselves.

Daniel pressed his open palm against the glass. "This thing with Felicity is...*different*," he said absently. He didn't know the how or why of it, and wasn't sure he wanted to. The funny hollow feeling he'd carried around in his gut since meeting her expanded a few more centimeters.

He ran a finger under his suddenly too-tight collar. Thoughts of Felicity occupied his nights, interrupted his sleep.

He'd be damned if she interfered with his daily schedule. He turned from the window just as a short knock sounded.

The door opened and his father stood at the threshold, the old man's expression grim. Daniel took a deep breath. *What now?*

"Your mother wanted me to remind you about golf tomorrow."

"She didn't think I got her two voicemails and the email?"

"She let you off easy. Four voicemails and two more emails on the BlackBerry." His father grimaced. For a brief moment Daniel felt the shared empathy of being lovingly, but persistently harangued by his mother.

He returned to his desk and logged into his email. "I'll let her know I haven't forgotten," he said, hopefully bringing the visit to an end.

"So you'll be there?"

"I said I would." He hit send. "Done. Now, was there anything else?" Daniel leaned back insolently in his chair.

"We need a fourth. Robert, what are you doing tomorrow? Can you join us?"

Daniel was sure his shocked expression matched Rob's.

"Sure, Mr. Mac. I'll be there with bells on."

"Good." Michael Mackenzie gave a brief nod and left.

Rob picked up his mug again and peered into it. "What the hell did you say was in this shit, again?"

଼

"What's that?" Lise pointed at the paperback in Felicity's open knapsack.

Damn. "A friend bought it. He thought I'd enjoy it," she mumbled, blushing.

"May I see?"

Felicity handed the book over and watched Lise's eyebrows rise. Her stomach sank. She knew what was coming, the gentle words of discouragement, and she rushed to the defensive.

"I've been practicing those exercises you said to." She rummaged through the knapsack for the dictionary Lise had given her during their first tutorial. "See? I marked each word I had a problem with and looked it up."

Lise reached across the library table and patted Felicity's hand. "You done good, kiddo, but we're not quite through with the Brothers Grimm."

Felicity heard the gentle rebuke. She riffed the dictionary pages.

"Hey." Lise waited till she looked her in the eye. "I love romance novels. The thing is, I'd love for you to get the same enjoyment I get from them. Not struggle with every other word. Where's the fun in that? We're not there yet, but—" Lise squeezed her hand, "—we will be. And then I'll have someone to swap books with. Okay?"

"Okay." Felicity returned Lise's encouraging smile.

"Now I do have one question…"

"Yes?"

"My husband and son give me no end of grief because I read romances. I always tell them to read one before they level any more opinions. That always shuts them up," she said smugly.

Lise's expression changed.

Uh-oh. Felicity knew that look.

"Sooo…"

Cheryl wore it a lot.

"…who is this treasure amongst men who buys you romance novels? Boyfriend?"

Daniel, her boyfriend? She hadn't given too much thought

to what it meant to be spending so much time with him during the last three weeks. But *boyfriend* had a nice sweet sound to it. A nice, sweet, safe, non-sexual sound.

"Not officially."

Lise laughed softly. "You're pouting. I take it you want things to be official?"

"Like with a capital 'O'? Oh, yeah." Felicity squeaked with embarrassment. Did she just say that to her tutor?

"Felicity, darling, if you keep looking at me like that, I'm going to be very insulted. I'm married, not mummified. In fact I may be able to offer some advice to bring him up to scratch."

"I don't think he's a 'bring to scratch' type of guy."

"Nonsense." Lise waved dismissively. "All men are trainable. You just need to know how to go about it."

"And how's that?"

"Sneaky."

Felicity laughed, not completely convinced that Daniel was trainable. She started chewing on a nail, but Lise tapped her hand away from her mouth.

"That's a really bad habit, dear. So what do you think the problem is?"

"Me."

"Don't be silly."

"No, really. The first couple of times we got close, things happened real fast. Too fast. I told him we needed to take it slow."

"And he's respected your wishes. He sounds like a really nice guy. His mother obviously raised him right."

"Well I wish she had raised him just a little bit wrong."

Lise snorted. "So now you want to speed things up again?"

Felicity nodded.

"But you don't want to seem cheap and easy?"

She nodded again.

"Men like cheap and easy, dear," Lise said with sigh. "But there are other ways." She thought for a moment. "Lingerie is always effective. Black or white. Men are such simple creatures, you throw colors at them and the poor dears get all confused. They start drooling and panting, then before you know it your hair's a mess, they're asleep and you want to kill someone. Black and lacey is the way to go."

"Black and lacey?"

"Trust me."

Chapter Eight

Felicity settled her head on Daniel's shoulder and felt his arm adjust, drawing her closer. Then his thumb resumed stroking along her bare arm. Distracting her. She wanted to pay attention to the movie's plot, not his touch.

Even though the drive-in at The Docks waterfront entertainment complex was filled to capacity, the backseat of his truck, with its tinted side windows and cushy leather seats, could have been as far away from the other vehicles in the lot as the stars in the sky overhead.

They both reached into the popcorn at the same time and Felicity giggled up at Daniel. His responding smile did crazy things to her vital organs. "You enjoying the movie?"

"It's not as bad as I thought it would be. Better than the last chick film you dragged me to," he mumbled.

She pulled away slightly. "Why didn't you tell me you didn't want to see this one?"

"Because you wanted to, and I needed to catch up on my sleep. Besides, you'd never been to a drive-in before." He pulled her back against him, then added softly, "And I wanted to make you happy." He dug another handful of popcorn from the bag and returned his attention to the screen.

What the? He dropped a bombshell like that——the first time he'd even come close to admitting she meant something to him——then went back to watching the movie?

Yet, there was something about his absolute stillness that told her he wasn't taking in the action on screen anymore than she could at the moment.

Over the thundering of her heartbeat, she heard herself say, "You do. Make me happy. No one's ever cared about me being happy before."

She had his full attention now, and this time she was the one who looked away. Something impelled her to go on. "My parents never seemed to have time for me. I always seemed to be in the way, or a disappointment, or a big puzzle they weren't sure what to do with."

She shrugged as if she could shrug away that deep-seated sense of rejection and abandonment. Even when she dropped out of school and moved out, they never tried to stop her. Never came looking for her. And it was always her fault when they lost contact.

"I never had a birthday party. Oh, my mom made my favorite meal and dessert, but it wasn't the same without friends over, and there never seemed to be any money for real presents. Just the cheap stuff from the corner store, that lasted about week before they broke." She swallowed, but the words would not be held back.

"The first birthday that ever meant something to me was on my sixteenth birthday. I took myself to the movies. I don't even remember the movie now, but I remember that I did something special for me." She looked at Daniel. "I knew then that I would never have to depend on anyone else for my happiness. I could do it for myself." Except now he was undoing all her hard work, she was becoming too addicted to feelings he stirred in her. He made her want to believe, again, in fairytales.

"But...it's not the same." Daniel said, his gaze searching. It was like he'd read her mind.

"No. It's not."

"This is all new to me too," he said enigmatically and looked back at the screen, running a hand through his shoulder-length hair.

Felicity heard the familiar hint of frustration in his voice, and had a good idea of what he meant by newness. Then he was staring into her eyes again, and his were bright and hard.

In the semi-darkness Felicity picked out the lines of tiredness that fanned out from the corners of his eyes. She felt a stab of guilt, remembering his joke about catching up on sleep. She knew he worked long hours. Half the time she couldn't get a hold of him on his cell because he was in some meeting or other.

But he was here now because of her. A riot of emotions blossomed inside her, crowding out the guilt. His gaze was laser sharp and full of heat, and when he spoke next he almost sounded angry.

"You've turned my world upside down, you know that?"

"Good. I think your world needs some rocking." Her voice was just as hoarse as his. Then she took his hand, the one resting on her arm and deliberately moved it to cover her breast. "*Tonight*," she added, pressing his palm to her.

For the longest time they sat frozen, gazes tangled while the projection light flickered over their faces, telling a different story from the one that reeled out in the dark tense intimacy between them. Finally, his fingers pressed against her flesh—molding, squeezing, rubbing and rolling, until she melted into him. Felicity moaned, and he drank it down in a bruising kiss that promised much more than the spar and thrust of his tongue. Why, oh why, had she waited so long to take the initiative? They fumbled with buttons and zippers in the dark, and gasped for breath, and things became wet...soft... hard...harder.

And Lise was right about the black lace...

They must have parted, left the backseat and stumbled drunk with whipped-up need into the front. They must have buckled up the seatbelts and driven out of the lot onto the main street. Little tidbits of nonsense must have been exchanged during the trip back to her place. Who knew? Who cared? All she was certain of, as she climbed the stairs up to her flat, was that tonight dreams would come true.

Black and lacey. That's what Daniel was remembering now as he followed the delectable swing of Felicity's jean-clad ass up the stairs. The light from the movie screen shining through the fogged up windows of his truck, the scents of leather, perfume and musky arousal saturating the damn air. The feel of her warm, slightly shivering body underneath his fingers as he pulled up her top to expose *black lace.* Then the lace was pushed aside to reveal...perfection. Full, creamy, honey-tinted flesh, tipped with erect dusky temptation.

Daniel's mouth dried up, but he fought to hold onto his sanity, going over the words he'd rehearsed in his mind on the long drive over here. The words he had to say—should have said before. He only now understood the extent of his cowardice, and his feelings for Felicity. He'd been kidding himself, thinking she was just some female he only wanted to do. If she had been, the possibility of losing her wouldn't be twisting this rusty blade of fear in his gut.

They walked down the narrow hall, each footfall playing chance with creaky floorboards as their muted shadows undulated along the uneven walls in a slightly erotic dance. And the closer they got to her flat, the deeper their desire grew into a rich stew of anticipation and anxiety.

Felicity unlocked the door, trying to control the tremors that raced through her limbs. Then they were standing inside the small vestibule, facing each other, with too much to say and not enough words.

"So do you want to ravish me here or in the bedroom?" she joked, ready to snap into a million tiny pieces as Daniel continued his inscrutable totem routine. She was betting his expression wasn't the only thing stiff on him.

His mouth slanted into a smile, her heart tilted along with it and she reached out to him. Daniel captured her hand, softly kissing the palm.

"There's some things we should talk about first," he said, a bit hesitantly.

She understood. The whole birth-control thing was always a bit awkward. She started to confirm things were taken care of on her end, when he repeated himself. Then he averted his gaze as he took a step away from her.

His withdrawal and the peculiar note in his voice made her ease back against the door, dread seeping into her belly. The look in his eyes chilled her even more. *Oh shit.*

A thousand penicillin-related things crossed her mind. "Okay." Felicity cleared her throat and crossed her arms, wedging stiff fingers beneath her underarms. "So talk."

Daniel raked both hands through his hair, a ruddy wash of color tinting his face. "I don't know how to say this—" he broke off.

Oh shit. Oh shit. Oh shit. "Just tell me," she said; then her nerves stretched to breaking when he still didn't say anything. "Say it!"

"I have to evict you."

"Wait— *What?*" She pressed a fist to her stomach.

Daniel swore. "I didn't mean for it to come out like that—"

"I don't understand..."

He dragged his hand through his hair again. "It's not just you. All the tenants have to go. That was the original plan when I bought this place. Then things got out of hand..." His gaze focused on her mouth, making clear exactly what had gotten out of hand.

"I delayed it as long as I could, even toyed with the idea of changing my plans. But things have to go ahead." He reached out, she flinched and his color deepened. "Notices will be in the mailboxes by the end of the week. I just wanted to tell you myself."

"Why? So you could rub in the humiliation personally, in case you missed a spot?"

"No!"

She turned to fumble with the lock. "You can consider me told."

Daniel's hand closed over hers; the strength of his touch, the heat of his body, sucked the anger away. "I didn't mean to hurt you." His voice was barely more than a whisper stirring soft against her ear. "I'm sorry." His voice went lower and she felt his lips press gently to her hair. Then he took hold of her shoulders and eased her around. "This is business. If it were up to me, I'd be locking you up in here, not asking you to leave." He cradled her head in his hands, holding her gaze. "Hell, I'd never let you go," he ground out.

Felicity searched Daniel's expression. She must have been blind. Her mind playing stupid tricks on her. There was no softness here. Just lust. Her pain mutated into anger as she cursed herself a fool for wanting to believe in more.

"Don't flatter yourself. How can you let me go, when you never had me?"

Releasing her, he held her gaze, then showed her for the liar she was as he dipped his head slowly, giving her ample opportunity to escape...*if she wanted to.*

His mouth brushed hers in the merest caress. "I want you."

This must be what drowning feels like. It was so much harder to struggle than to just give in. And she was drowning— in the overwhelming need to be closer to him. Felicity twisted her head aside, eyes clenched tight as if not seeing him would make him, this moment, less real.

"That's too bad, because I don't want you," she choked out.

"Is that why you're rubbing up against me like you can't wait to have it?" he murmured, rolling his hips until she gasped in pleasure.

His soft laughter made her curdle with shame of her weakness and his knowledge of it.

She jerked back, wanting to remove the self-satisfaction from his face. "Bastard."

He caught her hand on the upswing, pressing the captured wrist against the door as he crowded her against the hard wood, sliding a thigh between her legs. Unable to stop the impulse, she rocked against his leg, feeling herself grow wetter. Then Daniel shifted slightly, pushing her up more fully against his erection and she heard herself moan like some animal in heat.

"Next time you call me a bastard, say it like you mean it," he said hoarsely before he sealed his mouth to hers. She met him measure for measure, back arched, spinning out of control and needing much more than this.

"Felicity, do you know what you do to me?" he rasped, releasing her wrist before he buried his hands in her hair again, angling her head as he deepened the kiss. One hand swept down, fingernail scraping across a stiff aching nipple and she whimpered into his mouth as he cupped her. Touched and teased her. Stroking and squeezing. She started begging then, and he shushed her gently, trailing hot wet kisses and tiny love bites down her neck.

His lips blazed a path down over the curve of her breasts until his eager mouth fastened onto a hapless nipple through her cotton tank top and started sucking. *Hard.* Felicity's legs gave out and she settled on his thigh, riding him for all she was worth, until sensation shot through her and she cried out.

Daniel raised his head, the curtain of his sun-bleached hair only partially concealing his stark expression. A vein pulsed at his brow, keeping time with her racing heart as their ragged breaths mingled.

The lazy turns of the ceiling fan behind him teased at her unfocused gaze, pulling Felicity back to the reality of the situation. She was pressed up against the front door, her skin a patchwork of cooling brands from his hot kisses, her hips still gyrating with the echoes of pleasure and practically begging him to do her on the spot.

Dazed, she watched as he lowered his mouth towards hers again. More of his kisses and she'd be lost, letting him do what her body craved most. But as his tongue licked against her parted lips, she tasted bitterness on her own and something withered deep down inside her. She didn't want to be fucked. She wanted to be loved. With one last desperate cry, Felicity shoved him away.

"I want you to leave." The words tumbled from her broken, the way she felt. The way her dreams felt. She shoved at him again, feeling trapped by his warmth, by the need that still ran hot in her veins for him. When he eased away, she brushed past him and stumbled across the room. She barely heard the door snap shut behind him.

Felicity threw herself down on the unmade bed, hugging a pillow tightly to her chest as great, heaving sobs wracked through her. In time her tears dried, dwindling to soft hiccups and she sat up, scrubbing at her face with the heels of her palms as she tried to organize her thoughts on what had to be done. Should be easy enough, it was a routine she had down cold by now. Seemed she was always starting all over again with relationships, jobs, homes.

But this place had seemed different from the beginning. She'd known right away when she saw the dormer windows of this bedroom, that this was part of her fairytale—the little girl's room in the turret. This *was* her home. She'd chosen it. Now he'd taken that away from her, and so much more.

She couldn't be as detached as Daniel. It was just business he'd said. But it felt like betrayal.

Chapter Nine

Wincing at the shrill chirps of early-worm eaters, Felicity squinted up at a perfect summer sky, where wispy clouds traced curlicue patterns for a playful eye. Her? She'd just as soon poke that playful eye out with a sharp stick.

She went down the verandah stairs, sliding on sunglasses against the piss-yellow sun that shone so spitefully bright. Felicity didn't want to go to work today, didn't want to do anything except feel sorry for herself.

Sorry fact number one: The chances of finding an affordable rental that wasn't located at the corner of Tight Butt and Hard Poke were slim to none, judging by the classifieds she'd made her torturous way through over the last two days.

Sorry fact number two: She had no savings—so no first and last month's rent or moving costs.

Sorry fact number three—

The powerful rumble of an approaching car broke into her miserable musings and she whipped around, heart thudding. Her pulse settled when she saw a low-slung sports car instead of the big black truck she both feared and hoped for.

But as the silver Porsche cruised by, Felicity caught a glimpse of the driver, and if she'd been married to a man named Lot the effect couldn't have been more pronounced. She stood rooted on the spot, a pillar of dread, as the car pulled up to the curb. Seconds later Daniel exited.

Vanessa Jaye

Except this was a Daniel she hadn't seen before. He wore a snowy white shirt, dark tie and a charcoal-colored suit that fit his body with tailored elegance. His ponytail was more severely drawn back, matching his somber expression and adding an edge to his businesslike image.

Her hungry gaze roamed over him. There were new lines etched on either side of his mouth and smudges under his eyes that turned them to the darkest green. She felt a twinge of yearning that she quickly thwacked with self-disgust. *Hello? Bad-guy, remember?*

Daniel approached slowly. "You haven't returned my phone calls."

"We have nothing more to discuss."

"I owe you an apology."

"Accepted." Felicity nodded and attempted to walk around him, but he placed his hand lightly on her arm, halting her. She flinched and he let go.

"Do you? I can't blame you if don't. You were right, I'm an asshole and any other name in the book you want to call me."

Just what she always wanted: a Noble Daniel action figure. Felicity decided to end this before he got to the rending-of-garments stage.

"Look, what's done is done. Let's just leave it at that."

He shifted closer. "And what if I don't want to leave it, what we had?"

A part of her wrapped itself around his words, but the other part cringed at the memory of every single kiss and touch that had peeled away layer after layer of her self, until there was nothing left but the realization that he'd gotten past all her defenses.

Throat working, a continuous swallow of endless pain, she choked out, "I trusted you."

He winced, but he tipped her chin up, removing her sunglasses with his other hand at the same time. "I didn't want

102

to hurt you," he said in a hoarse whisper. "There just never seemed to be a good time to tell you about my plans."

"And what if we'd slept together, Daniel, when would have been a good time then?"

His expression said it all; she stepped back.

"That's what I thought. Could you move out of my way—"

"Okay, I already said I was a jerk." He grasped her arm again. "But I never hid the fact that I wanted you, Felicity," he went on in a low whispered rush. "Like I've never wanted another woman. It overrode my better judgment and complicated things. I'm sorry for that. But I'm not sorry for wanting to be with you."

She struggled for breath as all her senses were hijacked by the heat of his gaze, the possession in his touch. "What you want? Well it's not all about you, Daniel." She yanked her arm away. Hate spurted up and so did the need to hurt him, make him pay. For his wanting and making her want in return. For making her *believe*.

"I'm fighting this." The words popped out of her mouth, but the minute they did a sense of power surged through her. "I'm fighting you. I'm not moving."

"Don't be stupid—"

"I am not *stupid*! Don't call me that," she shouted. "I may have been a fool..." She trailed off, because she still was. Because it was unbearable to look at him, at that mouth and know the devastating pleasure it could bring. At his eyes and remember how it felt to lose herself in their warmth. Those eyes were cold now.

"You can't win," he said, his voice shards of ice.

"Just watch me."

Daniel straightened his tie, there was a flash of emotion in his gaze that could have been sadness. Most likely it was pity, because he said without a hint of his earlier softness, "The Notice of Termination will be in your mailbox tomorrow." He handed back her glasses.

"Bastard."

He quirked a brow and shook a finger at her. "You know, I think you're trying to tell me something." He turned abruptly and strode back to the Porsche. "You have sixty days to vacate the premises, Felicity."

"Don't count on me going anywhere."

"Under other circumstances, those words would be music to my ears." His grin was hard, his gaze burning, stripping her naked where she stood. Felicity crossed her arms around herself and his mask fell back in place.

"Sixty days," he repeated and slid behind the wheel.

Moments later the car tore down the street, leaving her even more ticked—*he gets the last word and the grand exit in the friggin' Porsche? Frug!*

℘

She'd been rash. She squirmed with the memory now. It was a small wonder Daniel hadn't laughed in her face when she'd issued her challenge. Now, with several minutes until the end of her break, Felicity perched on the freezer in the back change room, nibbling on a hangnail as she waited for Cheryl.

A couple of hours of trampling across sticky gray carpeting, serving beers to men with equally sticky fingers, had a way of focusing this girl's mind. She needed money, lots of it and fast. So she'd come up with a plan, because desperate times called for desperate measures, right? She squealed when the door suddenly opened.

"Well the hell with you too, chickee," Cheryl said, walking over to the vanity.

Felicity let out a little nervous laugh. "Sorry, I was thinking."

"Sounds painful." Cheryl's wry gaze met hers in the mirror.

There was no time like the present. Felicity braced herself, squeezing her eyes shut. "Cheryl, I want to strip" is what she meant to say. What actually came out sounded like, "*Shariwannastrip*", on helium.

"You want to share what?" Cheryl froze mid-lip gloss application.

"I. Want. To. Strip."

"That's what I thought you said. Are you out of your fool mind?" Cheryl spun round, arms akimbo and looking magnificent in her electric blue lingerie set.

"No you don't want to strip. Get up off of that freezer right now—the cold must be traveling up your butt and giving you a brain cramp."

"I'm serious."

"Girl, I will use your head like it's a tambourine and I just found salvation. Hopefully knock some sense into you."

Felicity jutted her chin out.

Cheryl threw up her arms. "Then strip at home before you take a shower. Or strip the sheets off your bed. But," she pointed at Felicity, "if I ever see you up on that stage? The only thing that's gonna be stripping, is skin offa your backside."

"Is it so bad then?" she asked weakly.

Cheryl sighed and crossed the room. "Move over." When Felicity shifted, she climbed up beside her.

"What's the story?"

Felicity told her.

"That bastard!" Then as she stared into Felicity's eyes, her expression softened. "You okay?"

"Getting there, but that's why I want to try dancing. I need the cash."

"Have you thought about a roommate?"

Felicity thought about her past adventures in flat sharing. The constant guarding against a slip-up that would betray her. The inevitably pitying looks, and whispered ridicule, her stomach cramped. Not to mention the lack of privacy, and let's not forget the deadbeats who were always late with their half of the rent. Who mooched your food and borrowed your clothes, returning them weeks later with mysterious stains. Forget it.

"I don't want a roommate," she said firmly. "Now, c'mon, tell me what I may be getting myself into."

"It's different things to different people, Fil." Cheryl shrugged. "Some girls get sidetracked. Know what I'm saying?"

She nodded. In the short time she'd worked at the club, she'd seen girls come and go. For some The Uptown was just a pit stop on a downward spiral into their own personal hell. She swallowed, rubbing suddenly damp palms on her thigh.

"Getting up on that stage, particularly the first time in front of all those strange men... Do you really think you can do it?"

She'd been asking herself the same question for the last two hours as she worked her tables. Normally Felicity focused on taking orders, and paying close attention to the different-colored bills and different-sized coins as she made change. But for once she noticed how all those strange men's expressions were carefully neutral, while their eyes told the truth. Eyes that touched and probed and fondled.

Pushing aside her unease she countered, "How do you do it?"

"For the same reason you want to—money. I make a nice chunk of cheese doing this and I figure I got a couple more good years left before my titties droop so bad I can tweak my nipples between my toes. Then it's retirement time."

She eyed Cheryl's small, firm breasts—which seemed to be holding up the two flimsy scraps of blue satin, rather than the other way around.

"Only way you're going to be doing that type of tweaking, is if you're double jointed."

Cheryl waggled her eyebrows.

"Get out!" Felicity gave her a playful push. But she wasn't entirely sure her friend was joking. She'd seen her act.

Cheryl hopped down from her perch. "Think about your decision long and hard. And then think some more. Just remember I'm a feature dancer. I do my routine and that's all I do to pay the rent. Those other girls—and by 'other' I mean 'you', if you're serious about this—make most of their money from private dances...and sometimes other things. Think you can handle that, Miss I-Wanna-Be-A-Strippa?" Cheryl winked before she sashayed back to the vanity and resumed touching-up her makeup.

As Felicity left the change area, feeling much worse after their talk, she swore she heard a low-keyed "fool" muttered at her back.

℘

"That bastard!"

Three for three.

Lise was pure outrage, her green eyes snapping with anger. "Well you can't let him get away with this."

Felicity stopped pushing the cart. They were shopping for groceries at a Loblaws superstore—another one of Lise's exercises. Normally, Felicity went to one of the small greengrocers along St. Clair Ave., where she could quickly walk the short aisles and pick out her needs by sight. This place was something else. The million different signs and endless shelves of products gave her a pounding headache, never mind the way her feet still ached from her shift. But Lise's outburst brought a smile to her mouth.

"Well, there's not much I can do, is there?" Felicity picked a box off the shelf, making only a halfhearted attempt to sound out the brand name in her head.

"But he toyed with your affections!" Lise pointed out in a tight voice.

She put the box back, thank God for logos and pictures. "I doubt that's covered under the Landlord Tenant Act."

"Then we'll just have to find something that is."

"Lise, I really appreciate you being ticked off on my behalf," she mustered up a smile, "but he's right, I won't win."

"So this is your response, giving up without trying?"

"I'm not a quitter. You know that," Felicity said quietly, on the defense.

"I do know." Lise gave her hand on the cart a little squeeze. "That's why you should fight this. At the very least it could buy you some time. You did say you needed to save more for moving..." Lise said all innocence.

She *could* use more time to save.

"And in the meantime you can make his life sheer unadulterated misery. I'll ask one of my husband's associates—"

"Wait! I can't afford a lawyer."

"No, no." Lise waved her protests away blithely. "We're just going to get some tips on how to make this joker really hurt." Her eyes glinted with determination. A bit of it rubbed off on Felicity.

"Yeah, make the joker pay." She held out her hand. "Let's do it!"

Lise ignored the hand and wrapped her in a hug. Felicity felt warmth blossom deep inside her. The last time someone had hugged her with any affection was...*Daniel.* Her heart lurched to a stop and she squeezed the other woman tight, then embarrassed, she released her and laughed to cover up her awkwardness.

"I think you're looking forward to this more than me," she said, noting the pleased flush on her tutor's face.

"Sweetheart, I live for these battles of the sexes."

Things happened pretty quickly after that, with Lise directing the show. Felicity spent a frustrating afternoon down at City Hall, picking up the proper forms. Fortunately, an accommodating clerk helped her with the paperwork, so she didn't have to bother Lise with it. Unfortunately the plan to organize a tenant's association never got off the ground.

Moog was going on tour with his band, so he'd been ready to give up his lease anyway. Mrs. Rogers, the cat woman from downstairs, was resigned to move in with her sister. And the immigrant couple upstairs were from a place where troublemakers "disappeared" in the middle of the night. So no help there.

Felicity nibbled on a cuticle as she peered out the window checking for Stuart's SUV. She was thinking about the difference a month and a half made. Had she actually contemplated stripping? And here she was still taking Daniel on in a battle he'd ultimately win. But she was buying time. And today she'd buy a little more with a bit of mischief her partner-in-crime had cooked up.

A rare-for-her-lately smile tugged at her mouth, but it was tinged with sadness. It wasn't all fun and games for Lise. There were too many times Felicity had looked up to see sympathy in her tutor's gaze—she *knew* Felicity still hurt.

ଞ

Daniel sat on one of the raised concrete vents that lined Queen Street, separating the green space of Nathan Phillip Square from the sidewalk. He placed his can of pop down beside him as he bit into one of the juicy kielbasas he and Rob had just bought from the roadside van. His partner was making similar short work of his own sausage.

"Cheers." Rob held up his coke. "Here's to renovations starting next month."

Daniel tapped his can against Rob's. "Don't go celebrating just yet. Something tells me my tenant from hell isn't quite finished roasting our nuts."

"Chestnuts roasting on an open fire—" Rob started warbling.

"Quit it." Daniel put the can down beside him on the ledge and double-checked that his tie was tucked in. Last thing he needed was to show up at the office with grease spots on him.

"Whatever you say, Scrooge. The point I was trying to make is, it's the end of the line." Rob jerked his thumb towards the famous curved towers of City Hall behind them. "Once you give her the copies of the Application to Terminate and the Notice of Hearing, badda-bing, badda-boom. Game over."

"Then badda-bing, badda-boom, she files another dispute and this little war continues." Daniel looked down at the meat in the bun he held, his appetite fast disappearing. How the hell had it come to this?

Two months ago he was spending at least two evenings a week on Felicity's flea-bitten couch, with her snuggled up against him while they watched TV. Then there was the impromptu trip to the zoo because neither of them had been since they were kids; he smiled remembering their shared laughter when she'd had to flee one of the suddenly amorous peacocks that roamed the grounds.

And what about the Saturday she'd dragged him to the mall to shop for a new pair of jeans to replace the ones that the latex paint hadn't come out of after all? Normally he would've opted for a root canal before he'd go shopping with a woman. *Normally.* His smile faded.

Nothing had been normal when he'd been with Felicity. He

could see that now. Daniel tore a chunk of bun off and threw it at a group of nearby pigeons.

"Hey, don't go feeding the vermin. They're all going to come over here."

"I bought *you* lunch, didn't I? But now that you mention it, you are sitting a little too close."

"Blow me."

"Bite me."

Rob belched. "Sorry." He took a long, noisy swallow of his pop. "Look, even if Felicity disputes this, it's still the end of the road. Man, I don't even know how it got this far, but she has no more cards to play. End of the month she's out on her keister."

"You know, you don't have to sound so goddamn happy about it." Daniel let the reins he'd been clenching so tightly slide a bit.

"That's right, buddy," Rob said real quiet. His dark eyes narrowed and bored into Daniel as he wiped at his mouth with a napkin. "I was wondering when you'd get around to placing some blame."

The thunderous rumble of a passing streetcar complimented the rage buzzing in Daniel's head. Hell yeah, he so wanted to dump a whole shitload of blame on Rob. Instead he looked around for a nearby garbage can and lobed in the remains of his meal. He took another minute to steady his breath. Finally he said, "Sorry, guy."

"Accepted."

Silence, deeper than the sounds of the city, enveloped them.

Daniel picked up his pop, but he didn't drink. "You're right. I want to blame anyone else for my fuck-up." He still wasn't looking at Rob, so it was easy to add, "I think I lost something special."

"You can try explaining to her again."

Daniel laughed mirthlessly. "Yeah, right. You think she wants to listen to me after all this?"

"You could always lay siege."

"What?" Frowning, he turned to Rob.

"Lay siege. You know, all that old-fashioned crap. Chicks just eat that stuff up, man. Wear her down. Do the flowers, the chocolate, the *mea culpa* thing—you know, all that shit."

Once again he had to wonder at his friend's apparent success with the opposite sex. "That's your advice? Lay siege—"

"*Gesundheit.*"

"—and all that shit?"

"And all that shit." Rob nodded emphatically with each word, a smile flashing from the framework of his goatee. Then his expression froze and he plucked the can out of Daniel's hand. "No time like the present." He jerked his chin; Daniel's gaze followed.

Felicity. Emotion fisted into his chest. He watched sunlight slide in a silky sheen over her chestnut hair, then the familiar swing of her hips as she walked to the lunch van, and the fist turned into a blade of pleasure that sliced through him.

He wasn't aware of standing, only knew he was drawn to her like a moth to an inferno.

"Felicity," he said when he was close enough to touch her.

She spun round, eyes wide in a blanched face. *And she melted.* For one precious moment he saw her gaze soften and her lips part. For one hellish hanging-on-a-prayer second her body swayed towards him. Then she recalled what he'd done and who he was.

"What do you want?" she snapped. "Or did I save you a trip to drop-off the latest round of paperwork?" Her mouth twisted with an edge of bitterness he'd never seen before.

"It didn't have to go this way, Felicity."

"So, it's my fault you're an asshole?"

"Look, we've already established I'm the bad guy here, I'll get out my black cape and you can nail a cross to your door."

"There's just one problem with that." She assumed a look of mock horror. "Oopsie. I don't have a door. At least I won't if you have anything to do with it."

"Felicity, there are other apartments."

"But that was—is my home, Daniel. *My home.* You ruined everything," she said in a broken whisper that almost broke him.

Then it clicked, really clicked. All her little comments about the neighborhood, and her pleasure and pride in decorating the tiny flat came back to him.

He understood about having something to call your own. About putting your heart, sweat and dreams into it, and having someone want to take that away. Like his father wanted to do to him. Like he'd done to Felicity.

Chapter Ten

"Excuse me, folks, what can I do you for?" The lunch van guy stuck his head out the service window, intruding on their brittle little drama.

Hanging onto the edges of herself like they were parts of a too tight garment, Felicity ordered fries and a couple of colas.

When Daniel didn't move, she turned on him. "Is there something else?"

His lips thinned, but he didn't say anything, just reached into the inside pocket of his suit and pulled out a thick white envelope that he passed to her.

She'd called it, hadn't she? Had she really been hoping there was another reason he'd approached her? She pushed aside her pathetic disappointment and took the envelope from him.

Felicity stepped back, a clear signal for him to leave, instead she was the one brought up short as she bumped into another body. She turned to apologize, but the words died on her lips.

"Ma," she croaked in surprise.

"Felicity. I thought it was you, but I wasn't sure. I—we," her mother glanced behind her, "haven't seen you in so long."

She followed her mother's gaze to the man standing several feet away. His open windbreaker emphasized the broad shoulders and barrel chest that demanded obedience. His iron gray hair, still in the same old military buzz, was as uncompromising as his demeanor. *Him.* Bitterness welled up unchecked.

"Don't," her mother said in the same whispery voice that used to tell bedtime stories and promised things would get better, until Felicity was old enough to recognize the fairytales and promises were one and the same. *Lies.* Only she hadn't truly learned that lesson. If she had, she'd never have believed in Daniel.

She turned away but Daniel was still standing there, open curiosity on his face, until his eyes met hers, that is. Then the change in that deep green gaze caused her heartbeat to machine gun and her stomach to roll. She quickly looked back at her ma, who rushed on in a torrent of words.

"Your da's been at it again with the neighbor about the fence. He's come down here to have a word with our city councilor." Her ma tittered jerkily, playing with the top button of the faded yellow cardigan she wore over a neatly pressed blouse and pleated skirt.

"I wish he wouldn't fuss so. Such a fuss over nothing." She colored, shooting a guilty look at her husband who'd started towards them. Hurriedly she asked, "So how are you then, Felicity?"

"I'm fine." She forced a smile.

"You could always come back. You know, back to the house."

How was this for irony? She was being forced to leave the home she loved, and invited back to one she loathed. "I don't think that would be such a good idea, Ma."

"I know you and your da have had your differences, but he only wanted what was best for you. You have to understand that Les was disappointed in your behavior."

"It wasn't my behavior, it was me."

"Well, if you'd been a bit calmer, acted more ladylike, things would've been just fine."

Her mother had never understood.

"Well, look where I have to come to lay eyes on me own flesh and blood." There was no joy in her da's greeting, but Felicity tried to keep up appearances.

"Hi, Daddy."

"'Hi Daddy, Hi Mummy', now is it? You have a funny way of acknowledging your parents." Leslie Cameron looked her up and down. "When was the last time you darkened our doorstep, or called to see how we were getting along? As a good daughter would see fit to do."

"I call," Felicity began heatedly. "I called…"

The last time she'd called her parents had been months ago.

"Your ma and me know just when you last condescended to call. Seems as if you only do so when you've gotten yourself in a spot of trouble."

"I was not in trouble."

"Janice said you wanted to come home."

"I didn't—"

"Are you calling your ma a liar?" he snapped.

"I didn't say that either! You're putting words into my mouth."

"Well someone has to put them there, seeing as there's nothing in your noggin."

"Felicity?" Daniel stepped closer. Of course, she'd been aware of him all along, but now she felt protected by his solid presence pressing lightly against her back and the quiet comfort in the way he said her name.

"Hi, I'm Daniel Mackenzie."

His outstretched hand was ignored by her father. "Have a new one already, eh? What happened to that Stuart fella?"

"I'm Felicity's landlord." There was an edge to Daniel's voice that she barely caught as she swallowed a hysterical bubble of laughter. He said it like it meant something, when it meant jack-all.

"Landlord, is that right? Well so was her last one, in a manner of speaking." Leslie Cameron dismissed Daniel as he addressed her. "Why don't you do the decent thing for a change? Empty-headed or not, you've got your mother's looks; at least get a ring on that finger instead of whoring around. Even your ma was smart enough for that."

Janice Cameron's face blanched and humiliation washed over Felicity for both of them, but she felt Daniel leaning into her, antagonism practically vibrating off him. She turned, placing a hand against him. "Daniel—"

"Perhaps I didn't make myself clear. Your daughter is my tenant. What gives you the right—"

"Daniel, please," she begged.

"What gives me the right?" Leslie Cameron raised his voice and Felicity shrunk miserably against Daniel, aware of heads turning. "I'm her goddamn father." Her dad jabbed a thumb into his own chest. "That's what gives me the bloody right. And don't think that crawling up between her legs gives you the right to start questioning me!"

Felicity shriveled at the attack, clapping her hands over her ears. Not wanting to hear anymore. Not wanting to hear it again. "Stop it! Stop it!"

Her breath came in heaving wracks as she pressed back, but Daniel's presence was now a hindrance rather than a comfort. She had to get away. "I gotta go," she hiccupped, turning away with stumbling feet.

"Be off with you then, you never want to hear me talk, that's why you are where you are," her da yelled after her.

Chilled to the heart and feeling like she would shatter under the hurt, she stopped and turned to face him.

"No, Daddy, I heard every word you said. That's why I'm where I am." Felicity spoke till the pain stole away her voice. She held his gaze until he made a gesture of disgust and stalked off.

She watched them go, her ma's last glance a hook to the gut that tore and tore, unreeling years of hurt. She was barely aware of Daniel's approach.

"I'm sorry."

"So you said." Felicity transferred her stare to him, feeling dead inside. Feeling small and alone.

His expression tightened. She knew she was being unfair. He'd tried sticking up for her, which was more than her ma had ever done.

"I just want to go home," she said, looking around for Stuart, then she blinked as her vision blurred, and just kept right on blinking. When Daniel's arms came around her, every bone in her body locked in place, but as she stared stone-faced at the buttons on his shirt, he weaved his fingers through her hair, easing her head to his chest and he held her. That's all, but it was everything.

She refused to cry. She wouldn't cry.

She wrapped her arms around his waist and let the steady beat of his heart anchor her.

Her mind was a void, except for the measured counting of each breath she took as she soaked in his scent and wallowed in his strength. Allowed herself to lean on someone else, just for a little while...

Daniel held her, or more accurately, held on, since everything else seemed to tip further out of whack. He was pissed and desperate, sad, happy and scared shitless, all at the same time. Buried under an avalanche of emotions.

He was used to losing himself in his work, whether it was poring over contracts or blueprints, they were things he could analyze and control. Relationships were messy and uncertain, always demanding that you give more. And what if all you had to give was never good enough?

Daniel felt Felicity tense, as if she'd read his mind, and panic flashed in him. What could he say to make her stay? He opened his mouth; nothing came out.

"Stuart." She pushed away from him.

"Stuart?" he repeated stupidly.

"He drove me down here to file the—" She broke off. "Oh, and my order is ready."

Daniel saw the fry guy waving at them from the window of the lunch truck, and then he scanned the crowd around them. Rob gave him a double thumbs up, but it wasn't Rob his gaze settled on. It was the turd who'd just walked past where Rob was sitting. Stuart strutted down the street with his shirt opened and his pants practically falling off. The guy looked like a tool. A tool with killer abs.

"That didn't take long," Daniel said, jealously strangling his voice as he locked eyes with tool boy.

"No it didn't. The food's probably cold by now," she said, totally oblivious. "Listen, thanks for just now."

Daniel stretched his lips into a tiny closemouthed smile and nodded. "No problem."

He watched her walk away. Stuart greeted her by slinging an arm around her shoulder; then the turd threw a smirk in his direction.

Daniel was grinding his teeth so hard, sparks should have flown out his nostrils and set his tie on fire. He headed over to Rob, who was making *what-happened* gestures.

Damned if he knew.

Rob shook his head in bewilderment. "Dude?"

"That was her ex. They have a history together."

"So? You guys have history too."

"Not the type of history you're thinking of."

There was a long enlightening pause.

"Dude," Rob said again, but this time he made it sound like a eulogy to Daniel's manhood.

Daniel pursed his mouth and looked away from the pity in his friend's eyes towards the towers that loomed in front of him. He frowned. Obtaining building permits was part and parcel of doing business, but City Hall bureaucracy had taken on a new painful dimension in this battle with Felicity—

She'd said something about Stuart driving her down here to file...

"Rob?"

"Yeah."

"How are your nuts feeling?" Daniel pushed his jacket back, resting hands on hips as he continued to stare at the municipal building.

Rob slowly stood and turned towards the parenthetical towers. He swore softly. "I'd say they were feeling pretty toasty right now. What do you think she did?"

Daniel could feel a muscle ticking in his clenched jaw. "Let's go back inside and ask, shall we?"

ℰℭ

He was playing with her toes. Not a good sign if she was reading her signs correctly. The foot rub was as good as Felicity remembered, but she didn't want to sample any other tricks Stuart had up his sleeve. Or in this case, down his pants.

"Stu, what are you doing?" She moved her leg away.

"What do you think I'm doing?"

"Getting ready to leave?" She gathered the CDs they'd been listening to and climbed off the bed. Stuart could be a good friend for hanging out—and this was one day she needed a friend; the nightmare at City Hall still had her head throbbing— but he made a sucky boyfriend. She wasn't even tempted to play footsies, spread-the-kneesies then bump-the-uglies with him.

Placing the stack of discs on the CD player, Felicity shut the music off. "It's time to leave, Stu."

She walked out of the room, ignoring his dramatic begging with her own bit of dramatic eye-rolling. When he finally came out of the bedroom, Felicity had the apartment door open.

He stopped in front of her, placing a hand on either side of her head as he leaned in. "I wish things were different between us," he grumbled, his voice at a seductive pitch. Then he drew out the big guns and gazed *soulfully* into her eyes.

Felicity suppressed the spurt of laughter. He was *sooo* predictable. "Horizontally different?" she teased.

"How about a goodbye kiss then?"

"No."

"Aw, c'mon." He pressed a series of soft kisses along her jaw when she averted her face. "Just one," he wheedled.

Felicity sighed, "Fine." She closed her eyes and puckered up. Making it clear just how totally unenthusiastic she was.

Stuart went in for the gold. Nibbles, licks, the works.

Through it all she felt like an old beater jacked-up on the front lawn—*unmoved.*

When his hand closed around her breast, she'd had enough. "No, stop." She pushed at him. "Stuart, stop it!"

Suddenly Stuart wasn't there. He was sprawled on the floor, halfway across the room.

Daniel stood between them.

"What the hell are you doing, man?" Stuart jumped back to his feet.

"Looks to me like Felicity didn't enjoy being mauled," Daniel pointed out reasonably. When what he *reasonably* wanted to do, was shove Stuart's head so far up his ass the next time he gargled he'd give himself a colonic.

"Who gives a shit what it looks like to you? What do you know? Fil and I go back years. We fight, she cools off, then I—"

Daniel brought his face within inches of Stuart's. "Then you'll stay the fuck away from her."

Felicity's ex squinted up at him, then looked at her. Daniel shifted, a wave of red hot emotion swelling up inside of him. He didn't want this asshole looking at her or touching her. When Stuart's narrowed gaze zeroed in on him again, Daniel could practically see the little twerp's mind doing its tiny rotations.

"*Oooh*, I get it. You think her crying on your shoulder earlier, downtown, actually meant something." Stuart shook his head, biting down on his bottom lip as malicious pity shone from his eyes.

The fog cleared from Daniel's brain. What did he know about them? Felicity didn't talk much about her ex. Hell, she didn't talk much about herself period, and he'd accepted her reticence, because it had kept the distance between them.

Feeling like he had Chuppa-Chup stamped on his forehead, Daniel straightened and, because he couldn't help it, looked over his shoulder at Felicity.

Her eyes widened in a deathly pale face. "Stuart, no!"

The sucker punch connected, but that was the last advantage——including the advantage of breathing——that the little prick was going to have for a long time.

He aimed for those pretty-boy abs; Stuart doubled over, but Daniel caught him before he crumpled completely to the ground.

He slammed him up against the wall. "Get the fuck off of my property, before I throw you off."

The fact that it was impossible for Stuart to move, the way Daniel had him pinned to the wall with no inclination to let go, was beside the point. He thought he heard other voices but ignored them as he studied buddy-boy's face, which was a deeply satisfying shade of red.

"Hey, Dan, I believe this is my dance." Rob wedged his shoulder between them, then forced Daniel back with a none-too gentle push.

"What the f—"

His partner gave him a deadeye stare. He knew Rob had just stopped him from doing something reckless, but he wasn't going to thank him for it.

"Okay, you sorry sack of shit." Rob glared at Stuart who was on his hands and knees gasping for breath. "Move your ass out of here." He grasped Stuart under the arms and hauled him to his feet, then let go with a shove that sent the little bastard reeling. Daniel clenched and unclenched his hands; his fingers were missing Stuart's throat.

Rob took the trash out and Daniel was left alone with Felicity. He trained his gaze on her and, if it were possible, she paled even more. His stomach churned, his heartbeat raced and there was a burning behind his eyes.

What if he hadn't insisted on confronting her right away? Rob had tried to talk him out of it, but Daniel would have hitched a cab ride if his partner hadn't given him the lift. She was visibly shivering now and he went to her.

Daniel came to a stop in front of her. His hands cupped her neck, then moved to cradle her face, smearing gentle caresses across her mouth with his thumb. He brushed a tendril of hair away from her face as his expression softened and he pressed a light kiss on her brow. "You okay?"

She could only nod, her eyes drawn to his face, where it had started to swell and discolor. "Oh God," she whispered, and saw a muscle jumped in his jaw.

"I should go after that asshole right now. Look at you, you're trembling." He started to chafe her arms in long strokes,

Vanessa Jaye

moving closer until his body heat overcame her chills. "God knows what he would've done if I hadn't come by."

"What?" Felicity tried to make sense of his words. She was still freaked-out by everything that had just happened, Daniel's sudden appearance, then Stuart throwing that first punch. She shook her head, none of it made sense. Stuart wouldn't risk messing up his pretty face. He was literally a—two-timing—lover, not a fighter. He wasn't violent period.

"Stuart wouldn't hurt me. He's not like that," she said out loud, more to herself than to Daniel.

His hands came up again to frame her face. "You just keep telling yourself that."

"No," she said in a stronger voice, sure at least of this one thing.

"I don't believe this. You're sticking up for the guy?" Daniel's brows lashed together. "He was assaulting you. You told him 'stop', and he didn't."

He was too close. Now that the shock was wearing off, she could smell him, his cologne, his scent. It was in her nostrils, on her skin, coating her tongue. She licked her lips and his eyes followed.

Daniel was motionless, only his eyes were alive and piercing through her. "Was that my mistake?" he asked in a low slow voice and came closer, his hips brushing against hers.

Electric need popped her veins and she started to tremble once more. Fingers shaking as she traced the shape of his mouth, growing mesmerized as those lips parted and he took one of her fingers into his mouth, twirling his tongue around it as he suckled her.

He moved his hips, pressing forward, easing back, again and again in a gentling rhythm. Then the pressure increased, and he was only moving forward, grinding harder and harder. She moaned as he trailed kisses along her jaw then buried his face in her hair, his rapid breath bathing her ear in alternate rushes of warm air. Wanting more she gyrated against him and groaned in frustration when he eased back.

"What hold does this guy have on you? Do you still love him?" He seemed to choke on the words. "Is that why you're protecting him?"

"I'm not protecting him. I told you, he's not like that."

"Really? What's he like then, Felicity? I can be just like him...*for you.*"

She stiffened at the dark edge in his silky whisper. "Daniel?"

He sealed her eyes shut with sweet heat, kissing each lid, before he brought his mouth to her ear again. "It's okay, baby. You can tell me what you like." He rubbed against her again.

"Yes," she hissed, turning to liquid despite the hint of danger in his voice.

"You like that, huh? How about a little rough play—does that turn you on, too?"

It was more than a hint now. Beneath the desire, he *was* angry. She stopped moving. "Daniel, d-don't do this."

He shushed her, pressing his mouth into her hair. "Because if you need a little push over the edge, I'm your man, Felicity." She felt his hot lips against her brow and shivered. "I'm way over the edge now, baby. Come join me."

"No." She turned her face away. "Not like this." *Not without love.* She stilled.

Daniel stopped at once. His promised kiss withheld. For several anguished moments, the only sounds she could hear were his harsh breathing and her own heartbeat racing from the truth.

Finally he stepped back. His mouth curled into a distorted smile. "Now, see how easy that was?"

He left her standing there, stunned.

Wondering how she hadn't realized before now that she'd

fallen in love with the man.

Chapter Eleven

"Turn around again. Slowly this time."

She did.

"Okay, now take off the coat." Cheryl was all business.

Fumbling, Felicity untied her belt, then pulled the trench open with a jerky motion.

"Honey, are you sure you want to do this?"

"I am going to do this."

Cheryl raised a brow, but thankfully refrained from any more lectures.

"Well, don't worry none about the audience. You're looking mighty titty-licious in that outfit. You'll be a sure fire hit."

Felicity made a face. What she looked was trashy and tacky. Her tight white hot pants left half her butt hanging out and nothing to the imagination. It was a wonder a G-string fit under the shorts, but underwear was a safety-must due to the impending danger of zipper nip.

Then there were the matching under-wire bra that pushed her cleavage up so high she could use her nipples as nose plugs, and the white PVC trench coat that had the texture of a giant condom wrapper. She felt like public transportation. Cheap and accessible.

Cheryl was right. She would be a success.

"Okay, now remember, the first song you keep the coat on,

flash some leg, use your slit— I mean the slit in the back of your coat, of course." Cheryl's mouth twitched.

Felicity narrowed her eyes. "Of course."

"Song two, the coat gets ditched, use the pole, bend over a lot and give them a good look at the booty. Then song three is the money shot, get rid of the bra, unzip the shorts, and show them what your mama gave you."

Felicity closed the coat again, wrapping her arms around her waist. "I know what you're doing and it's not going to work. You've never talked about stripping in this way before."

"I can joke about it because I know the reality, hon. But just in case you still had a few illusions left, I'm here to strip them from you. See? That was a joke right there. Actually, more of a pun really."

"You're not making this any easier."

"I don't want to make it easier."

"I need to do this." She took Cheryl's hands in her own. "I love you for what you're doing, but right now I need your support, please."

Cheryl's face remained stubbornly closed, then finally she heaved a sigh. "Somewhere in hell, I just made a front row reservation." She opened her arms and they embraced. When they parted Felicity emitted a suspicious sniffle.

"What?" she asked defensively. "There's something in my eye."

"There's a lie in your eye." Cheryl checked her watch. "Almost show time."

Felicity moved back on wobbly legs, her steps made more uncertain by her four-inch heels.

"Are you sure you can dance in those things?"

She nodded.

A flash of emotion showed in Cheryl's face. "C'mon, let's practice a few moves." She started singing one of the latest dance hits, moving fluidly to the imagined beat. "C'mon, girl, work it! Let's see you shake that money-maker." Her movements turned into an exaggerated version of the *twist*.

A reluctant smile tugged at Felicity's lips as she half-heartedly rotated her hips.

"That's lame, Fil! Lame." Cheryl made a face of disgust. "Do the *running man!*" She demonstrated. Felicity followed her example, but not very well.

"*Crank that Soulja Boy!*" They broke into a fit of giggles when Cheryl's *Superman* sent her flying, unintentionally, across the room.

"*Moonwalk!*" There was hardly any room to, but they tried with hilarious results.

"*The Watusi!*"

"*Raise The Roof!*"

They had *limbo'd* right into a *tango*, when one of the strippers popped her head around the door. "Fil, you're up next, sweetie."

At which point Felicity did the *running man* straight into the bathroom and did the *funky chicken*.

But without the *funky*.

෮෮

The music came on, strobe lights pulsing through the darkness and then, "*Gentlemen, we have a very special treat for you tonight. Please welcome, new to our Uptown stage...Miss Candeee Kane.*"

She didn't look at the audience, just kept her focus on making it up the stairs. Funny how small the stage seemed when you weren't actually standing on it. Now she felt like she was standing in the middle of Carnegie Hall about to play the kazoo.

Felicity closed her eyes and took a deep breath, thankful for the half glass of wine Cheryl had made her drink. She let the music, along with the alcohol, course through her veins and started to move to the rhythm, doing a little shimmy before strutting across the stage.

"You go, girl!"

"Whoo-hoo! Shake it, baby!"

That chorus of familiar voices made her brave a closer look at the front row. A lump leapt up in her throat at the sight of several tables filled with other dancers, and she swallowed the ball of emotion.

She knew just who to thank for masterminding this display of solidarity, sitting smack dab front row center, the loudest of the rowdy group—Cheryl.

Felicity broke into a grin and the shadowy male shapes beyond the lights receded from her consciousness. With her confidence upped a notch, she danced on to the whooped up appreciation of her friends. *Her friends.*

Felicity's grin widened and she spun round to face the mirror, watching herself smoothly untie the belt before she turned again and flashed them. A wave of female catcalls swelled up. Then with a saucy wink, she trailed the coat off her arms and lassoed it off to the side.

A new song came on. The sultry beat and eroticism of the singer's husky voice filling her mind with writhing imagery. And that's when she forgot about her audience.

Forgot about everything except...*Daniel.*

She ran her hands through her hair, letting it cascade through her fingers. She felt free, sexy, powerful. *His.*

Slowly, she slid her hands up her body. *Imagining they were his hands.* She reached for the dance pole and undulated downward, her body demonstrating its yearning. *She wanted him. Right there.* The hard smooth metal felt hot under her palms. *She wanted him. Right now.* And as the lights blazed down on her, she licked at her parched lips. *Almost tasting him; wanting to in the worst way.*

No one heard her moan under the incessant beat. No one felt the energy coursing through her as she dipped and twisted, strutted and posed. Then as she slowly straightened, she caught her reflection in the mirror along the back wall. The woman who faced her was almost unrecognizable.

In the shiny white bra and shorts she looked *begging* hot. Her hair was in a wild tangle, her skin flushed and eyes gleaming. She placed a hand on her belly, slowing her movements as the song wound down...*and her fantasy faded away.*

The music changed again. Felicity turned to face her audience. Her mouth paralyzed into a half-smile as she reached for her bra straps and slowly drew them down her arms.

Up until now she'd blocked out the rest of the room. Tony serving drinks to regulars at the bar, a group of businessmen seated off to the left, and the two tables of frat boys in their team bombers.

Her gaze searched out Cheryl's, and her friend gave her a thumbs up, but Cheryl's face was blank. *She knew.*

Felicity's gaze skidded away as she reached for the bra's closing.

℘

"Here you go, honey; your favorite."

Daniel accepted the large slice of cheesecake from his mother. It almost salvaged the last two hours from being a total write-off. He cast a quick glance at his watch, deciding that he'd give this latest attempt at "quality family time" another forty-five minutes of his life.

Then some instinct caused him to glance across the table,

and he found Deirdra's deep blue eyes studying him as they had done frequently throughout dinner. Was she supposed to be an extra buffer for the evening? She gave him a slow smile and he experienced a twinge of alarm. Or was his mother meddling in his love life? Both she and Deirdra should know better.

When it came to his personal life, he made the choices on who he wanted to be with, and when it ended. Or at least he had until Felicity. Dark hot hunger twisted in his gut.

"Darling, you're not eating," his mother prodded.

"I was just thinking about—" *touching her, kissing her, losing her...* He stabbed his fork into creamy cake, "—a few loose ends that need tying up."

"Not the Maple deal?" his father demanded.

Daniel ate a forkful of dessert, buying time to keep his cool. Thirty minutes more and he was out of here. He could keep the peace till then. "No, not the Maple deal. Besides, you were the one who took the last meeting with him. Is there anything you want to tell me?"

His father grimaced, and Daniel couldn't help but grin. He had a pretty good idea what the reason was for his dad's expression. "Where did he drag you to this time? No wait, let me guess." He leaned both elbows on the table and thought about it.

"The last place Fred held a lunchtime meeting was at some hole in the wall noodle shop down in Little Korea. It was the type of place that kept you checking your bowl, in case a health 'n' safety violation crawled out of it. Or in."

His mother and Deirdra let loose a chorus of "ewws".

His father made a face, but there was a trace of humor in his voice. "At least he took you someplace where they had adequately dressed employees."

"Oh? And where did Fred take you, sweetheart?" his mother asked with a twinkle in her eye.

"The type of place I haven't been to since my bachelor party."

"Really? I thought you said the boys took you to a casino."

His dad busied himself with a large swallow of wine under his mother's sharpened stare and Daniel exchanged amused glances with Deirdra. For the first time in hours he was enjoying himself. She leaned a bit closer, touching him lightly on the arm.

"So what had you distracted, if it wasn't the Maple deal?" Deirdra asked.

"One of the projects me and Rob have on the books," he said, his good mood slipping away.

Silence met his statement.

A scowl had settled on his dad's face and Daniel braced himself as the old man's mouth opened to blast—

"Ow! Dammit, Elle!" Michael Mackenzie jerked in his seat, then frowned at his wife as he reached under the table to rub at something out of view.

"Watch where you place your foot, dear, it may land in your mouth." She patted his hand.

"One of your clients being difficult, sweetheart?" Daniel's mom addressed him.

"Not a client, a tenant," he answered reluctantly.

"A tenant?" The ladies spoke in unison once again.

Daniel rubbed one brow, a headache developing. "I purchased a property last spring with the intentions of doing some upgrades then flipping it. It's a big old Edwardian, the brickwork reminded me of Grandma's house."

Elle Mackenzie smiled mistily. "I loved that house."

"Yeah, me too." Something caught in his throat; he cleared it. "Anyway, the plans were okayed with the city and we had a hole in the scheduling to fill." He shrugged. "I have a crew to keep busy earning a living, so I sent out the evictions, giving the tenants more than enough time to move." He stopped again on a wisp of guilt.

"And one of the tenants doesn't want to leave?"

Daniel twisted his mouth into humorless smile. "That's putting it mildly. She's downright determined to put me through hell on this." Some of his melancholy dissolved under a returning wave of anger.

"Rob and I have wasted hours down at City Hall counter-filing against all her trumped up claims." He picked up his fork and jabbed it in the air. "You know she didn't bother turning up for a single hearing?"

"Oh, people like that disgust me." Elle Mackenzie made an impatient sound as she scooped up a small morsel of cake. "Just stirring up trouble for trouble's sake."

That's exactly what Felicity had been doing. Daniel's ire burned brighter. "And the kicker was when she petitioned for the house to be listed on the city's Inventory of Heritage Properties."

His mother frowned. "Heritage Properties?"

"It's run by Preservation Services, they monitor redevelopment and renovation activities. Making any kind of changes to a property that affects the historical character is all but impossible once it lands on that list," he ground out.

"If she'd been successful, I'd be royally screwed right now. Thank God the other tenants didn't join Felicity in her little campaign."

"Felicity?" Elle's fork paused mid-air.

"My tenant."

"Oh."

"She sounds like a vindictive bitch," Deirdra said.

"Hey, don't call her that!" he snapped. "You don't know her. She's just angry about losing her home." And being betrayed by him.

Deirdra pulled back. "No need to take my head off, Daniel. People get evicted every day. What makes her so special?"

Everything.

"Speak to Nat Turner at the firm; he's the expert on property management and development."

"No!" his mother interrupted, a little pale and wide eyed, as Daniel also absorbed the shock of his father's offer to help.

She reached for her wine. "I really don't think that's necessary, dear," she said weakly. Leave it to his mom to point out Michael Mackenzie's overkill tendencies.

"It doesn't matter anyway. As of this morning the Sheriff's Notice was delivered. Felicity Cameron has two weeks to move out." *Then he'd never see her again.* The words filled his head and a sudden yawning darkness spread through him.

"Well that's all right then," said his father.

"Good riddance," Deirdra agreed.

"Oh dear." His mother drained her wineglass.

Daniel did likewise.

Chapter Twelve

After a forty-five minute shower, which left her feeling cleaner on the outside at least, Felicity went out to the deck. It was a new ritual she'd established to help her feel a little cleaner on the inside, also. The fresh night air was an antidote to the phantom scent of stale tobacco that seemed to cling to her no matter how thoroughly she bathed. And the view of the rooftops helped to wipe from her mind all thoughts of small curtained booths where "private dances" took place. She gripped the mug of herbal tea harder and leaned back in the rickety lounger, legs pulled up tight and hidden under her old thick terrycloth robe.

Hunching her shoulders, she inhaled the fragrant steam wafting from the cup before she took a sip. Yet despite the robe, the tea, the late summer night, she shivered. Felicity clenched her teeth together, mentally ticking off the calendar she kept in her head. By the end of this week she'd have enough for a first and last months' security deposit. By the middle of next week, moving costs.

Then she'd give it another three months tops, just to get a small nest egg going before she quit and found a straight job. Felicity thought about the little décor shop near the club. She wouldn't mind working somewhere like that, and maybe Lise would be a reference for her. Guilt zinged her—she'd blown off the last couple tutoring sessions, and hadn't returned Lise's phone calls. But just the thought of reading anymore fairy-tale crap pissed her off. Life was not a fairy tale. It was a Tarantino film.

As she studied the star-studded darkness above—forgetting about guilty consciences, dingy cubicles and staring eyes—her fragile peace was interrupted by the buzzer. She tried to ignore it, but the person wouldn't let up.

Felicity hauled herself out of the lounger and stepped over the classified section she'd skimmed through earlier, then opened the creaky screen door Daniel had never gotten 'round to fixing. Her mouth twisted. *Gee, I wonder why?*

The buzzing stopped when she was almost at the apartment door. Great. Why didn't they think of that five minutes ago? She turned, heading back out to the deck, when the phone started ringing. What the hell? She put her mug down on the coffee table and snatched up the receiver. "Yes?"

"Why don't you answer your buzzer?"

Her heart slammed to a stop in her chest as she white-knuckled the handset. "What do you want?"

"We need to talk."

"Actually, no, we don't. I'm about to go to bed."

A heavy pause met her words, and then he asked in a low growl, "Alone?"

The possessive note hit her deep in the belly and she pressed a fist there to suppress the roll of sensation. "That's none of your business."

"Let me in."

"No."

He hung up and she hurried over to the window, peering through the blinds in the hopes of catching one final glimpse of him. Her senses were so tuned to detect the slightest movement below or the faintest sound of a car starting, that the metallic tumble of the door's lock didn't register. And by the time it did, Daniel was calmly shutting the door behind him.

"Looking for someone?"

Felicity released the blinds with a snap, a combination of nerves and nausea roiling through her gut. "This is still my apartment, Daniel. I know my rights now, so you can just get your illegally entering ass out of here." She folded her arms across her chest to show she meant business.

Daniel mirrored her, his whole attitude saying: *Make me.*

What his movements made her do, was commit to memory the sight of his broad chest and shoulders encased in a chocolate brown suit and snowy white shirt, and the implied strength of his arms that strained the expensive material.

Daniel was checking her out, too. His gaze lingering on her face, her bare feet, then back up to her chest where the neck of her robe gaped open.

"Could you make this quick and just leave?" She adjusted her robe and retied the belt. "Why are you here?"

He pulled a folded sheet of paper from of his pocket and held it out.

Her irritation warred with a healthy dose of panic and any sense of caution she felt at being alone with him fled. "I already got the eviction notice. What's this now?" She stalked up to him and plucked the paper out of his hands, her own shook with anxiety as she opened the sheet.

Felicity sucked in a breath on the stabbing hurt that came as she viewed the neat list of addresses, names and phone numbers. "Well," she croaked out faintly, but couldn't raise her watery gaze from the printout. "Can't wait to get rid of me, huh?"

"Just the opposite," he said quietly.

She waved the paper at him in lieu of words, all tears dried now.

"You misunderstand. I know the rental market's tight, I just wanted to help. That's a list of some buildings held by a few of the firm's clients. I've vetted them personally, you just have to call to set up a time to view the units available."

"Well thanks for all your help." Felicity let the sarcasm drip from her voice as she carefully folded the list and slid it into her pocket. "And thanks for dropping by." She stepped towards the door, but he grabbed her arm.

"Wait."

She looked up at him, wanting to hate him, but only feeling the opposite as her body drank in the taste of his touch.

"Wait," he repeated softly. "That's not all. I didn't just want to help you. I didn't want to let you go. At least this way I'd know where to find you."

She shut her eyes and swallowed at the hope lodged in her throat, choking off her breath. "Don't," she pleaded.

"Why? What do I have to lose now?" He turned her to him, and she felt the heat of him more fully. "If I say nothing, you'll leave." He came closer, a whisper of fabric that brushed the back of her hand.

"But if I said that I can't get you out of my mind, can't sleep at night without dreaming about you, or get through a single day without thinking of you..." His voice deepened to a dark aching tone that slithered through her blood till the ache penetrated every part of her being.

"That just standing here beside you could bring me to my knees with the need to be with you. That I'm sorry I hurt you and would go down on my knees right now, if I thought you'd give us another chance." He stroked the side of her face and her own knees threatened to give out. "If I said all that, and asked if I could love you, what would you say, Felicity?"

She breathed in his scent, fought with yearning, and wrestled her heart. Of course he didn't mean love the way she felt it...

"Yes," she whispered and opened her eyes to stare up at him. "I'd say yes."

He seemed shocked, then a slow smile spread across his

face. "Really?"

"Rea—"

His mouth was on hers, devouring, hot, wet and hungry, cutting off words, feeding insanity. Soon two pairs of frantic hands were pulling at clothes—untying, unzipping, unbuttoning—either wedged below a waistband or cupping firm velvety flesh.

First he was back-stepping her across the room, headed for the bedroom, then they were spinning round and round, till with heaving too-short breaths he was the one walking backwards.

They hit the bed in a partially-clothed heap that knocked some of the urgency out of them. Daniel rose up on an elbow and she stared into his eyes, noting the ring of blue-gray around his pupils that she'd never noticed before.

He brushed her hair away from her face, his finger strokes causing gossamer streams of desire to sluice down her spine. Then he slowly ran a work-worn palm down her neck, stopping just above the crest of her breast. A feeling, thick and bittersweet, pressed down on Felicity's heart, seeking entry, and she ached with the wanting of it.

"So what does this mean?" she asked, knowing she shouldn't.

"Does it have to mean anything more than we want each other?"

She felt his fingers spread out and edge under her robe. "I've never been in love," he said carefully, not pretending that he didn't understand what she was really asking. "Don't even think I know how to."

But did he want to?

He bent closer, pressing his mouth to the corner of hers. "What I do know...is how to *make* love. How to give pleasure and how to take my own," he whispered hotly against her cheek.

"I know the magic of taste." He trailed kisses down the curve of her neck that ended in a kittenish lick. "And the tease...of a single touch." She felt his hand on her breast and a thumbnail scrape over her nipple. Felicity gasped and this time he plucked at her then rolled the nub between finger and thumb.

"It wouldn't be just sex, Felicity. Not between us." He must have felt her stiffen slightly because his voice was ragged when he said, "Tell me to stop..." His voice dropped lower, barely more than a stirring of warm air against flesh. "And I will." He made no other movement.

Neither did she.

Then he was pressing her backwards onto the mattress, his face hovering over hers, his eyes gleaming through their thick fringe of lashes. "It's way too late stop now, isn't it? We both know it. We both want this."

His mouth covered hers, warm, firm, persuasive and she opened to him, reveling in the sweet punishment of lips that touched her so reverently, so lovingly, when she knew it was merely lust.

"This is enough, then," she whispered when he broke their kiss. A few golden locks of hair had escaped his ponytail and she twined their silky texture about her finger. "If I can't have more, I'll settle for this."

Daniel stared down into her eyes, wanting to make wild promises, make her believe that whatever this was between them, it *was* more than sex.

He buried his face in the cascade of her loose tresses, breathing in the fresh clean scent of her. Hiding from her eyes and from himself. He knew at some point he was going to hurt Felicity. Despite what she'd just said, he could tell, by her eyes, she wasn't settling—she still wanted more, more than he was prepared to give.

But he couldn't put aside this selfish, powerful want. The

anticipation of finally making love to her was like a needle's promise to an addict. He craved her, her touch, her kiss. Everything.

Daniel sealed his mouth to hers again. He drank in her sweetness, siphoned off her passion, then fed it back to her. Her lips were like wine, heady and intoxicating, the skin below her chin slightly salty beneath his tongue, the curve of her neck flavored with her perfume. She was a feast and he would be a glutton tonight.

He rose up on his knees between her splayed legs and stripped off his shirt, then he pushed off her robe.

"Beautiful," tumbled from his mouth. *Mine,* echoed in his thoughts, but he didn't want to think; he just wanted to feel and taste.

His next kiss was complete and merciless, demanding total surrender.

And Felicity gave it.

She was filled with sinking want as his mouth devoured and delivered, tasted and nipped. He gentled with his tongue, incited with his lips, trailing wish-soft kisses down her neck as he moved lower.

Wet openmouthed heat pressed across her breasts till Daniel took a nipple between his teeth and bit down gently. Felicity arched off the bed, cursing under her breath as her hands raked through his hair, holding him closer as he suckled deeply.

Daniel cradled her ribs in his hands, his thumbs tracing lazy circles on her sides before his calloused palms swept down over her hips, then up her inner thighs. Bracing her wide open as he hooked his thumbs under the crotch of her panties.

"God, you're so wet. So fucking hot." He stroked his tongue into her mouth as the rough tips of his thumb pads rubbed lightly over her.

She squeezed her eyes shut, but she could still hear his

heavy breathing, still feel the weight of him and the springy hairs on his chest scratch softly against her naked flesh.

He traced circles round her throbbing nub, over and over again, varying the firmness and speed, drawing her arousal out like a fine tensile wire almost to breaking. Felicity moved her hips forward then away, *seeking, seeking*—

With perfect timing Daniel gave her just what she needed. He parted her flesh, thumbs pushing into her clenching body. Rotating his digits to pull apart and press, then delve deeper while his tongue snaked around her mouth, mirroring the movements of his hands.

Felicity felt the coiling craziness build inside her, and she moved frantically, her ears filled with the sounds of their lovemaking—the muffled slide of damp skin, the smack of wet hungry kisses and their mingled breathy moans.

He moved his hands from her hot soaked center, swallowing first her groans of protest then of satisfaction as he settled fully onto her.

She raised her knees, spreading her thighs further, as the complete length of his thick hard cock lodged against the sodden lace at her crotch. He pressed down firmly, grinding against her, causing every muscle, every nerve, in her body to gather in on itself in a dense crushing mass of sensation.

Then, exquisitely...*nothing.*

A pause...before...the raw explosion of orgasm.

Daniel ate at her mouth, feeding off her cries; so hard he was almost ready to spill.

He rose up on his knees and looked his fill. Damn, she was hot. Beautiful. *His.* From her full breasts with the nipples still glistening with his kisses, to the damp scrap of material bunched between her slit. Daniel traced a finger down the plump cleft, pushing into her sweet little body and was gifted with a guttural moan as she pumped her hips in response.

He pulled his hand from her wetness and holding her gaze, slipped the finger into his mouth, then slowly withdrew it, sucking off her cream.

She reached out to him. "Please."

"I aim to." He stood up, toeing off his shoes as he reached into his briefs and eased his cock out. He stroked himself as Felicity's blatant, hungry, expression egged him on.

"I call sharesies." She licked her lips, sliding her panties off.

Hell if he didn't wonder how that lick would have felt for real. Daniel groaned and squeezed the head of his dick. He wouldn't last a minute with her the first time, but it would be a minute of Paradise.

Then it would be a very, very long night.

He started pushing the thigh-length BVDs down past his hips. "You have protection?"

She seemed flustered for a minute, but nodded.

As he removed the last of his clothing, she flipped over on her stomach and started a part-wiggle, part-crawl across the bed. *Damn!*

He was a mere man, flesh and blood. How was he supposed to resist temptation like that? He went after her, capturing her around the hips as she reached into the drawer of the bedside table.

He took a nip out of one firm ass cheek, and kissed it better as he guided her up onto her knees. Then he urged her legs further apart as he angled his head to delve into the folds of slippery flesh with his tongue.

He lapped and probed, drank in her sweetness, until she was moving against his mouth with increasing urgency, her moans and mewls causing him to grow painfully harder. He wouldn't last if he didn't stop now.

So he did, and laughed softly at her dismay. Daniel came over her then, his chest pressed against her back, his cock trapped between the damp heat of their two bodies and took the

144

foil package from her hand. He stopped her when she tried to turn over.

"No," he whispered into her ear. "Like this...at first."

He felt a shudder run through her at his words and then she was arching her back in invitation.

"*Yess*," Felicity all but panted.

Fuck. He tore open the wrapper, covered himself, then thrust hard and deep into her.

And almost died from the mind-numbing unadulterated pleasure. Hot. Wet. Tight. *Fuck*.

He pressed forward a little deeper, trying to stave off the frenzy of lust building inside of him. Then with a grunt of surrender, he pulled out almost completely before plunging back into her drenched heat. He set the pace; Felicity followed. Her delectable ass meeting his groin with a satisfying slap each time.

Sweat trickled down between his shoulder blades as his heart raced to a tempo twice as fast as the strokes he pistoned into her. He moved his hands from her hips to her waist. Turned on by the erotic contrast of his tanned hands against the smooth paleness of her skin as he lightly guided her movements to his rhythm. Another spike of pleasure tapped into the nape of his neck, twining its fine garroting tentacles around his veins. He changed tempo, gyrating rather than pumping, and was rewarded with Felicity's moans of gratification echoing his own.

He could take no more; yet more was what his body hungered for—more, deeper, harder, faster. Daniel yelled out, surging into Felicity with a powerful upthrust, sure his chest would burst open with the effort. She let out her own yell of enjoyment, but still moved on him, winding and winding. *She was going to kill him with pleasure.* He grabbed her hips, held her in place. He was buried to the hilt, but it wasn't deep enough, he wanted to be right inside her mind, body and soul.

He wanted to crawl right up under her skin. He wanted to be one with her.

Daniel was gasping for breath, on the brink of his orgasm—but not like this. He needed to see her expression, needed to find his reflection in her pale gaze, mingled there with fulfillment. He pulled out.

"Roll over. I want to see you." His voice was guttural with urgency, his hands sure as they guided her. When she was on her back splayed before him, he slid his hands under her ass and lifted her to his mouth.

Daniel feasted, licked and probed. The greedy sounds of his pleasure were drowned out only by her rising ecstasy. Finally, savoring the taste of her, he wrapped his lips around the bobbing button of engorged flesh and suckled while his tongue tried to tame it, stroke it, love it.

Felicity's hips bucked under him, but Daniel held her firmly clamped to his mouth as her cries grew more pleading. He was cresting also, flush with the heady pleasure of possession. Enflamed by the sound of his name tumbling from her lips, and the feel of her hands buried in his hair as she moved with manic rhythm. A roar filled his head, he was going to lose control—*now!*

He tore his lips away from her swollen slickness and went up onto his knees; swinging her legs to rest on his shoulders, he quickly slammed into her. Thrusting so hard and fast their bodies shoveled across the sheets until sensation crashed into his spine and he let go, pouring himself into her clutching heat as she came also. He was lost in her gaze, caught in her embrace and all that he was, all that he had, belonged to her at this moment.

Daniel just about collapsed on her, and felt Felicity's arms wrap around him. He captured her lips, drinking in her loving, and couldn't stop. He fed off her fulfillment, wanting it for himself and to give her more. But there was something else he sought, it was intangible and elusive yet now seemed as necessary as the air he breathed in. And deep inside, he was certain only Felicity could give it to him. He felt himself swelling.

"Again?" Her eyes were wide.

"Oh yeah." He kissed her several more times, then got up and took in the picture she made—skin flushed, hair wild, lips swollen, eyes shining. He'd done that to her. "Wait right here," he ordered and went to the bathroom.

His reflection filled the medicine cabinet mirror as he bent to the wastepaper basket by the sink. He hadn't fared much better than Felicity, his hair hung in tangled skeins, his complexion ruddy.

Daniel leaned in closer, noting the four crescent-shaped marks on each shoulder and a smug smile split his face. He looked like he'd been used hard then kicked under the bed.

He could get used to this look.

Then he caught his own gaze and jerked back. His eyes were glowing, fevered…wild.

Daniel sobered up real fast. There it was—dwelling deep in his gaze—that vague need that had plagued him since their first kiss. The feeling lurked, crouched like a hungry beast in the depths of his expression, and what it hungered for was Felicity. Every emotion, every thought, every bit of sinew down to the marrow of her bones—all of her.

She'd done this to him.

He ran a hand through his hair then turned on the tap and bathed his eyes with cold water. He focused on what he wanted to believe. No matter how incredible it felt—or how much he wanted to make love to her over and over again—what he was feeling, in its most distilled form, was lust. An obsession at the most. Nothing more.

He ruthlessly squashed the flare of emotion that blazed up at the thought of this ending, and went back into the bedroom.

Chapter Thirteen

Daniel spent the next hours gorging himself on the pleasures of her body and urging her to do the same with his.

And when he was done, Felicity didn't know herself. Only that she was his now, body, heart and soul.

It was at that point, when her voice had gone hoarse with repeated pleas and her body almost crippled with ecstasy, he'd relented and allowed her to rest. Then wrapping her in his arms, he fell into a deep, exhausted sleep himself.

Body still humming, she flexed experimentally, and his arm tightened around her, with the leg he'd thrown over hers, pulling her closer. She snuggled back, washed in contentment. Opening herself so fully to the magic of this night had been the sweetest thing. And even though she knew the only part of him that throbbed for her wasn't *his heart*, it could be. In time.

To the steady rhythm of Daniel's breathing, she fell into dreamless oblivion until, with the sky still shadowed shades beyond blue, he roused her with long lazy caresses and warm, sleepy kisses.

Afterwards, he got up to leave. Something about an early meeting—like she was paying attention to his words instead of the smooth ripple of his muscles as he dressed. Bone tired, she rolled into the spot he'd warmed all night long and smiled sleepily when he kissed her goodbye...

"No, no, no, noooo." Felicity tunneled under the covers as the rumble grew louder, then she jack-knifed up in bed, heart thudding with terrible understanding.

She flung back the sheets, lunged for her discarded jeans and T-shirt on the floor and pulled them on. Scrambling round the room like a crazed woman, she finally got one foot into an orphaned slipper and the other into a waylaid running shoe. *Oh God, she was going to be sick.*

She rushed through the flat, wrenched the door open and hurried down the hall, flicking sleep-tangled curls away from her face as she hit the stairs.

On the last step she came to a stop. There seemed to be an army of tool-belted men milling around downstairs. Through the open door she saw Daniel out on the lawn with Rob. From their gestures it was obvious they were arguing. Without further thought, just existing as a mass of pain, she flew outside.

As she approached the two men abruptly broke off their low-level shouting match. She spared Rob a brief scornful look, but it was Daniel's presence that halted her. By now tears blurred her vision and each breath was sheer torture.

"Felicity—"

She slapped him. Knocked the lies from his lips before he said them. Then, shattered, she spun and raced back towards the house.

"Felicity!"

In her rush, she sent a workman tripping into the driveway as a vaguely familiar sedan started to pull in. A horn tooted, the man cursed, and she mumbled an apology but took the stairs two at a time, aware that Daniel was hard on her heels. She made it to the flat and had whipped round to slam the door shut, when he came crashing through it.

"Wait! Hear me out!"

"I don't want to hear anything from you! Get out! Getoutgetoutgetout!" she screamed. Get *out of my sight, out of my head. Get out of my heart.* "Oh God." She doubled over, wrapping her arms around herself.

His arms joined hers, holding her stiff body to his, and slowly his words penetrated her fog of pain.

"Rob pushed the scheduling up without consulting me. Normally it wouldn't be a problem—another job fell through and we had to keep the men working. But he didn't know about last night. He didn't know I was with you." Daniel's grip tightened as he cursed.

"Not that that stopped me from tearing into him."

The argument outside. "The truth?" she asked tentatively, her pain subsiding.

He eased away, tilting her face up to him. His gaze was serious. "The truth. I know we got off on the wrong foot with the eviction, but from here on in, as long as we're together, I'll never lie to you or make promises I can't keep." He paused and she understood the warning in that silence. He was reminding her that he didn't love her. Felicity lowered her eyes, fear of the hurt to come, garroting her heart.

"I also expect you to be truthful with me."

He did, did he? Well that was a big fat lie right there, because he obviously didn't want to hear the truth about her feelings for him.

"Hey."

Felicity raised her eyes, and her pulse did a little hopscotch at the sight of his smile.

"Kiss and make up?"

She laughed, relieved. Willing to pretend the danger didn't exist. "I'm beginning to think you're insatiable."

"Only beginning to think? Looks like I'll have to work harder at convincing you," he murmured, fitting her more firmly against him.

She "*hmmmed*".

He kissed her. And any more *hmmms* she had to express were swallowed up in the satisfaction his mouth delivered. When he broke the kiss, his eyes gleamed from beneath lowered lids. "Why don't I stay up here awhile?"

"What about your men?"

"They're not invited." He kissed the tip of her nose.

"Someone might come looking for you," she whispered, a little more excited than she should be. She moved her hands up to his broad shoulders, loving the feel of his big strong body.

"No one would dare," he said, cupping her breasts, flicking her nipples into aching stiffness with his thumbs.

A low liquid groan rumbled from deep in her throat, and Daniel laid another of his mind-draining kisses on her. He snaked an arm around her waist, holding her tight against his growing hardness while his other hand kneaded her breast, giving her nipple the odd delicious pinch to keep things interesting. Felicity lifted one leg and locked it around his. Pretty much started humping him on the spot.

"Oh dear!"

They sprang apart at the exclamation and looked towards the open doorway.

"Lise, w-what are you doing here?"

"Mom!"

"Mom?" Felicity repeated weakly.

"I hope I'm not interrupting?" Lise sounded coolly off-hand, despite the bright flags of color at her cheeks and the blatant curiosity in her gaze.

"Of course not," Felicity rushed out. Why would she mind getting caught like a dog on a hydrant with— "He's your son?" she squealed.

Daniel frowned. "You two know each other?"

"We're members of the same book club," Lise exclaimed. "See? No mystery." She—*Daniel's mother!*—walked up to him and kissed his cheek. "Stop frowning, sweetheart. You'll get lines like your father."

That comment made him scowl deeper before he realized what he was doing and cleared his brow, but his gaze remained narrowed. "What book club is this?" he asked in a dangerously pleasant voice, a muscle ticking at the corner of his jaw.

Felicity couldn't make her mouth work. *His mother!* Then the realization hit with all the subtlety of a two-by-four that she'd never known Lise's last name. And because of her reluctance to discuss her private life, she'd never referred to Daniel other than this guy she was seeing, or, after the humiliation of the eviction, *that bastard.*

In either case, she would leave all the fast talking to *his mother!* She bit back a groan and tuned into Lise's attempts to cover their scheming butts.

"—you and your father like to tease me about my romance novels, but then I met Felicity at the library—you remember I do some tutoring there?"

Felicity's stomach heaved, and she made an abbreviated movement to stop Lise from revealing *anything*, but one look from the other woman reassured her. She exhaled in dizzy relief.

"—Well, then, we girls got to talking."

"About what?" Daniel crossed his arms.

"Why, about reading and books, darling. Honestly, what else would we talk about? Please pay attention." She didn't even blink. *Bravo.*

"Oh!" Surprised comprehension dawned on Lise's face. "Are you thinking about the discussion at dinner last night? I'll admit that the name 'Felicity' caught my attention, but I didn't think you could be talking about—"

"That's all sorted out now." Daniel cleared his throat, adjusting the knot of his tie.

"Evidently," his mother said dryly.

Felicity's curiosity was piqued, but when he slid his gaze her way, she stopped wondering why she was a topic of dinner conversation as the resemblance between mother and son struck her. They had the same eyes. Lise's seemed larger and a brighter green because of her makeup. But Daniel's retained their piercing quality. A trait he put to good use now.

"I swear I didn't know she was your mother. I'm as shocked as you." To say the least.

"What's to feel shocked about?" Lise asked breezily with a wave of her hand. "Now that that's all settled, why don't the two of you come over for dinner? Just a nice little casual barbeque."

"Wait a minute, what did we settle?" Daniel asked.

"Darling, I really wish you would listen. We've all gotten over our collective shock, now we're all deciding when would be a good time for you two to come to dinner."

While Daniel pinched the bridge of his nose, Lise gave her a conspiratorial wink.

Felicity wanted to be her when she grew up.

They all settled on the upcoming weekend.

ଚ୍ଚ

"Nervous?"

"A little."

"No need to be. You already know my mother. And my father will be his usual charming self."

Felicity thought there was a trace of sarcasm in Daniel's voice, but wasn't sure. He reached over, interlacing their fingers with a reassuring squeeze and Felicity couldn't stop her idiot grin.

A little composure here, woman. She took a deep breath and focused on the stately parade of I've-got-more-money-than-God-and-I-used-some-of-it-to-buy-this-house homes. Daniel was probably taking this short cut through Forest Hill to avoid the heavier traffic on the main roads.

"We don't have to stay more than an hour or so. Just long enough to eat and chit-chat. Then we can leave. Go someplace quiet."

They'd stopped at an intersection and Daniel turned to look at her. There was no mistaking the heat in his gaze. He leaned over to press a brief hard kiss on her mouth. Others followed, each more lengthy than the one before. He eased away. "Forget the chit-chat, how fast can you eat?"

"It depends on if I chew...or just swallow," she said with a slow smile and watched his throat work.

"Oh man."

A car horn blared impatiently behind them and he cursed, straightening in his seat. She laughed softly, running her gaze over him, from the hint of stubble on his jaw to the powerful chest encased in a shirt that fit him like it had been hand-stitched on by clever little designer elves. Lucky elves.

He was perfect. In fact the last three days had been perfect. The only thing that sucked was her work at The Uptown, and the strain of hiding it from Daniel.

"I don't believe this!"

Pulled out of her reverie, she looked around for what had set him off. Her mouth slowly unhinged to the sounds of crunching gravel as they drove down a circular drive towards a two-storied Architectural Digest wet-dream.

"'Casual little barbeque' she said. I should have known better." Daniel parked, then returned the waves of a khaki cabal making their way up the front steps.

He turned to Felicity with a smile. "Well, we're here."

One hour later.

"He loves me." A velvety petal drifted to the manicured

grass beneath her feet, followed by another. "He loves me not."

"He loves me...." She hesitated, staring at the lone pathetic petal that remained. "He loves me not." Felicity dropped the decapitated stem to the ground and took a sip of her lukewarm cola.

The sounds of laughter drew her attention back to the flag-stoned patio and she spotted her so-called date near the buffet table. To be fair he hadn't voluntarily abandoned her. It was more a matter of her conceding defeat. From the moment she and Daniel had arrived, everyone wanted a piece of him—to ask his opinion, or tell him some latest development.

Finally she'd drifted away from the bewildering tide of big business legalese, and ended up on this stone bench in a little secluded corner of the landscaped garden, with only the nearby babbling fountain to talk to her. As for Lise, she'd barely had more than a glimpse of that busy lady.

Felicity eyed the other guests morosely. Everyone knew everyone else, belonged to same clubs, or owned cottages on the same lake. Her spirits sank lower. So this was Daniel's world.

She'd been so worried about keeping all her secrets safe from him, that she'd never *really* thought what his life was away from her. Then again his life seemed to be all about his work, and as far as she knew, when he wasn't with her he was working. Shows how much she knew.

She refocused her attention on the small knot of people surrounding him and made a face at the sight of the newest member of the group. Standing beside Daniel and hanging off his arm like a one-woman zebra mussel colony, was a sleek brunette introduced earlier as The Vivacious Deirdra. Mentally, Felicity had promptly christened her "VD".

"What are you doing over here all by your lonesome?"

"Plotting murder and mayhem," she said to Rob, who was walking towards her. Her relief at having some company was mixed with lingering resentment at his part in the evictions. But he was charming in a cheesy, always joking around sort of way, so it was hard staying mad at him.

"My type of gal."

As he sat down, her earlier handiwork caught his eye and he toed the small mound of petals. "Don't like flowers?"

Then he smirked. "I know what you were doing, you were playing that game, 'He loves me, He loves me not'." Rob batted his eyes.

"Nooo."

"Yesss. Here." He snapped off another flower and presented it with a flourish. "Best two out of three?"

"You mean my chances could improve?" She took the flower, and plucked off a petal. "Besides the first one is the only one that really counts. The rest is cheating." She plucked another.

"Not cheating, playing the odds. It's called perseverance."

"It's called deluded." *Pluck, pluck.*

"Only the deluded fall in love anyway."

"I'm not in love—"

Rob cocked a brow.

"I'm not." *Pluck, pluck, lie, lie.*

"Yes, you are."

Pluck, pluck. She looked back to where Deirdra was pressed up against Daniel like they were in a Tokyo subway station. His head was bent, seemingly attentive to her animated chatter, but he was looking around distractedly, until his gaze rested on Felicity. Relief flashed across his face, followed by a slight frown.

Felicity frowned back. It was a wonder Miss Static-Clingy still had both feet on the ground and not locked around his waist.

"I. Am. Not. In. Love." She tore off several petals at once. "What's the deal with Daniel and VD, anyway?"

Rob made a choking sound. "Listen I don't think you should be telling—what I mean is, Dan and I are close, but we don't...*ah*...discuss things of that nature." His face was flaming brighter than the rosebush beside him.

She knew it was unfair to put him on the spot like this, but she was hoping to at least read something in Rob's expression. "I'm not asking for details. Just if there's something I should know about her and Daniel?"

"Her?"

"VD." She whipped her poor peony in the direction of the brunette barnacle in question. "The Vivacious Deirdra."

"VD?" Rob's face went blank before he let loose a loud belly laugh that had heads turning in their direction. Including Daniel's. His brow looked downright thunderous.

She resisted the urge to stick her tongue out.

"You don't have to worry about Dan and VD—" Rob started laughing again. "Whoo boy, that didn't come out right."

Wiping away tears from his eyes with one hand, he laid the other over hers, stilling her unconscious twirling of the amputated peony. "Daniel knows how to deal with Deirdra. I think it's you he doesn't have one clue on. Poor bastard."

His chocolate dark eyes were still crinkled with humor, but a hint of seriousness crept into his gaze as he tucked a loose curl behind her ear.

"You two seem to be hitting it off."

Felicity jumped at Daniel's voice. How had he gotten over here so fast? She looked up. His expression was tight. Size 6 feet in size 5 1/2 shoes tight. He drew her to stand.

"I was just keeping Felicity company."

Daniel gave his friend a hard look, while pulling her closer. "So I noticed."

Her eyes narrowed. *He was jealous.* The realization should have made her gleeful, instead she felt like a toy that had been discarded till someone else wanted it.

He brought her hands up to his mouth. "Sorry, I left you alone," he said, before pressing soft kisses in quick succession against her knuckles. "Forgiven?"

The jackass. She pulled her hands from his. "You ditched me almost as soon as we got here."

"That's not fair. You saw how everyone wanted a piece of me the minute we arrived." He tried to recapture her hands, she tucked them behind her back.

What she'd seen was how VD wanted a piece of him. *Everyone had seen that.* Felicity bit back the accusation. The last thing she wanted was for him to see her jealousy, and guess the true depth of her feelings.

"You can keep your little apology. If it hadn't been for Rob, I could've left thirty minutes ago and you wouldn't have noticed."

"That's where you're wrong. I knew where you were, and I knew who you were with." He flicked a glance at his best friend that wasn't very *friendly.* "You wouldn't have made it as far as the front door without me stopping you." Daniel's serious tone held not even a wisp of the sweet-talkin' softness it had just moments ago.

A bit of wind went out of her sails. It was true, time and again she had watched him scan the crowd for her, and in fairness it wasn't just Deirdre who'd monopolized him. Felicity realized in a moment of clarity that she wasn't really angry with him, she was angry with herself. Why had she drifted away?

Because she'd been afraid he'd start to make the inevitable comparisons between her and the other guests. So she'd done the rejecting first. It was the story of her life.

Well, she needed to start a new chapter, or this story would turn into one of those sad tragedies where the heroine grows old, bitter and alone, then gets eaten by her cats when she dies in her sleep.

The starch went out of Felicity completely, and Daniel

wrapped an arm around her waist.

"Now, am I forgiven?" He dropped a gentle kiss on her mouth before she could answer.

She nodded and he kissed her again, deeper, entangling her tongue with his.

His brain-sucking technique worked. *Forgive him for what?*

"You two need to get a room," Rob protested.

"Exactly what I had in mind," Daniel said. "Catch you later, bud." He turned her towards the house. "Now to find my mother and say our goodbyes— Ah, perfect timing." Lise was coming down the path, followed by a distinguished-looking older man.

"Why are you three hiding yourselves away?"

"Not hiding," Felicity lied. "You have such a beautiful garden, and it's nice here with the bench and fountain."

"Thank you." Lise beamed. "We had a landscaper in for the initial plan, but I still like to come out here and putter about. I'm particularly fond of the peonies... Oh!" She froze, her gaze widening as she stared at Felicity's feet.

All eyes followed...to the thin carpet of petals that covered the grass. Felicity raised her head and opened her mouth, doing a fairly good imitation of a flycatcher.

"We were actually about to leave, Mom." Daniel came to her rescue.

"But you can't leave yet, we haven't spent a minute together."

"And whose fault is that? I thought you said this was going to be just the four of us," Daniel said with a hint of exasperation.

"I'm not the guilty party here. This is all your father's doing." Her mouth pursed as she glared at the man beside her. "Did it behind my back, too, then told me this morning *fait accompli*. The sneaky devil."

"Sneaky? That's a bit of the pot calling the kettle black,

don't you think?" he pointed out dryly.

"I'm not sneaky. I'm strategically stealthy."

Lise shushed their laughter, before addressing Felicity. "I don't think you've met Daniel's father, Michael. Darling, this is Daniel's friend I was telling you about, Felicity."

"Nice to meet you." Michael Mackenzie, eyes crinkling with a smile that held no warmth, shook her hand.

Her stomach folded in on itself. "It's a pleasure to meet you also, sir."

"Daniel's been keeping you a secret from us—" He flinched and looked down at his wife's casual hold on his arm. She smiled brightly up at his frowning face.

"What a silly thing to say!"

He returned his scrutiny to Felicity. "Have we met before?"

"I don't think so."

"Are you sure? You look familiar—" He broke off abruptly, and glaring at his wife, removed her hand from his arm.

"Are you through interrogating my date?"

His father pinned Daniel under a hard look. "I've triaged a conference call between us, New York and Maple in another half hour. But there're some things I'd like to go over beforehand."

"No one told me about any conference calls. We came here for a quiet little dinner. Not for an afternoon of Mackenzie Phillips and Bassett business. As I said before, I was just about to take Felicity home."

"I'm sure Felicity can wait." Michael Mackenzie's mouth curled slightly.

There was something about the way he looked at her that made her squirm inside.

"I'll make sure she's all right," Lise said, soothingly.

"And I'll be here too, bud," Rob offered.

If anything, Daniel's expression became more unhappy as

he looked from her to his friend.

"Let's get this over with." He dropped his hand from her waist and, not waiting for his father, stalked away.

Michael gave his wife a quick peck on the cheek, then for a brief second, over her shoulder, his hostile gaze focused on Felicity.

Chapter Fourteen

After the Mackenzie men left, Rob went in search of some more beer while Felicity and Lise toured the garden, though, Felicity noticed, Lise steered clear from the peonies.

Exchanging giggles, they recounted the shock of their close call, and reviewed all the (now obvious) clues they'd missed in connecting mother and son.

"So things are going well with you and Daniel?" Lise's smile could only be described as self-satisfied.

"No complaints," Felicity said, but couldn't stop her gaze from searching the patio area. There was no sign of VD.

"What's the frown for?"

"Nothing—" Lise's sharp look demanded the truth. "It's just that Daniel never talked about his background." She swept a hand out to indicate the house, the people, the wealth. Her fingers brushed against a leaf of something that she started to fondle until she was pulled away.

"I'm not surprised." Lise sighed. "My son keeps a lot to himself. Part of that has to do with the situation between him and Michael." She rubbed between her brows.

"This latest decision of Daniel's to leave the firm has made things so much tenser. It hasn't been this bad since the wedding."

A bout of dizziness hit her and Felicity braced herself against the trunk of a birch. "Daniel was married?"

Under the sun-dappled shadows, pain flitted across the older woman's face. "Almost. He called it off just days before. They'd been together ages, but—" she grimaced. "I've probably said enough if he hasn't said anything himself."

"Of course."

"It was a long time ago." Lise squeezed her arm reassuringly. "And he's never gotten seriously involved since." She made an impatient sound. "I talk too much. I've upset you."

"No, you haven't! It gives me a better understanding of him." Felicity scraped together a smile.

Lise's gaze was long and probing, before it softened. "I think you already understand him. He needs that."

Felicity's mouth trembled with the strain of appearing unconcerned. All she understood was the completeness of Daniel's statement that he'd *never* been in love. And, now, how big a fool she might be in hoping she could change that.

The women walked on, their talk not so lighthearted as before, but soon the demands of hostessing pulled Lise away, at the same time Felicity's bladder made demands of its own. Following directions she found the main floor powder room, but it was occupied.

Many minutes later, shifting from one foot to the other, she raised her fist to give the door a severe rapping. Hell, it wasn't as if the chick had bought the bowl. *Share!*

"There's another bathroom upstairs you could use."

Felicity cringed at the voice that scuttled down her ear canal. Like all VD, this one arrived unannounced and was just as unwelcome.

Deirdra revealed a set of even white fangs. "The other one's probably vacant. Come, I'll show you. Besides, the one upstairs is much nicer," she added in a conspiratorial whisper.

Felicity hesitated a moment longer, hoping to hear the flushing sounds of her salvation from beyond the powder room door, but no such luck.

"I'm over here a lot. I'm sure Lise won't mind if I show you the other bathroom."

Okay I get it already: You. Are. Precious.

Frowning, she followed VD up the Scarlett O'Hara stairs and then down a hall strewn with oriental rugs over hardwood flooring. Deirdra opened a door and stepped through, but on the threshold of the very masculine room, done up in pale blue-grays and deep chocolaty browns, Felicity hesitated.

"This isn't a bathroom."

"No, this used to be Daniel's bedroom..." Deirdra's full pouty lips formed a smirk. "The bathroom's right through here." VD crossed the carpet, her shoes leaving little icy diamond-shaped imprints.

Felicity crossed the room after her, reminding herself that VD had probably been over here "lots of times" for other business get-togethers. They passed through an open dressing area, then entered a large airy room. Deirdra pointed one elegant finger towards a door on the opposite wall.

"Thanks," Felicity gritted out, walking with as much dignity as one could muster while "holding it".

Several minutes later, she exited the small exquisitely appointed cubicle, feeling like a new woman, but her relief was short lived when she saw that VD was still waiting for her.

"Can I ask you a question?"

Felicity turned on the tap and warily met Deirdra's sapphire gaze in the mirror.

"How's the house coming along?"

"The house?" Felicity's hand stilled on the soap dispenser.

VD ran her hands through her hair, fluffing it. "I know I shouldn't ask. Daniel made me promise not to drop by, but I'm dying of curiosity. You live there now, don't you think it's *the* perfect house to raise a family?"

"Family?" The numbness started at Felicity's extremities,

and made its slow journey up her limbs.

"Of course. Daniel told me all about his plans. The renovations and the evictions. He and I are very close."

Mechanically, Felicity continued rubbing her hands together under the water.

"Working with him after the break-up was hell." The other girl's eyes suddenly became bright and watery. "But we've known each other forever, plus about hundred years ago, Michael and my dad went to Harvard together." VD blinked several times, patting under each eye as she turned her face this way and that in the mirror.

"It almost killed me to let him walk away, but neither one of us was ready to make a big commitment. Daniel is...well, he's very physical. I think you understand...for men like him, one woman isn't enough." Her hard dry gaze met Felicity's.

Felicity looked down at her hands. Not a single soap bubble remained but she found the repetitive motions soothing. If she felt anything at all, it was an overwhelming need to be clean.

Deirdra leaned forward, carefully wiping a finger along the edge of her bottom lip to remove a slight smudge. "I realize now, that while he may have strayed from time to time, in the end it means nothing. Nothing at all." Her gaze slithered to Felicity again, her expression becoming contrite.

"Oh, I've upset you. That wasn't my intention. So sorry." She tapped Felicity's arm. "Ready?"

"I'll—I'll be down in a minute. You go ahead."

"All right, see you downstairs." Deirdra smiled brightly and fluffed up her hair one last time, before sashaying from the room without a backwards glance.

Felicity stared hollow-eyed at her reflection. Thinking of weddings that had almost been and family connections. Thinking about the way Daniel made love to her. Like a man possessed. *"He's very physical...one woman isn't enough."*

Numb, Felicity retraced her steps back out to the hall. Deirdra claimed that Daniel loved women. But he didn't love them. He used them.

Hearing voices in the foyer downstairs, she paused as she looked over the banister to the foyer below. The last thing she needed was someone catching her up here.

It took a split second to recognize the couple at the foot of the curving staircase. The man's back was towards her, but the brunette's deep blue eyes flicked beyond his broad shoulders and met Felicity's. Deirdra's pause was infinitesimal, but long enough for her mouth to curl into a satisfied smile.

Moving even closer, she ran her fingers through Daniel's hair and pulled his head down towards her. Daniel's hands settled on Deirdra's hips.

Their mouths met.

For Felicity it happened as if in torturous stop-action motions. She went back into the bedroom, closed the door, and somehow made it over to the bed, where she sat and waited for the world to right itself.

All too soon tendrils of sound came to her from the hall, feminine giggles and masculine murmurs that grew louder the closer they came.

The door swung open, revealing the writhing twosome. Mortified, Felicity watched as the man, his hand filled with the rounded swell of his partner's ass, lifted the woman almost off her feet to press her closer. He maneuvered them a few steps into the room without breaking their embrace, then with a practiced motion, swung the door shut again with his foot.

Caught in this nightmare like a deer in the headlights, Felicity couldn't tear her eyes away as one large tanned hand released the captured booty, and came up to bury itself in the woman's mass of dark brown curls. His mouth was devouring as he bent his head further to place searching kisses in the girl's cleavage. Then he shifted his face slightly to the side, and

Felicity saw a flash of teeth just before he captured the protruding tip of his mate's generous bosom. The brunette's gasp of ecstasy caused Felicity's womb to clench in stinging empathy.

Felicity must have made a sound because the man froze and looked up through the screen of dark hair that flopped over his brow. The glaze of lust cleared from his eyes when he saw her.

"Where the hell have you been?" he roared. His hands fell away from the object of his recent attentions, sending her stumbling, unceremoniously on her ass.

"We've been looking for you everywhere." Rob made to step forward, before coming to the belated realization he would have to step over his playmate to get to Felicity. He stopped and reached down to help her. "Geez, I'm sorry, uhm, Jacqueline?"

The girl glared at him, slapping his hand away. On her hands and knees, she struggled to pull down the hem of her dress that had ridden up past mid-thigh. "Just get away from me."

"Please, let me—" His hand was slapped away again. "Listen, ah, Julie—"

"That is *not* my name, you big oaf." Standing now, she shoved at the solid mass that was Rob's chest and almost toppled over again. The irate female clawed at his arm to steady herself.

"Cripes!" He pried her off of him, then tried to cradle her hand. "Baby, I can explain."

"I am not your baby." The brunette pulled away from his grasp and stalked to the door, taking her goodies with her.

"Janice?"

"Jerk." The door slammed.

He whipped around, finger pointing at Felicity. "You. Come with me."

His expression was priceless. She lost it. Wracked with

laughter and tears streaming down her face, she flopped back on the bed. Somewhere in the back of her mind, she knew the situation hadn't been funny at all. It was sad.

That girl could have been her with Daniel. Dropped on her ass like a hot potato. She stopped laughing and stared up at the ceiling but the tears still trickled down her face. At least Daniel knew her name. She hiccupped a few more giggles.

The mattress sank down a bit. She turned her head towards Rob. His earlier frustration was replaced with concern.

"Hey, you all right?"

She nodded.

"Daniel's been looking for you. You have him worried."

Right. "Take me home, Rob."

"No offense; I know you'd like to make amends for what just happened, but you're no consolation prize."

It took a moment for his meaning to sink in. "Oh!" She grabbed a pillow and started clubbing him. "You really are an oaf. You should be so lucky, you—"

Laughing, Rob deflected her blows easily.

"Ugh." With one more wallop, she flung herself back down.

"That's more like it," he said. "I like the fighter much better." He wiped away a last tear that spilled from the corner of her eye.

"I really have to leave."

"Now?"

She nodded.

"Want to talk about it?"

Felicity closed her eyes in silent refusal. After a minute, the bed shifted.

"Okay, come on."

She opened her eyes to see Rob standing beside the bed; he took one of her hands and urged her up. "Anyone you want to say goodbye to?"

Lise. But she didn't want to run into Daniel or Deirdra or Michael Mackenzie. Daniel she'd deal with later. "No. Let's go."

They left the room in silence, went down the stairs, through the foyer and swiftly out the front door.

"This way." He guided her down the drive with a hand at her back. They passed Beemers, Benzes, any number of SUVs, and Daniel's low-slung silver Porsche.

Finally they came up to a motorcycle. Tongues of fire were airbrushed onto the gleaming black finish and the chrome shone with mirror-like intensity.

"A Harley," she exclaimed, surprised.

"Nope. A Dakota Travis original. Nineteen seventy-seven model. S & S 113 cubic inch V-twin engine on a Daytec rigid frame." Rob fondled the handlebars as if he were caressing a woman. And she had more than a fair idea of how he went about doing that.

"Hop on." He handed her a helmet.

She put on the head gear and eagerly straddled the bike. A ride on this powerful machine was just what she needed to blow every care—except the sort related to crashing—from her mind.

"Ready?" Rob climbed on in front of her and patted himself down several times. "Damn!" He looked at her over his shoulder. "Looks like I left the keys somewhere."

"Where?" She wanted to get away from here. From Daniel, his exclusive pedigree, and his VD.

Rob dismounted. "Don't worry. I must've dropped them in the bedroom." Grinning, he took the helmet off. "Just sit tight, I'll be back in a flash."

"Rob. Don't tell Daniel."

He winked as he held up one hand. "Scout's honor."

He strode quickly back to the house, disappearing through the double doors of the inner sanctum.

Minutes ticked by. Each opening of the door caused Felicity to catch her breath. She only relaxed when Rob appeared in the front doors again. Smiling, he held up his keys as he approached her.

"Okay, we're all set to go. Except for one more thing."

"What?"

"Did I mention that I never made the Scouts? It was a very small fire, but they kicked me out anyway."

Felicity processed Rob's gibberish, searching for a point of reference. She got it. "You rat." She scrambled off the bike.

"One day you'll thank me."

"Rat."

"If Rob's a rat, what does that make you?" The question came from behind her.

Felicity bared her teeth at Rob. He winked back. She should have known rats would stick together.

He jerked a thumb over his shoulder. "I'll be over there while you guys hash this out." With that he turned on his heel and walked back to the house.

Daniel perched on the motorcycle. "Did it occur to you to tell me you were leaving with my best friend?" he asked conversationally, his voice dripping ice.

"Did it occur to you that making out with your ex-girlfriend, where your current date could see, wasn't such a hot idea?" she countered.

Daniel blinked, and flushed. "That was an accident."

"What does that mean? She slipped and her tongue fell into your mouth?"

"It means *she* kissed me. I was distracted looking for you—"

"Yes, I could see how hard you were looking...for the right grip on her ass."

"That wasn't how it was. I'm not denying that Deirdra and I had something. But that was a long time ago."

170

"Actually, it was only half an hour ago."

"I promised you I would never lie to you. I'm not lying now." His expression went all earnest. He'd probably practiced it in the mirror. Or on every girl he'd ever kissed by accident.

His fingers sought hers out, prying one hand away from the helmet she hugged to her belly. "The only woman I want to kiss accidentally, or otherwise, is you." He leaned closer. "And I don't care who catches me doing it."

Then he *was* doing it. His tongue, lips and teeth doing it to hers.

She should know better, really she should. But try telling that to her heart. Or to her body that came alive at his touch.

"A room, people. Get one," Rob interrupted.

"Best piece of advice I've heard all day." Daniel straightened and pulled her towards the Porsche, barely giving her enough time to shove the helmet into his partner's hands.

Ten minutes later Daniel pulled into the driveway of Southview. Five minutes after that they found a room.

He rolled over, skin slick with sweat, his mouth full of tasting her. "Do you like this?"

"*Yesss.*" She held on tighter, damn near out of her mind with liking. He slid in, touching deeper than flesh could go.

"Good," he whispered, slowing. "Let's make it last."

And he did....

§

Cold dread seeped through the edges of her sleep. *Something was wrong.*

She struggled through smudgy layers of half-remembered dreams as Daniel's voice penetrated her consciousness.

"Felicity, get up, c'mon wake up, baby. C'mon."

"Don't," she mumbled as he shook her more forcefully; then the shrill of an alarm registered and wakefulness arrived like a runaway train. Heart slamming against her ribs, Felicity's eyes sprang open and began to sting.

"D-Daniel?"

He yanked on his pants, then bent down, grabbed her clothes from the floor and shoved them at her. "Here, get dressed. Fast."

Somehow her shaking hands cooperated and she dressed quickly, her watery gaze glued to Daniel as whispery shiftings, like dry leaves, crackled in her ear. She finished and just stood there, frozen, till he drew her into a brief hard hold.

"It's okay." He pressed a quick kiss on her forehead then hustled them towards the window. "Fire— I can't tell where. But we need to get the hell out of here."

His voice sounded calm and controlled, but she felt the racing beat of his heart.

Daniel wrenched open the window. He turned back to her just as a loud crash ripped through the interior of the house.

Felicity jumped, her screams drowned out as the fire's susurrations suddenly whooshed into a roar.

Daniel read the stark fear in her expression. Felt it score him to the bone. "This way. I'll go first, then help you out."

She nodded, but suddenly lunged into him, wrapping her arms around his waist. A feeling pierced his chest—sweet and clear, and wholly alien. Words trembled on his tongue, words he didn't know, had never said before. Another crash shook the floors and walls, and the moment was lost.

He eased her away, swung both legs out the window and paused before jumping to the porch roof. He skittered down the steeply pitched slope, feet scrabbling for a hold against the shingles. Daniel twisted and grabbed the roof's peak. A second away from tumbling down through the billowing smoke onto the lawn below.

He quickly found his balance and scrambled closer to the exterior wall, right beneath where Felicity sat on the sill.

"Come on, baby. It's just a small jump." He held his arms up to her. "Trust me."

She shook her head. The air thick and swirling around the terror mask she wore. He fought the urge to use brute strength just as she turned on the ledge, shooting a look of terrified resolve at him over her shoulder. Her shaky limbs found toe-holds in the wall's mortared ridges as she held onto the sill.

Daniel reached up to steady her, help bear her weight and her trembling lessened. *He had her.* She pressed back against his chest and her nails dug into his arms, but he would bear pain a thousand times worse if it gave her any comfort.

"Just one more time, sweetheart, and we're home-free, okay?"

She nodded, her death grip loosening. He released her and in a half-crouch scooted to the edge of the roof. A swift inhale and he dropped to the lawn, folding into a front roll that sent every bone in his body jarring.

He leaped up and sprinted back to the veranda. Scaling the balustrade to help Felicity down. She had one foot braced on the eaves trough, the other leg dangling until he captured it.

"Hurry up, baby." He stretched to brace her.

Too late. The eaves trough ripped away with a sharp crack, raining bits of debris down on them as it tore her out of his grip. Arms pinwheeling through the air, her shriek died abruptly as she got body slammed backwards onto the lawn.

"Felicity!" Daniel jumped down and was on his knees beside her before he'd drawn his next breath.

When she moaned weakly, he sent up a prayer of thanks, but the sounds of oncoming sirens underlined there wasn't even time for the most cursory of examinations.

"Do you think you can get up?"

"Y-yes." She blinked up at him, nodding.

"Hold on." Daniel lifted her. He had never held a more precious burden.

The revelation almost caused him to stumble.

He jogged around the dumpster parked on the grass and across the street. Gently, he laid her down on a neighbor's lawn then quickly checked her over.

Along with cuts and scrapes on her hands and legs, she had a small gash on her forehead and the smooth belly he'd worshiped last night was now marred with a large abrasion. Even with the reassurance of these minor injuries, black terror still squatted heavy on his chest. All he could see over and over again was the moment she'd hit the ground like some rag-doll.

People gathered around and Daniel tried to answer their questions patiently. But he wished everyone would just back the hell away. He had one frayed nerve left and it was currently dealing with his latest discovery: He was in love with Felicity.

Chapter Fifteen

"How'd it happen?" she asked hoarsely, staring at the fire while he stared at her.

Damned if he knew. Considering it took a burning house for him to finally get what his heart had known all along.

Daniel almost laughed at the bitter irony. Last night he'd been so driven, so inventive... But no matter how many times he'd wrung pleasure from her yielding body, she never said the words he hadn't even known he needed to hear, *that she loved him.* And why should she? When everything he'd ever done or said had been to emphasize that he wanted her physically, with no emotional entanglements.

As the sirens grew closer, his weary scrutiny shifted across the street to where months of work for his crew literally went up in smoke.

"I don't know," he finally answered her question. "It's an old house. The guys were working on the electrical in the basement yesterday." He rubbed his jaw. Made a brief attempt at estimating the damage and gave up. Couldn't say he gave much of a shit at the moment.

Instead, as the fire trucks arrived with a last deafening wail, he brushed back the hair from Felicity's beautiful face, then thumbed away a tear on her cheek.

His heart contracted. If he hadn't been here last night... Fear mushroomed in Daniel's throat. Fear of what he'd almost lost. And for what he might not be able to make right.

While he struggled for words, people surrounded them—firefighters, policemen and paramedics—all asking questions. Daniel's answers were clipped; his attention was glued to Felicity as the medics examined her.

Beneath the soot, she was pale, and even with the blanket draped around her, she was shaking. But with her chin raised, she continued to stare at the burning house. Almost as if she was staring it down, as she bore her pain.

This was the woman who had his heart. A fighter—strong, giving and passionate.

Minutes later, the ambulance carried her away from him.

ജ

"Nothing broken," the doctor said, writing out a prescription for some painkillers. "The scratches will heal up nicely. Take it easy on the shoulder, and stay off the ankle as much as possible for the next couple of weeks." He tore off a sheet from the pad and handed it to her. "All things considered, you're pretty lucky."

Yeah. Lucky. She was alive. And homeless. And everything she owned was destroyed. Dazed, she nodded when he paused in his patter, but her brain had shrink-wrapped itself around the devastation of her loss. Nothing else seemed real.

Finally, the doctor left her to get dressed, which she did carefully, wincing as her abused muscles protested any movement at all. She scrubbed at her tears, they weren't going to help. But, really, was she ever going to catch a break? Just once. It was doubtful anything had survived the fire. She had nothing left. *Nothing.* What was she going to do now?

She stared into the middle distance. All that was going through her mind was the memory of horrible sounds of the fire, the heat and smoke. Each breath she took burned in her lungs and scraped her throat and nose raw.

Then she thought of Daniel. He'd make her feel safe again. If only he'd hold her again, she could draw the strength she needed to go on.

A few minutes later, the bright orange curtain parted and a nurse entered the closed-off examination space.

"Here we go." She propped a pair of crutches against the bed. "Your boyfriend picked these out. I told him they weren't necessary, but he insisted," she said with a smile.

"He's not my boyfriend."

"Your husband?" The nurse cast a swift glance down at Felicity's hands. "He's a very worried man, I told him you'd be out soon."

The RN left while Felicity stared at the crutches and felt a wisp of tenderness tickle her throat.

With everything finally buttoned or zipped up, she made her way back to the waiting area. Her gaze skimmed over the occupants to Daniel, who sat in the farthest corner away from everyone else. Coffee cup cradled in his hand, he was hunched over in one of the hard plastic chairs, his face haggard and streaked with dirt. Irrationally *she* wanted to comfort *him.*

When he saw her he sprang to his feet, dropping the paper cup onto a table. For a foolish moment, as his strides ate up the distance between them, she thought he was going to sweep her into his arms. And the fierce pure need she had for his embrace made her stagger back.

He blanched as his feet slowed to a stop. "So what did the doctor say?" He slid his hands into his pockets.

She swallowed her disappointment. "I'll be good as new in about a week. He wrote something out for codeine, if I need it."

"We can pick it up on the way home."

"Home?" A spark of hope lit inside of her. "Does that mean the fire wasn't that bad?"

"No, it *was* that bad. They've sealed the building until the cause is discovered. So far the evidence points to some ancient wiring down in the basement." He shook his head. "Anyhow, the structure is unsafe. No one can get back in."

"Then how can I go home?"

"You're coming to the condo with me."

"Your place?" Her eyebrows reach new heights.

Daniel tipped her mouth shut, cupping her chin. "I let you stay in that house and it almost cost you your life." His features were sharply drawn and his voice only a hoarse whisper. "This is the least I can do."

Oh great. She couldn't have his love—but guilt? Bring it on, baby. As tempting as it was to drop her pride like a chewed piece of gum, she didn't. "I can't stay at your place."

"Why not?"

Because it only took a friggin' house burning down around your friggin' head to invite me over? "I have other plans."

"What plans?"

"I can stay with—" She blanked. She couldn't stay with Cheryl and her man in their tiny loft. Her parents? She cringed inwardly. "—I can stay with Stuart, until my new place—"

"Stuart?" He paled. "No! There's no way in hell you're going to Stuart."

"You can't tell me where I can and cannot go. You're not the boss of me—" He tugged one crutch away and dropped it to the floor. "Hey! Wh-what are you doing?" She reached for it and almost lost her balance. When she grabbed onto him, he took the other crutch and sent it sliding down the hall.

"Are you crazy?" she demanded.

"Yes." Daniel swung her up in his arms.

"Put me down!"

"No." He strode towards the door, assuring the nurse at reception that everything was just dandy.

Helpless, Felicity nodded confirmation to security. As the automatic glass doors were sliding shut between them and bemused people in the waiting area, she yelled, "He'll be back for the crutches!"

℘

"You haven't eaten," Daniel pointed out. His pissed-off expression, the one he'd been wearing since they'd left the hospital two days ago, got more pissy.

She reached for the cold toast and dutifully took a bite as he loomed over her, so close she could smell the mingled scents of his soap and aftershave. He was dressed in pinstriped navy pants but his crisp white shirt was tails out, and his hair was loose on his shoulders.

She turned her head to stare through the floor-to-ceiling windows at a lake view that had lost its wow factor a while ago. The dry bread stuck in her throat.

He obviously didn't want her here. Robo-host only came by to bring her a solitary meal on a tray. Spending just enough time to inquire about her comfort before disappearing through the bedroom door again.

Why insist she come here, only to practically ignore her? She heard him sigh, followed by his retreating footsteps.

"I'm going into the office this morning for a couple of hours. You can reach me on the cell if you need me."

"I'll be fine, thank you." She looked up in time to see him pause at the threshold. He thumped the wall and left.

"This is ridiculous." Coming here had been a big fat dancing Mistake-o-gram. She put the tray on the floor, got up and limped over to the phone. Even Stuart's had to be better than this.

"C'mon, c'mon." She pressed the receiver to her ear.

The line stopped ringing and his answering machine clicked on. "*Wazzup? Leave the digits.*"

Idiot. She was rolling her eyes when she heard the phone at the other end pick up. "Stuart? Is that you?"

"No, this is not Stuart," Daniel said coldly and slammed the phone down.

"Crap." She dropped the receiver back into its cradle, and flopped back on the mattress, running a trembling hand through her hair. What was the big deal? She didn't owe Daniel anything. That reasoning didn't stop her heart from leaping to her throat when the door swung open minutes later.

She sat up and faced him. He stood in the threshold, one hand resting on the jamb, while the other held on to the ends of the tie now draped around his upturned collar.

"My mother is on the way up to see you." His voice was bland enough, but his mouth was all twisty.

"Daniel—"

"Hellooo?" Lise's voice echoed from down the hall.

"Back here, Mom." His brooding gaze never left Felicity's face.

"Darling." Lise came into view, and Daniel released Felicity from his scrutiny. His mouth relaxed for the first time since yesterday, and she watched a magical dimple appear in his cheek as he kissed his mother in greeting then submitted to having his hair brushed back from his face.

Lise turned to Felicity, tsk-tsking as she crossed the room, almost hidden from view behind an extravagantly large bouquet of peonies. "How are you feeling?" she asked, sitting on the bed.

"Okay."

Lise tilted her head to the side. "Just okay?" Her mouth curled up into Daniel's smile as she patted Felicity's cheek, and said in a conspiratorial whisper, "Well, don't you worry about a thing; I'll see that he treats you right." She winked.

Oh goody. Nothing like having his mommy make him play nice. Felicity nodded to the flowers. "Are those for me? They're beautiful."

"Of course they're for you, silly. I cut them myself from the garden this morning." Lise placed the bouquet in her lap.

"I suggested you might like them. Since you admired them so much at the barbeque."

Felicity looked over Lise's shoulder. *VD.* Standing in the doorway beside Daniel. Felicity stretched her mouth into a smile. "What a thoughtful gesture from you. It's so...surprising."

Deirdra's eyes narrowed into slits, but she smirked as she placed a hand on Daniel's sleeve. "When Dan told us about your predicament, we just had to come over to see if there was anything we could do to help." *—you get the hell out of here,* VD's hard gaze added.

"Did Dan pass that list of available rentals on to you? I helped him with the research."

Felicity's gaze flew to Daniel.

"Deirdra is more familiar with that part of the firm's portfolio. She got the info compiled faster than I could," he said.

"I sacrificed my secretary to get the particulars together as soon as possible," VD bleated.

"Sounds like you really put yourself out on that one, Deirdra," Lise said dryly.

"It was no trouble at all. In fact it was my pleasure."

No kidding. "Thanks. I appreciate it." *Bitch.*

"So, did you find something?" Deirdra persisted.

"Felicity has options I didn't take into account," Daniel interjected smoothly, knotting his tie. "You should get those flowers in some water soon. If you ladies will excuse me? I have a few things to take care of before I leave for the office." He turned on his heel and left.

"He's absolutely right. Here, give those to me." Lise swiped the flowers from Felicity's arms. "I'll just pop these into a vase and be right back." She sailed across the room and out the door.

Those Mackenzies sure knew how to make a fast exit.

"Great view." VD slithered over to the window.

Felicity agreed, but she kept her eyes on the girl not the view. VD trying to make nice-nice was a load of crap-crap.

VD turned, her shapely form backlit in the sunshine streaming through the window. Felicity squinted, trying to make out her expression. The phrase *"Ve haff vays off making you talk"* ran through her mind.

"Wow, a fire. You must have been scared to death." Deirdra gave a delicate shudder. Like a rattlesnake shaking its tail.

She moved to the dresser opposite the bed, where she checked her flawlessly applied makeup—and probably her fangs too—in the mirror.

"Wasn't it a stroke of luck that Daniel was with you when the fire broke out. At three in the morning, was it?"

Felicity felt a smile tugging at the corners of her mouth; this chick brought out the worst in her. "It was a stroke of something...several strokes in fact."

VD's Cadillac-lush mouth tightened into a Cabriolet-moue.

Swish, two points me.

Averting her face, Deirdra looked down, trailing one manicured nail along the top of the chest of drawers. "This is a nice guest room, isn't it? I helped Daniel pick out this dresser. We went away for a long weekend, antiquing and...other things." She leaned back against the large piece of furniture, obviously not caring if any dust ended up on the short, tight black skirt of her suit. Hard blue eyes met Felicity's. "Several other things."

Feeling ill, Felicity's vivid imagination quickly filled in the details of "other things".

VD's mouth coiled into a satisfied smile.

"We also stumbled upon the workshop of this funny little man; Serge, I think his name was. Daniel ordered a bed from him that weekend."

Deirdra glided over and eased down on the mattress as she spoke. Her cloying perfume hung in the air like roach killer.

She crossed her slim legs, resting her elegant hands, fingers interlaced, on a bony knee.

In comparison to the other girl's polished sophistication, Felicity felt like the before candidate for X-treme Makeover. Her hair was only finger-combed, she wasn't even wearing lip-balm, and she still had on the oversized T-shirt that she'd borrowed, and slept in, from Daniel.

"It's quite a bed...don't you think?"

Felicity was mute, her heart labouring to beat, one, more, time.

The other girl studied her for a long moment. "You haven't seen his bed have you? Now that's interesting...Daniel tired of you already?"

Felicity's face burned and Deirdra leaned in for the kill.

"I told you before, one woman isn't enough for him. So don't kid yourself in thinking that you meant anything more to him than a piece of ass, just because he yelled out your name as he came."

"And whose name does he yell when he's fucking you?"

"He'll say my name where it counts. At the altar. Then you can crawl back to wherever you came from. Just like the rest.

"So enjoy the *guestroom*, sweetie."

ॐ

Daniel entered his study, softly closed the door, then crossed the carpet to his desk where he picked up a pencil. The

183

pencil snapped.

He flung the pieces from him before raking his hands through his hair. *She was going to leave.* And there wasn't a damn thing he could do about it!

He started pacing. It had taken sheer willpower, more than he'd known he possessed, to stay out of the guestroom since he'd brought her here. But his ear had been tuned to her bedroom, anticipating her call for...*anything.* A call that never came.

She thanked him politely, her eyes not quite meeting his, for each meal he brought in. And thanked him again, just as coolly, when he returned for the empty plates.

Every lukewarm expression of appreciation made him want to reach out and drag her mouth to his. Force a response from her. Explain with his body what he was too afraid to say out loud.

Stopping in front of the window, he grunted; he couldn't just barge into her bedroom and flip her legs up over her head.

Although, the plan held certain merit.

He shook his head. No, he'd just end up killing them both if he tried to articulate in lovemaking what was in his heart.

Daniel went back to his desk. He reached for another pencil as he sat down, and began drubbing it deep in thought. *Tap, tap, tap, tap.* The scheme to put in place had to be non-threatening, but quick. *Tap, tap, tap.* He had to get Felicity to let down her guard, let him get close again. *Tap, tap—* Woo her!

He dropped the pencil, breaking into a smile. Turn on the charm, seduce and conquer. He frowned, sounded like something he'd heard Rob say once.

Daniel stood up, sorting through his files. The sooner he got to the office, the sooner he could get back here and put his plan in action. Moving one file in particular revealed the phone hidden underneath and as quickly as his spirits lifted, his mood darkened.

He slammed the file back down on the desk, sending several documents fluttering onto the carpet and he let loose an expletive that ended with "Stuart".

"Daniel!"

"Not now, Mother," he ground out, coming from the behind the desk. He hunched down to scrape up the mess.

His mother placed a peony-filled vase beside the phone, then bent down to help him pick up the papers. Daniel dropped the gathered files onto the desk to be sorted later. His plans for Felicity had just been moved up a couple of hours. No way he was leaving her alone in the condo with the phone.

"So who is this incestuous Stuart?" his mother asked.

"A client."

"I don't think so; you usually describe clients in anatomical terms."

Daniel pressed his lips together, refusing to smile. "I believe that was an anatomical...action."

"Still, it's not nice language, Daniel."

"Yes, Mother." He dropped a kiss of apology at her temple.

"Speaking of which...." she said in that *idle* way of hers that sent danger signals flying through his synapses.

He retreated around to the other side of the desk. "We weren't speaking of anything." He busied himself with documents that suddenly couldn't wait to be sorted after all.

"Stuart wouldn't be the surprise option Felicity has, would he?"

Daniel shoved several files into his briefcase, before shutting it with a decisive click. "I wouldn't know."

"Well, do you want to know what I think?"

"Not particularly." But he surrendered and sat.

"I think you should do your best to keep her right here. It's quite obvious to me that's what you both want."

Daniel reached out and plucked a petal from one of the peonies. "Well think again." He plucked another one. "This is the last place Felicity wants to be, I practically had to beg—"

His mother's eyes widened in surprise and he shut up. *What was he saying? And to her of all people.* He groaned at the dawning expression of pleasure that replaced her surprise.

"I don't want to talk about it," he growled. *Pluck.*

Her smile widened.

"Things are complicated." *Pluck, pluck.*

Her smile vanished. "Stuart?"

He was somewhat mollified that the name had the same effect on her as it had on him. And she didn't even know the schmuck. "Stuart," he confirmed.

When she appeared on the verge of offering advice, he held up a hand. "Let me handle this, okay?"

She dropped her gaze, fussing with the flowers.

"Mother?"

She plucked a petal. "Okay, sweetheart," she answered demurely, pinching off another petal. "Oh!" She looked up, eyes wide. "There is something else I wanted to talk to you about."

He let out the breath he'd been holding. His mother could be persistent when she chose to be.

"Your birthday's coming up in two weeks; I'd like to throw you a party."

Case in point. "No! Absolutely no parties. We made a deal when you booked Ferdinand the Face-Painter at the last party."

"Daniel, you were ten!" She rested her hands on her hips.

"Exactly. Do you think the guys ever let me live that down? You gave Rob a lifetime's worth of material in that one day."

"Well how about the party we threw for you three years ago?"

"For me?" His bark of laughter was humorless. "Dad threw

a party for Mackenzie Phillips and Bassett, and somehow my name got on the invitation as guest of honor."

"Now Daniel—"

"Now nothing." He tapped the desk for emphasis. "No party."

"Well, how about a nice little quiet sit-down dinner?" She clasped her hands to her bosom, her voice spiced with a *soupçon* of wheedling. "Oh, and drinks afterwards? But please don't argue with your father about the wine selection this time."

"Fine. Dinner is fine." He conceded. He wasn't fooled for a second, his birthday was the perfect excuse for another one of her attempts to get him and his dad together.

Daniel grimaced. Some happy birthday that was going to be, spent facing Michael Mackenzie across the dining table.

"That's settled then." She swept the vase up from the desk, and moved swiftly to the door. "I've got to put the finishing touch on my plans. There's so much to do!"

Her unbridled joy gave him a jolt of alarm. "What plans?"

"Why-why the menu, darling. And the cake and flowers and-and—" her gaze shifted around, "—your gift! All sorts of things."

"I don't need a gift."

"Oh, phooey. I have the perfect gift in mind. You'll absolutely love it, sweetheart." She beamed at him. "Come, come now. Let me pop these flowers in Felicity's room. I'll have to fly after that."

A bit more enthusiastic at these words, Daniel rose and hurried after her. He loved his mom dearly, but now that she was on her way out, it couldn't be soon enough for him. When she and Deirdra were gone, he could focus on Felicity—she, who hadn't poked her nose out of the bedroom since she got here. The first phase of attack was to get her out of the guest-fort.

Smiling, he loosened his tie. That showed just how crazy

this situation was, he wanted to get Felicity out of the bedroom, so he could get her *into* bed.

There was more to it than that of course, but bedrooms and beds figured big in his plans. With a decided swagger he reentered Felicity's room.

Chapter Sixteen

"Would you look at these peonies, aren't they lovely?"

At Lise's singsong entrance, the malice in Deirdra's eyes glossed over and the brunette got up.

"They do look wonderful. Isn't that the vase you brought back from your trip to Paris last year?" VD's voice was pleasant and friendly. So unlike a minute ago.

"Yes, it is. I thought giving it to Daniel would encourage him to have some fresh flowers in this waiting room he calls a home." Lise looked around the stark space. "I mean really, darling, can't you at least do something with the walls? Just a little color." Lise held her thumb and finger close together.

"White's a color." Daniel leaned against the door frame, arms crossed over his chest. He'd loosened his tie, and for some reason seemed to be more relaxed. When his gaze swung from his mother to meet hers, Felicity blinked, tempted to look over her shoulder for the person he was staring at with such warmth.

"White is a cop-out," Lise retorted. "Don't you think so, Felicity?"

"Me?" She tore herself away from the sensation of drowning in Daniel's gaze, and looked around the sparsely furnished room. There was a chair slip-covered white and the bed was dressed in white linens. The only other pieces of furniture were the plain wood dresser and nightstand. He'd mentioned once, when he was spending a lot of time at her place, that he didn't spend a lot of time at his own. It showed.

She assumed an iffy expression. "Maybe he *did* play it safe with the eggshell in here. But he really went to town in the bathroom. Bone-colored tiles, off-white on the walls and ivory towels." She slid a sly glance Daniel's way and saw two dimples carved into his jaw. Her heart skipped a beat.

Lise laughed and wagged a finger at her. "I like you."

Felicity grinned.

VD sucked a lemon.

Then Lise checked her watch. "Oops. Will you look at the time? I have to run." She came over to the bed. "I know this was a short visit, but I'll be back." She bent down to kiss Felicity's cheek. "We have to talk," she added in a whisper, a twinkle in her eyes.

"Okay," Felicity agreed cautiously. Lise's *twinkles* usually meant *twouble.*

"Deirdra, I'll drop you back at the office."

"I thought I'd catch a ride with Daniel," VD replied.

"I'm not going in today. Something's come up that needs my immediate attention." He stared at Felicity as he spoke, pulling the tie slowly from his neck. "I'll be here for the rest of the day."

"Oh." VD sounded nonplussed. "But I wanted to confer with you on Tillman Steele...?"

He was shaking his head. "No can do."

VD resumed her lemon sucking.

"But if you want to set something up for tomorrow—"

"Lunch?"

"Sure."

"Wonderful." VD purred; her lemon turned into lemonade.

"Come along, Deirdra," Lise said. "See you later, Felicity."

"I'll see you out." Daniel threw an arm around VD's shoulders as they followed Lise out of the room.

Felicity's spirits plunged to a new depression level: 10 Below, then parked themselves in the farthest darkest corner where somebody had taken a piss. And that somebody would be VD.

Half an hour later found Felicity staring at the phone undecided. She'd already called The Uptown, to explain to Tony about the fire and her ankle. He'd given her until next Friday to get back to work. What a guy. Not that she could afford to take any more time off anyway, but now she had to decide about staying here. Her head told her to go. Her heart, and a sense of shove-it-up-yours-Deirdra, told her to stay.

"So are you planning on hiding in here forever?"

Felicity jerked round at the sound of Daniel's voice. The business attire had been replaced with loose fitting jeans, hung low on his hips, and a denim shirt, unbuttoned with sleeves rolled up. The hard ridges of his chest and stomach and the corded strength of his forearms were totally on display. She swallowed, feasting on the way his tanned skin shone through the fine gold hairs dusting his body.

"I'm not hiding. I haven't been given clearance to leave my quarters," she said with a touch of sarcasm.

He frowned. "Is that how you feel, like a prisoner?"

She shrugged. "What do you expect? I feel like I'm intruding."

"It looks like I've been a bad host. But give me a chance to rectify that." He came to her, his hand held out. "Starting right now."

Felicity stared into his watchful gaze. Staying in here and keeping her own company would probably be the smarter and safer thing to do.

Unfortunately she didn't do smarter/safer very well. She

191

put her hand in his, then suppressed a shiver as a wave of goose bumps swept along her arm and trickled down her back. It was the first time he'd touched her since arriving at the condo.

"Okay?"

When she nodded, he helped her to her feet and passed the crutches to her. "I'm sorry you've felt unwelcome. Just know that my home is your home, for as long as you wish."

She seriously doubted that, given his track record. But she couldn't help thawing a bit more in the face of that crooked little smile that rocked her heart.

Limping awkwardly beside him, they left the room and went down the airy hallway that opened up to the great room of the condo. For the first time she got a really good look at the place. Sunlight flooded through the gauzy white fabric that draped the floor to ceiling windows, beyond which she could see a large terrace and, further out, the vista of Lake Ontario and a cloudless sky.

The room was huge. One wall was taken up completely by a shelving unit that housed some exotic-looking artifacts, a bar, and, from her years with Stuart, what she recognized as a kick-ass stereo system.

Anchoring the center of the room was a low slung sofa upholstered in a rich chocolate brown leather, flanked by two chairs named after one of those dead French kings, and a large rustic coffee table. The other end of the room was dominated by a compact kitchen area, separated from the main space by an oversized island.

The rest of it was...space. Empty *white* space.

Felicity stepped back, intending to turn around again but found herself pressed against Daniel's hard body.

"Whoa." He grasped her arms and recall shimmered through her veins, of the last time they had been chest to back with their bodies pressed together. His voice whispering and urging from behind, his mouth buried in her hair, suckling at her nape, trailing kisses down her spine. Felicity's knees went wobbly.

"Are you okay?" He held her tighter.

"Y-yes, I'm fine." Briefly, she closed her eyes and breathed in his aftershave, overcome by memories that were much too real—the smell of him, the feel, the taste.

She fought the need to lean back into him and moved away, clearing her throat several times before she could speak. "So, what do you do around here for entertainment?"

She looked over her shoulder, turning on her good leg to face him. His eyes were hooded and the skin seemed stretched taut across his cheekbones. With his thumbs hooked into the belt loops of his jeans, the pants settled further down on his hips.

Her eyes followed the happy trail of bronze hair from his navel down into the shadowy regions just below his waistband.

Before her eyes, he turned hard.

And she turned to liquid.

"I find ways." He focused on her mouth then skimmed over the cotton T-shirt she wore, the heat in his gaze beading the tips of her breasts.

A muscle ticked in his jaw and he moved abruptly towards the wall unit. "There's lots to do in the area since we have tourist designation. And on the rare occasion I don't bring work home with me, I read, watch a good movie, or listen to music." He pressed a button on the stereo and in an instant, soulful crooning infused the space.

"Otis Redding, right?"

His back to her, Daniel nodded. Felicity limped over to the sofa and sat, allowing the words of the song to wash over her. A little tenderness would be her complete undoing right now.

"Felicity?" The sadness in her expression hooked into Daniel's chest and drew him to sit beside her. Slowly, he reached out and framed her face in his hands. His thumbs exploring the softness of her skin as he gently urged her closer, till he settled his mouth on the lushness of hers.

She opened to him with a little whimper, and the muscles in his shoulders bunched under the will not to crush her to him. Never let her go. Arousal accelerating into overdrive, Daniel plunged his tongue in her wet warmth, entwining her tongue, swallowing her greedy moans. Then with an agonized moan, he broke away. *Easy does it.* He forced the thought through his passion-fogged brain, even as every nerve in his body snarled in frustration.

Deliberately, he slowed his breathing as he stared into her face. He saw confusion and passion in her eyes...and something else, something warm and yearning, just before her lids swept down. It was a glimmer of the truth.

"Felicity?" He nudged her chin up, willing her to look at him. After long moments, she raised her eyes again. They were guarded. Daniel felt his jaw tighten. Had he seen a hint of her true feelings, or did he just imagine it? Just want it so damn much? Abruptly he stood up.

"Let me show you the terrace."

She hesitated for a moment before accepting his help up from the deeply cushioned seat. They stepped out onto the terrace. As they crossed to the railing, his hand settled into the small of her back, but he was sorely tempted to let his palm slide down over the sweet curve of her ass.

He folded his arms across his chest, hands securely sandwiched between biceps and torso. *Must not touch.*

Felicity leaned on the railing, face turned skyward. "I didn't realize we were on the penthouse level."

Her eyes lit up as a gentle breeze played in her hair, lifting several wisps, then trailing one lock across lips that were parted in pleasure. He reached out and smoothed the hair away from her face. He wanted to capture that sweet mouth again.

"I like my privacy. No neighbors except the ones downstairs." Daniel leaned forward dropping his voice suggestively. "No one to hear your moans."

He watched the muscles in her throat work, saw her eyes darken. What the hell was wrong with him? This wasn't wooing. He might as well grease his hair back, throw on some gold chains and unbutton his shirt, for all the finesse he was showing. Wait a sec—

His shirt *was* unbuttoned.

The upbeat sounds of Motown drifted out from the condo. Something about a guy being a clown. That would be him: Horny the Clown. Stuck tooting his own horn for the foreseeable future.

"Look, I apologize; that was a stupid thing to say." He dropped his hand. "I'll show you the rest of the condo."

"How much more is there?"

"Like I said, no neighbors. The whole floor is mine."

Her eyebrows rose. "Must be nice."

"I bought in from the beginning. The developer is a client and a friend of the family."

"Of course," she said wryly and hopped in place, adjusting the position of the crutches.

"Are you up to it?" he asked, concerned.

"It's going to take a lot more than a little fire and a twisted ankle to lick me."

Lick me. Not a good phrase for a man in his present condition to hear. Daniel fisted his hands in his pockets, hoping to give his semi-erection a little more room.

"After you." He inclined his head for her to go ahead of him. There really wasn't much to show her except a few more under-furnished rooms.

He had the necessities—chairs, tables, beds. And he'd cared enough to choose unique pieces that were interesting, but now, walking through the condo with Felicity and seeing his home through her eyes, he was aware of what was missing. The throw pillows and fresh flowers. A woman's touch.

Her bland compliments on the nice white walls weren't lost on him either. He hesitated at the door of his study, rethinking his position on nesting.

"You don't have to show me your office."

Daniel looked down at Felicity. "I have nothing to hide from you." He tried to hold her gaze, but she looked away again. *Damn it. Take it slow, clown boy.*

He pushed open the door and ushered her in. "I'm particularly proud of the walls in here. I chose French Vanilla Fadeout for its stimulating properties—"

Daniel earned himself a poke to the ribs that he twisted away from, then he quickly moved out of tickling range when he saw her eyes narrow and the almost evil grin that curled her delectable mouth. The last time he'd seen that look there had been a paintbrush in her hand. He wasn't taking any chances—even with her on crutches.

"And through here—" he walked across the room to another door, "—is the master bedroom..."

Felicity wasn't following along; she'd stopped in the middle of the room, staring at the wall behind his desk. His mother had insisted the degrees he refused to display at Mackenzie Phillips and Bassett find a proper home here.

This was the only room he'd allowed any signs of nesting, and his mother, true to form, had run with the ball. There were framed family pictures, some of happier days between him and his dad, on the credenza, and a bunch of useless tasseled cushions on the small two-seater. A Persian rug under the desk and a potted fern were the final pieces of clutter she'd snuck in before he asked for his key back.

"You sure have a lot of degrees," Felicity said quietly, shooting him a look from the corner of her eye.

He shrugged. "It looks more impressive than it really is, considering my mom framed and hung every single award I've earned since age three."

Felicity snorted. "Maybe I should try that."

He wondered at her hint of bitterness. "You didn't finish your degree?"

"Didn't start it. I decided the school of hard knocks, with a major in crappy jobs, was an easier route."

The dark thread in her voice roped his heart. She looked a little lost, a little vulnerable standing in the middle of the room. He remembered the odd comments she'd made from time to time, painting a picture of a lonely childhood. He hadn't pried, picking up on the pain in her eyes and the proud tilt of her head, but he'd gathered that money had been an issue growing up.

But not as big an issue as love. The scene with her parents played through Daniel's mind, her father's harsh words and the way she'd kept so still, felt so brittle, in his arms afterward.

That same brittleness was there now, telegraphing that she didn't want to be touched. He would respect that, *for now*. But he did move closer, right into her line of vision by leaning against the desk.

"You're interested in interior decorating, right?"

She met his gaze. "Yeah." The admission came reluctantly, as if she didn't want him to have even that small bit of knowledge, he thought ruefully.

"You have an eye for it. Besides your sad lack of appreciation for the infinite possibilities of white."

The tightness in his chest eased at her smile.

"So it's not like you're going to be a waitress for the rest of your life. You can go back to school, or gain experience working in a design studio or shop. Or you can start up something freelance."

Felicity rolled her eyes, a look of bemusement on her face. "And who would hire me?"

"Me," he said, surprising himself for a split second, but it made perfect sense. Now he had to convince her.

"Why so shocked? You have talent. I've seen what you did with your place on a budget. Well, I've got a way bigger budget."

Color rose in her face, and sensing her pride might cause some resistance, he quickly added, "Plus, I've got some experience in the field and connections within the industry. I can be like a tutor."

"A tutor, huh?" She seemed to find this amusing, but she was still wary.

"You doubt my tutoring abilities?" He let a suggestive note trickle into his voice.

She giggled in response. "Oh, I think you'd be a natural," she said. Then, "You really think I can do this?"

He stood up and rested his hands on her shoulders. "I know you can."

She gave him a blinding smile, then her smile dimmed. "You don't know how much I hate my job."

"I have an idea. My third year at U of T, me and my dad were barely on speaking terms. I moved out. Luckily, I had a small trust from my grandmother that helped pay for tuition, but the rest I had to ante up myself with odd jobs."

She cocked her head to the side. "Construction?"

He nodded. "Which in light of my present situation, almost makes those years training and working in law seem like a waste of time."

"I know all about wasted years." She sighed, looking at his degrees again, and started nibbling on a stubby fingernail. He'd noticed her nails before, ugly, raggedy and bitten to the quick. He loved all ten of them.

"I moved out when I was sixteen," she said, taking him by surprise. "That's when I quit school. I thought anything would be better than being at home, and-and school, well it wasn't for me." She looked at her bitten nails a little too studiously.

"It must have been hard."

"Yep. But that's life. Right?" Her tone said she didn't want an answer, she was done sharing.

He was disappointed, but reminded himself, *patience.* There'd be time, later, to share their pasts, their disappointments, their dreams.

Their futures.

"Sometimes you make one little careless decision, and it changes your whole life."

She was looking at him. *Sweet.*

"Then you realized that maybe you made the wrong decision."

Shit. She was still looking at him. No, wait, she was looking at the wall again. Daniel pulled her hand away from her mouth. "So when do you want to start? We can probably get some things done this week. If you're up to it."

"You're serious, aren't you?"

"I told you before, Felicity, you can take my word as bond." He squeezed her hand and watched as she went from confused to cautious, then just as her features were softening into something more, the phone rang.

A curse ran through his head as he released her and went to answer the call.

"*Daniel?*"

"Deirdra." He saw Felicity stiffen. "Hold on a second." He moved the mouth-piece away. "This will just take a minute."

"You go ahead." She backed up, hobbling towards the door.

"Here, let me help you."

"No, thank you, I can find my way. Thanks for the tour."

For someone with a limp she moved pretty fast. The door shut behind her. *Thank you for the tour. Breakfast was delicious, thank you. Thank you, I'll be fine.*

Just when he was making progress.

Screw thank you.

Chapter Seventeen

Felicity lay down on her bed, chewing on a nail while jammy sensation slicked her gut. *Fear.*

But this fear...this was about achieving dreams, or losing them. This was what she'd felt when she'd walked out of her father's house at sixteen, knowing that she was more than he'd said.

Her heart plunged then buoyed back up on the possibilities. A lot of what Daniel did straddled the finishing end of decorating, and he did have the connections. This could really happen!

Her gaze flitted around the room, her mind coming up with a thousand alternative decorating possibilities, until she lit upon the dresser and mirror. The one VD had checked to see if she still had a reflection. Felicity's high came crashing down.

She rolled onto her back, straining with bionic intensity to pick up on Daniel's conversation with his ex as she bit at her raw cuticle. Her attempted snooping was rewarded with the sound of bare feet padding down the hall. The footsteps stopped at her door and she tensed.

"I'll be going out this evening, Felicity. Probably be gone for most of the night. Going to give VD some of that hot monkey lovin' I gave you—" She shut off the imaginary voice in her head as Daniel's footsteps retreated back down the hall.

Felicity resumed biting her nails. Why was she tormenting

herself like this?

Because she wanted to be the one wrapped in his arms, being kissed by him and feeling him hot and hard moving inside her. She stopped nibbling and sat up, indecision plaguing her. She was an idiot to even be thinking of making love with him again, when she was just another piece of ass to him. If she believed Deirdra.

Thing is, she didn't want to believe her. *Stupid bitch in too much makeup.*

A loud crash came from somewhere in the condo, followed by a string of curses. She grabbed a crutch and limped as fast as she could to investigate.

"Daniel? What happened? Are you okay?" She reached the main room and spotted him in the kitchen.

"I'm fine. Can't say the same for the antipasto." He stooped down, disappearing below the counter.

Curious, she went around the island and stopped short at the sight of the mess on the floor.

Daniel went down on his haunches, a garbage bin by his side as he picked out the bigger pieces of china from the assortment of spilled meats and vegetables, and dumped them into the receptacle.

"What's that?" The sound of a tinny voice calling Daniel's name had her frowning.

He straightened up and grabbed the phone off the counter. "I'll call you back...no, no, it's fine." He glanced at Felicity. "Now's not a good time to talk. Yes, I'll see you later."

"Are you going out?" The question slipped out as he hung up. She couldn't help herself. Visions of Daniel and VD engaged in hot monkey-lovin' were trapezing through her mind.

He looked over his shoulder as he grabbed a short-handled brush and dirt shovel from under the sink. "No, why?"

"I thought you were talking to Deirdra. It sounded like you were going to see her later..." She shifted under his suddenly sharp gaze.

"That was my mom. I needed her advice on something." He stopped, flushing. "I thought you'd like a home cooked meal instead of another soup and sandwich deal for lunch."

Felicity looked around; there was a skillet on the gas range, and a colander in the sink filled with mixed greens. A slow smile curved her mouth. "What were you making?"

"A mess."

"Maybe I can help?"

"No!"

Her jaw dropped at his quick vehemence, and he chuckled. "I remember your macaroni and cheese."

"At least my food was cooked *before* it ended up in the garbage."

"And your point is?"

She stuck out her tongue. "Do you need help cleaning up, at least?"

"This is exactly what you can do." He stepped over the crap on the floor, then guided her to a barstool on the other side of the island. "Sit here."

Daniel removed a wine glass from the overhead rack and placed it in front of her. From the fridge, he retrieved a bottle of wine.

"You'll like this; nicely rounded, crisp, with some pleasing fruity notes in the aftertaste." He poured her a glass.

She barely suppressed a smile, before taking a sip.

"What's so funny?" He set the bottle down and leaned forward, resting his elbows on the counter.

"All I know about wine could be summed up in four words: red, white, baby duck."

"Then I'll just have to take the time to teach you a little bit more about wine while you're here." He sounded lazy. He looked dangerous. His gaze drifted from her eyes to her mouth.

Daniel reached out, his hand covering hers as he deliberately turned the wine glass so that the exact spot she'd drunk from was facing him. Then forcing her hand up with his, he raised the glass to his lips and drank.

Over the edge of the goblet Daniel watched Felicity's irises deepen from silver to pewter and a flush bloom across her cheeks. Her tongue darted out, wetting her lips, making arousal tug at his groin.

Was the plan to *do* her, then woo her? Or vice versa? He was getting confused. He swallowed and put the glass down.

"Color—the clarity, the richness and the depth—are all very important elements of wine." He stroked the silken skin on the back of her hand. And felt her tremble. He wanted her to tremble some more, every part of her, under his hands, his mouth, his body.

He moved his caress to the rim of the glass, tracing slow lazy circles around it, then dipped his finger into the wine. He smeared the liquid across her mouth.

"It reveals a lot about the nature of the drink. Like making love, there are different experiences, different tastes, different levels of enjoyment.

"White wine can be intense, complex, exotic." Her clever little tongue darted out again, touching him, then warm lips parted and he felt the light suction to his forefinger. The tug of desire he'd been experiencing turned into a tight milking grip.

"Rosés," his voice went rusty with barely suppressed want, "are softly textured...sweet, warm, and sumptuous." By exquisite degrees, he stroked his finger into and out of Felicity's mouth, savoring the intense pleasure of slowly gliding against her wet tongue. Each suckle on his flesh made his cock harden and grow, while his 'nads shrank tight and hot up against his body. He groaned, pulling his finger out of her mouth, before he wrapped his hand around her neck and urged her to him.

"And red is earthy, elemental, deep, and...irresistible," he whispered harshly, before covering her mouth with his own. Tasting, plunging, exploring. A growl of frustration tore from his throat, he wanted to be closer. Needed to feel her sweet curves pressed against him.

Without breaking the kiss, he moved around the counter and indulged himself for a few amazing minutes eating at her mouth, until he remembered that he wasn't supposed to be pawing her. Groping wasn't good strategy for a long term relationship. He eased back.

"Is the lesson over already?" she whispered wistfully.

"A connoisseur never overindulges. They savor the experience." He dropped a final kiss on her nose and slid the glass closer to her. "Here, drink, while I work on dinner."

He went back to the sink and started washing the veggies for their salad. "You'll be quite pleased with what I have in store for you."

"*Hmmm.* Oh I'm sure I'll love every mouthful," she said huskily.

A reminder to himself not to pressure Felicity in any way was the only reason he wasn't performing handsprings back over to where she sat. *The only reason.*

By some small miracle they managed to get through the rest of the day without tearing each other's clothes off. As it was, they barely kept their hands to themselves. But there was a sense in the air of something fragile budding. Something new that shouldn't be rushed.

Instead they spent the time talking and teasing, watched a couple of movies and discussed what Daniel wanted for the condo. Felicity's confidence grew as he agreed with several of her suggestions or put his own spin on them. And the fact that he turned positively mule-headed on other suggestions—making her want to smack him—soothed any last doubts that he was just humoring her.

They decided to check downstairs in the shopping concourse for accessories the next day, before sourcing stuff at their individual favorite stores. Daniel had several pricey designer places in mind, while she planned to introduce him to the wonderful world of dust allergies at the little hole-in-the-wall places she liked.

After a restless, horny night, she spent a restless morning waiting for him to come home from the office, so they could get started. Then she realized she had nothing to wear.

With no other choice she called Daniel on his cell to ask if he could grab her a pair of jeans and a top at the Gap on the way home. He knew her size already and she'd repay him when she got to a bank machine.

So she timed her phone call when she knew he'd be having lunch with VD.

Sue her.

Felicity was out on the terrace, enjoying the view of the lake, when a strong pair of arms slid around her waist and warm lips started nuzzling at her ear.

She turned in his embrace and looked up into Daniel's smiling face, trying to suppress her happiness.

"Did you miss me?"

"About this much." She held her finger and thumb a smidgen apart.

"Did I ever tell you how great you are for my ego?" he asked as their bodies swayed to some imaginary music only the two of them could hear.

"Nope, you haven't, but I can *feel* exactly how great I am for your ego." She bounced her hips lightly off his.

"I can't argue with you there." He grinned. "I have a surprise for you."

Felicity reached down and stroked him. "No surprises

here," she teased.

"Not that, wench." He gave her a quick kiss then took her hand. "Come with me."

She followed him down the hall, limping slightly, but stopped cold at the threshold of her bedroom when she saw the bags piled onto the bed. "What's all this?"

"Your surprise."

"For me?" Unease rippled through her. "But I just asked you to pick me up a pair of jeans and a T-shirt."

"And I did that. Plus a few extras."

"I can't accept this." She looked at the famous names on the bags, not the least of which were several large bright pink and black ones bearing the exclusive name of Bloor Street's Holt Renfrew store.

"Daniel, I can't afford this."

"But I can."

Her mouth firmed into a stubborn line, but she eyed the bags again, tempted to at least look.

Daniel sighed and reached into the nearest one, pulling out a wisp of black lace. He held it up so she could see that it was a pair of thong underwear. "Besides, I think my hair dryer is in danger of shorting out..." His expression was wickedly amused.

She groaned and covered her face. She'd been hand-washing her panties in the bathroom sink, then drying them with his blow-dryer. This morning he'd caught her.

"Personally, as far as I'm concerned, you could go without. But..." He dangled the thong in front of her and Felicity snatched it out of his hand.

Caving in to temptation, she climbed onto the bed and tentatively pulled one of the bags, not from Holt's, towards her, telling herself she just wanted a look. She wasn't used to getting gifts. Growing up, money was used for practical things. And even though Stuart had been surprisingly good about remembering birthdays and other special days, it had never been anything like this.

The first couple of bags she went through held more lingerie, delicate bits of lace and delicious slivers of silk and satin. "I'm beginning to see a pattern."

He grinned unabashedly. "Look in those bags over there; I think they have some real clothes in them."

Felicity burst out laughing and attacked the last of the booty. She found the jeans, tops, a slinky white wrap dress with spaghetti straps, and two pairs of shoes—heels and flats. There were also several basic makeup items in a smaller bag. With the bounty spread out on the bed, she was again visited with misgivings.

"Don't even think it," he warned. "I still feel I could have prevented that fire somehow. Let me do this."

Some of her pleasure deflated. *Guilt.* He wasn't buying her gifts. He was assuaging his conscience.

"Okay," she agreed quietly.

Daniel rose from the bed. "Get dressed and we'll go downstairs if you're still up for it. I'll be in the study. Just holler when you're ready."

"No problemo." She conjured up her own smile. Then watched him stride out of the room with his characteristic lithe grace.

Felicity looked again at the pile of clothing. It was like looking at tinsel after Christmas. The magic was gone. And really, she couldn't afford any of it. She grabbed what she could afford to pay for—the jeans and top—and got dressed, determined that he would have to take the rest back.

As for Daniel, there was a decided spring to his step as he made his way back to his office. The wonder on Felicity's face, the growing excitement as she emptied each bag had made him feel like Superman and Santa Claus all wrapped up in one.

He knew her well enough to know it wasn't all about getting stuff. Or even getting expensive stuff. No, judging from what she'd told him about her past, it was just the fact that someone had thought enough of her to shower her with gifts. Some of his happiness faded. He had no right to feel angry at her parents. Not everyone had the financial wherewithal the Mackenzies had, yet did it take that much?

He thought back to his own childhood, to the few times he'd won his dad's approval, and the constant affection of his mother. Felicity had never had even that. He couldn't take her back in time and make her parents show her the love she deserved. But he could love her here and now, in every way he knew how. The gifts were just a small start.

Twenty minutes later, they were downstairs in the ground-floor mall adjacent to the condominium. Their first stop was at the ice cream parlor, where she and Daniel spent several minutes checking out the selection.

"What are you having?" she asked.

"Vanilla."

"Vanilla?"

"Vanilla is a perfectly acceptable flavor. It's classic."

"But it's so—" she searched for the right word, "—white."

"Make that chocolate," Daniel said to their server. His narrowed gaze challenged her to say anything. Anything at all.

She rolled her eyes, then asked for a double scoop of coffee biscotti and banana caramel ripple—which Daniel shot repeated glances at as they left the store. Grudgingly she offered him a taste, and he managed several greedy licks before she finally protested.

They took their time browsing, stopping frequently to give her ankle a rest. Eventually Daniel made several purchases, including a boldly colored tapestry by a local artist, and arrangements were made for the deliveries.

She and Daniel were circling back to the mall's exit when they nipped into a small store to admire some unusual silver jewelry. One ring in particular caught Felicity's eye.

"That's one of my favorite pieces," the store owner said. "Would you like a closer look?" At Felicity's nod, she opened the display case and removed the ring, then dropped it in Felicity's open palm.

"It's beautiful." Felicity turned the ring one way then the other as the fire within the cubic zirconia caught the light. "There's something about the design...it seems so...I don't know."

"Strong? Peaceful? Joyous?" the other woman offered.

Felicity smiled and nodded. "Yes, all those things."

"If you look closely, you can see the bands are actually two birds flying. It's representative of two spirits together, traveling towards a brighter future."

Now that it was pointed out, she clearly saw the wings. "Wow."

"When you think about it, all engagement rings have the same symbolism," the shop owner continued. "This particular designer made the interpretation a bit more literal. The diamond is flawless by the way; two point five carats," she finished, beaming rather pointedly at them.

"Oh." Felicity's sense of awe shrank down to *aww crap*. She handed back the piece of relationship kryptonite, then deliberately *ooh-ahh'd* over several necklaces and bracelets.

When the owner asked if she'd like to see those pieces, she declined. The only thing she wanted to see was the exit.

They left the store, Daniel silent beside her. And for once he didn't suggest where they should check out next. Blindly she looked around, desperate to escape the sudden awkwardness. Across the aisle another display window caught her attention, and her momentary embarrassment eased as she walked over for a better look.

Felicity's eyes darted around the showcase. *Unbelievable.* She glanced over her shoulder at Daniel who had his hands shoved into his pants pocket. His eyebrows rose innocently, the effect ruined by his lopsided grin.

"This looks familiar." She pointed at a slinky bra and panty set. "And so does this one and this one and that one. And, oh, look, the sales woman is waving at you."

"I think I paid for her kid's braces earlier today." His grin widened, but the heat in his gaze sent a shiver down her spine. The unease between them turned into another type of tension.

"I can tell you one thing, that kid's new smile won't even come close to the one I'll be wearing when I see you in that little number over there in the corner."

Felicity looked at the outfit in question. That little number was a fraction.

"I think that can be arranged." Her voice came out husky.

"Soon." Eyes darkening, he slowly bent towards her. "Tonight," he whispered in a low rumble, giving her the briefest, most unsatisfactory, kiss. "Now."

She looked around, and Daniel chuckled. "I meant upstairs. But I like the way you think."

She blushed. "It's all your fault. You've thoroughly corrupted me."

"Surely not *thoroughly...*" His measuring gaze made her stomach knot in anticipation.

"Let's go." She tugged at his hand and the humor in his expression increased as he snaked his arm around her waist to slow her down.

As they made their way back to the condominium lobby, Daniel recounted in a lowered voice exactly what constituted thoroughly corrupted in his book.

His finger hesitated over the UP button as they stood in front of the elevators. "Didn't you want to look around outside?"

Vanessa Jaye

"What's so great about outside? Trees, sky, grass, seen it all before." She pressed the button herself and gave him a *what are yah nuts?* look. The topography of Daniel's body was all the landscape she was interested in at the moment. When the doors opened Felicity stepped into the elevator ahead of him.

"Besides, I think I've given this ankle enough exercise for the day."

He instantly became concerned. "Why didn't you tell me it was bothering you?" Daniel pulled out a plastic card from his pocket and swiped it in the control panel. *Penthouse* flashed on the screen and the elevator started to move upwards.

She laid a hand on his arm. "I'm fine. It's a little sore, that's all. I'll just spend the rest of the day lolling around."

"I'll have to peel you some grapes when we get upstairs."

"My very own love slave?"

The smile slipped from his face and he drew her to him. "More than you know," he said gruffly.

"Excuse me? Are you going up?"

Daniel pulled back and Felicity looked into the inquisitive expressions of an older couple holding matching Schnauzers. The dogs started yapping and Daniel sidled into a corner, maneuvering her to stand in front of him.

As the elevator ascended, the reason for him using her as a shield became obvious—eight hard, blatant inches of obvious that he mischievously pressed against her ass periodically. Then to her utter shame she felt her nipples go bionic—bigger, harder and ready to pop through her thin top.

For several floors Felicity gritted her teeth in a false smile at the other occupants, who were staring at her and Daniel with unabashed amused curiosity. Even the dogs seemed to know what was going on and continued to whine and sniff loudly with their stupid little wet noses pointed at her and Daniel.

"Have a nice day, folks," he called good-naturedly at their retreating backs once the couple got off. The door closed on the

212

wife's tittering and several more yaps from the dogs.

Felicity whirled on him. "You—you—"

He kissed her. Again and again and again. She dimly heard the bell announce their arrival at the penthouse. And somehow they got off the elevator in a tangle of limbs, until Daniel was against the wall of the private foyer, his splayed legs framing her hips as she leaned into his groin. He pushed up her top above her breasts and his head dipped to lave attention there, raining suckling kisses on her heated flesh.

With feverish fingers, she unzipped his pants, reaching into his boxers to grasp the thickness of his cock. He groaned and captured a nipple. She moaned and stroked harder. And into all of this came the insistent buzz of the intercom.

"Ignore it, they'll go away." His words were muffled against her skin. But whoever was downstairs had no intention of going away. The ringing stopped briefly only to start up again. With an oath, Daniel tore his lips from her cleavage and slammed the side of his fist against the intercom.

"Yes!" he barked out, chest heaving. Eyes still holding her captive as his other hand took to roaming over her body, cupping each ass cheek in a possessive squeeze, before sliding between her thighs—

"Daniel, sweetheart, it's your mother," the scratchy voice emitted from the intercom.

He jerked his hand from Felicity's crotch and thumped his head back against the wall several times. With a groan, he closed his eyes and then took a deep breath, causing his chest to brush the wet tips of her breasts.

"Daniel, are you there?"

"I'm here." His expression turned wry as he looked down at Felicity, finally letting her go. He punched in the access code for the penthouse elevator. "Come on up."

They straightened their clothing, but even after he assured her she looked fine, Felicity still wanted to go hide in the bedroom.

"Oh no you don't." He halted her escape by snagging her wrist. "My mother's probably here to visit you."

"Do I look all right? My hair—"

"You look absolutely beautiful."

He leaned towards her again, and she held up a hand to ward him off. "Whoa."

He grabbed her hand and pressed it to his mouth, licking at the shallow heart of her palm.

"Don't do that!" She snatched her hand away.

The elevator doors opened, and Lise hesitated at the threshold. "I'm not interrupting?" She looked them both over with the same sly amusement the older couple had.

"N-no of course not."

"Whatever gave you that idea?" Daniel bent and kissed his mom on both cheeks.

"What indeed?" Lise patted him on the chest before turning to Felicity. "You're looking much improved. Daniel must be taking good care of you."

And then some. "We just came from a walk around the mall."

"You're positively glowing, my dear," Lise said, linking arms with her. She towed a limping Felicity into the living-room. "Nothing like some well-timed calisthenics to do you a world of good," she added dryly.

Blushing, Felicity shot a beseeching glance at Daniel over her shoulder. He just winked.

Jerk.

Chapter Eighteen

Felicity sat with Lise on the sofa, while Daniel reclined in one of the chairs, feet propped on the coffee table.

Lise made shooing motions. "I taught you better than that."

Shaking his head, he took his feet down. "There were supposed to be advantages to moving out on my own."

"And some of those advantages you took with you, like the civilized manner in which you were raised." She stroked some hair behind her ear and turned to Felicity with a smile. "Does this mean your ankle is feeling better, if you're getting around without your crutch?"

"Well, the nurse did say the crutches weren't really necessary." She snuck a peek at Daniel, who sank down in his seat sheepishly. "But I should take it easier for the next couple of days since I pulled an afternoon shift for Saturday."

"Surely you're not going back to work so soon?" Lise protested.

"I can't afford to lose my job. And I can't stay here forever."

"I've already told you, you're welcome to stay here as long as it takes," Daniel said, his expression now darkened.

As long as it takes for what?

He stood up abruptly. "Mom, would you like something to drink? Wine? Coffee?"

"Water, thank you."

He glanced at Felicity.

"I'm fine."

"I take it this visit also has something to do with Saturday night?" Daniel asked as he walked over to the kitchen.

"Yes!" Lise clapped her hands together. "I've gotten so much done since yesterday. Almost everything is in place for your birthday. We have reservations for four at Butterfly—"

"Wait a sec." He looked up from pouring out two glasses of water. "Reservations? I thought you said a small dinner at home." He rested the bottle on the countertop, subjecting his mother to narrow-eyed scrutiny.

"Oh." Lise waved his concern away. "I've got enough on my plate without whipping up a gourmet dinner."

"Gee, thanks, Mom."

"Now, Daniel, I didn't mean it like that. Only that with everything else—"

"Everything else?" He pounced again as he brought the drinks over, passing her one.

"Yes, everything else. I had to make a last minute appointment with Frederick—do you know how difficult it was to convince him to squeeze me in? I assured him I only needed a wash and a teensy trim. And then I had to—"

"Okay, okay. I'll take your word for it." He returned to his chair.

"And why wouldn't you?" Lise looked very pleased with herself as she took a sip of her water. "So you and Felicity should meet your father and me at the restaurant by seven-thirty."

"Me?" Felicity squealed.

"But of course. It's Daniel's birthday. I'm sure he'd want you to be there."

Felicity wasn't so sure. He hadn't said word one to her.

He must have read her thoughts, and tried to explain. "I

didn't say anything earlier because I was hoping my mother would drop her plans."

"And that was totally unrealistic of you, Daniel. You know me better."

"I'm not too fond of celebrating birthdays. The last two parties were fiascos."

"Now, now, darling, fiasco is such a negative word."

He sat forward, his focus on Felicity. "I want you to be there. Say yes."

It was the gentleness of the command that got her, and the warmth in his eyes. She said, "Yes," just as the phone rang.

Daniel returned her smile, then excused himself to answer the phone.

As soon as they heard him say *hello,* Lise leaned closer. "Listen, I need a really big favor," she whispered hurriedly, shooting glances over Felicity's shoulder at Daniel. "You have to get hold of the security pass for the elevator."

"But I don't have one." She lowered her voice to match Lise's.

"Yes, but you can get it."

Felicity nodded without having the faintest clue as to how she would get her hands on the card.

"He has an extra one. I used it when I decorated his study, but he took it back." Lise craned her neck, glaring at Daniel. "The ungrateful wretch."

Felicity turned to look at him also.

"Felicity!" The urgent whisper brought her attention back to Lise, who had slouched down further into the couch.

Felicity started giggling.

"Stop that," Lise commanded, even though she was fighting not to smile herself. "You'll need the extra elevator pass card for when you start back at work, right? So..." another pause for another surreptitious glance, "...on Saturday, I'll get the key from you at dinner, and while we're eating, the caterers can get in here!" she finished victoriously.

"Caterers?"

"Yes, yes. Pay attention, dear. I'm throwing Daniel a little surprise cocktail birthday party. Right under his very nose." The hushed tones of prudence barely contained Lise's glee.

"Are you sure about this?" Felicity ventured tentatively. "Wouldn't he hate a surprise birthday party?"

"I'm his mother, it's my duty to surprise him." Lise's smile vanished as she looked over Felicity's shoulder. "*Oh, here he comes!* —Darling, everything all right?"

He stopped behind the sofa, hands braced along the top edge. "You two had your heads pretty close together just now," he said, pinning his mother under a hard stare.

"I was telling Felicity about a really good book I just read. It was an espionage. The ending was quite a surprise."

"Oh, yeah? What's the title?"

"Details like that escape me, sweetheart." Lise stood, adjusting her bag strap on her shoulder. "Now remember, don't start anything with your father Saturday."

"I won't start anything, but I'll finish it."

"There'll be nothing to finish, because there'll be nothing started. This dinner is a celebration, not a challenge, and you will both behave yourselves."

Turning to Felicity, she heaved a theatrical sigh. "Men! So stubborn." But there was a hint of strain in her eyes that caused unease to curl in Felicity's throat. She remembered Michael Mackenzie's cold dark scrutiny at the barbeque. *Oh, yeah. Saturday night was going to be a blast.*

"We women have to stick together." Lise's conspiratorial twinkle returned.

Trapped. She couldn't back out of the dinner now. Then she looked at Daniel's shadowed expression and realized she didn't want to. He'd asked her to be there and she would.

"You can count on me," she said softly, sparking something deep in his gaze. She turned to Lise. "I won't let you down."

"Good. I've got to run again. But, Felicity, we really need to start our little book club up again. Next week, when you're settled? I've really enjoyed our time together, I don't want to lose what we've accomplished." Her tone was serious and pointed, but her eyes held real warmth. "Promise?"

"Promise."

Lise lightly stroked her cheek. "That's my girl." Then she stepped back. "Well, I really must be going. There's just—"

"So many things you have to do," Daniel finished dryly, seeing her out to the elevator.

Once Lise left with a final wave, he came back and sat down beside Felicity. "So what should we do that'll keep you off your feet for the rest of the day?" He waggled his brows.

She punched him on the shoulder, but her stomach did a loop-de-loop at the thought of picking up where they'd left off earlier. Then her stomach flipped again, this time with a rumble.

"Well I guess that answers my question." Daniel laughed. "Time to eat." He went over to the stereo, asking her music preferences, while she made a head start towards the kitchen.

As they prepped the food, working together like they'd been doing it for years, they debated where to put the new accessories he'd bought and stole kisses on the fly.

At one point, Felicity glanced over and caught him doing a little hip wiggling dance while he manned the grill, and she smiled. *This is the happiest I've been in a long time...*

Something twisted in her heart. A reminder that she had to guard against being lulled into the belief they were having a real relationship. But she could enjoy it while it lasted, couldn't she?

"Here, try this." He shoved a spoon at her mouth.

She tasted the sauce. "A dash more pepper, maybe?"

He stole a quick kiss. "Hmmm. No. I'd say that was spicy enough."

She laughed. Oh yeah, she'd enjoy every here-and-now minute to the full. Not waste a single one with worrying. And with that, she pushed all thoughts about the future from her mind.

This was the life. Dinner alfresco on a penthouse terrace. Felicity had the last of her grilled salmon, then pushed the plate away, rubbing her tummy with a sigh as she leaned back. Across from her, Daniel was sprawled in his chair, looking deceptively indolent, his eyes gleaming slivers between their thick gold-tipped lashes.

She took a sip of her wine, a two-year-old Chardonnay she'd just learned. Yep, there was that complex fruity stuff Daniel had been going on about. Tasted like *grapes*. She giggled.

"What's so funny?" His foot nudged hers under the table.

Felicity nudged him back then wiggled her toes under the hem of his jeans, making it partway up his hard shin. Daniel's smile froze in place and his gaze sharpened.

"You're not ticklish on your legs." Pouting, she removed her foot.

"Maybe you should try a little higher."

"Maybe I will. Later," she countered and took another sip, watching Daniel watch her.

He reached across the table, covering her hand with his own, his thumb caressing her in softly sweeping strokes. "Come on, we can lie on the loungers and enjoy the view." He pushed his chair back and stood, before helping her from her seat.

Daniel swung her up in his arms, then whispered in her ear, "And maybe enjoy other things too."

With easy strides he carried her across the L-shaped terrace to a more intimately scaled space, a private niche that was formed by the wall of the main room, the hallway and a third room. Squinting through the glass, Felicity made out a large heavily carved bed. *His.*

He settled her onto the nearest recliner and she pressed her palms down on the seat, lifting her body a fraction to scoot back in the chair, but pain bloomed in sore muscles and she dropped back onto the cushion with a grimace.

"Your shoulder?"

She nodded.

"Here, lean forward a bit," he instructed and swung a leg over the chair, straddling it.

Daniel's hands encircled her waist as he shifted so she was settled between his legs and her hips firmly wedged into the vee of his thighs. His fingers trailed against her skin, brushing her hair out of the way.

"Tell me if it hurts." His touch was gentle but firm as he began to work at her shoulder.

Heart thumping, Felicity nodded again, not trusting her voice.

Eventually his light kneading turned into gossamer strokes, at the nape of her neck, across her back and down to her waist—dissolving each knot of tension along her spine.

She tilted her face up to the sun's rays, her lids drifting closed in sensual pleasure as she swayed with the rhythm of his strokes. Felicity practically purred in contentment. "Mmmm."

"Feel good?" His mouth was at her ear, warm breath causing a cascade of goose bumps to sweep over her.

"Mmmm-hmmm." It felt more than good.

"I can make it feel better." Soft lips brushed against her skin, his voice filling her head with fantasy as he skimmed her waist in a smooth slide that swept up to cup her breasts.

Felicity caught her breath as he shaped his hands to her flesh, thumbs flicking the erect tips.

"Absolutely perfect." Daniel kissed her shoulder softly, capturing each nipple with a deliberate pinch, roll and tug.

No, not perfect. *Love would make this perfect.*

She whimpered and turned her head, seeking his kiss. He obliged, his tongue tangling with hers as he fed hungrily. When she would have turned around further, Daniel tightened his embrace. "Wait."

His hands moved to the fly of her jeans, quickly undoing them, before he helped her wiggle out of them. Leaning back against him, she kicked off the pants, while he rubbed his calloused palms over her tender breasts.

She shuddered. His touch made her feel complete, as if she were made for him. As if she'd found a part of herself she didn't even know was missing. He lightly twisted her nipples again and she moaned, rotating back on his hard cock. In response the thick length of flesh pulsed against her spine.

"Open for me, baby," Daniel urged, delving between her legs in broad sweeping caresses. Each stroke moved further up her thighs, pushing them apart until he was cupping her with a single finger pressed against her seam. Moist spasms of need came at his touch and she cried out at the same time he exhaled in a hiss.

Felicity looked out over the water. The whole world was hers at this moment, held in a heartbeat, captured in Daniel's fingertips. She felt alive, strong, free. But above the thudding blood rush in her veins, she heard another sound. In the distance a helicopter appeared over the lake and she tensed.

"They can't see us. There's just you and me...and this." His fingers repeatedly pressed against her and sensation flashed through her body in waves of escalating need.

"No one can hear those little sounds you're making...driving me crazy. No one can see the way I'm touching you." He pulled her panties aside, a finger dipping lightly into her swollen entrance.

He buried his face in her neck, pressing fevered kisses there. "You're beautiful, Felicity. I want to make you happy. Like this." He touched her softly, skirting where she was open and seeping. "And like this." His fingers moved again, playing with her inner lips.

"Look." He slid back the hood of skin. Air swirled across the exposed bead of her clit and she shivered, mesmerized as he ran a feathery finger over her. "You...are...beautiful."

Ecstasy threaded from nerve ending to nerve ending in one long pulling stitch as he continued to tease her. "*Please, oh, please*," she begged.

His mouth settled on the curve of her neck, suckling softly, moving upward until his tongue swirled around her ear. He blew gently, racing shudders through her. "I like it when you beg. Makes me hot."

He started rubbing, *faster, faster, faster*, but never with enough pressure! Felicity moaned. Her hips moving forward and back, seeking the rhythm that he held just out of reach. Then he pushed two thick fingers deep inside her and there was no holding back her cry of pleasure.

"Yeah, you like that don't you, baby?"

She moaned insensibly as he continued to stroke in and out and play with her clit. Trembling, pushed to the edge of delirium, she spread her legs wider, giving over completely to him.

Daniel pulled his fingers out of her body; his other hand cupping her protectively. "Christ, you're so wet. Do you know what you taste like?" He brought the fingers up to his mouth. "Like heat and cream and musk." Felicity watched his tongue snake out, licking off her essence. "Like this."

He wiped her mouth; the salty taste of herself was brief, before he was sucking on her lips, his tongue probing until she opened up.

Then his hand was back between her thighs, pushing in deep, while the heavy bar of his cock pressed against her ass and lower back. Daniel rocked with her, his breathing just as labored, his fingers buried to the knuckles, fluttering and stroking.

"You're so tight inside... Now, baby! Let go. I can feel you want to." He groaned and pushed another finger deep inside her. The feeling of being stretched was so *exquisite*...until he started rubbing firm, wet, frantic caresses on the swollen knot of nerves beneath his thumb. All her senses went crazy.

I love you. She bit down on her lip, but moan after moan dredged up from her soul as if to pry her secret out.

To the litany of Daniel's dark whispered urgings, she was cresting, flooded with pleasure, her body arching up from the recliner. And when the next breath came, it was almost too late.

Deliverance poured from her in a heaving mass of emotion and sensation until she had no more to give...

Not the least of which, was her heart.

Felicity collapsed back into Daniel's arms.

Daniel gathered Felicity closer, cradling her as the last shudder shook her body. He rubbed his jaw against her silky hair as he looked out to the sun-dappled lake, and darkness crept inside him. *She was leaving.*

Getting on with her life. What role would he play then—her lover and mentor? He wanted more.

He wanted her eyes to light up when she saw him, the way they did whenever she mentioned her plans for her new apartment. Or hear the same unabashed happiness in her voice when she talked about the things they'd done together, just like when she talked about shared experiences with her friend Cheryl, or, Daniel's jaw clenched, her ex.

He sensed she held an essential part of herself from him, a

part his gut told him he needed to reach. But how?

He could seduce her body, make her laugh, but how to touch her heart? *How to make her stay?*

Felicity sighed, snuggling against him. Daniel groaned. Her movements pulled him from his somber thoughts, and he was glad to let them go. He had a beautiful woman in his arms. *His woman.* And he wasn't through making love to her.

His hard-on nestled against the cleft of her luscious ass, and he flexed his hips forward, stroking her belly as he did so.

She rubbed her cheek against his chest and murmured something he didn't catch. Daniel bent his head forward. "Say it again?"

Felicity curled an arm around his neck and tilted her face up towards his. "I want you," she whispered in a much stronger voice.

If he was hard before, he was granite now. Tempered steel. *The bedroom.* It may not be worth the effort to try and make it that far; in the state he was in he probably wouldn't last long.

But he wanted Felicity in his bed.

"Let me up." He pushed her forward gently and rose in agony. His cock was painfully hard.

When she stood, he lifted her into his arms again, then carried her through the master bedroom's open French doors and headed straight for the king-size bed.

He'd ordered it several years ago from a master craftsman who'd told Daniel that his beds were made strong for the loving between a man and a woman, and with the generous size to hold the children that came afterwards.

Daniel wanted Felicity to be that woman.

He now regretted every other female who'd ever shared this bed with him. But none of them had ever slept here. She would be the first. And if it were in his power, this would be the first of many nights, and days, of loving, sleeping, and just being together.

He laid her on the bed, but she didn't loosen her arms around his neck, instead she pulled him down with her. Daniel gave in without a struggle, bracing his hands on either side of her to bear his weight before settling full-length on her body.

He grasped her hips and ground against her as he ravished her mouth. How could he ever get enough of her? Was a lifetime going to be enough? He didn't think so. Every touch woke a hunger deep in his soul for more; every kiss left him parched for another. He wanted to crawl right up under her skin, wanted to be so deep inside her, he'd find completeness.

Daniel left her only long enough to remove his clothing and hers, then they were pressed together again, bared flesh sliding and slipping, sweating and flushed. They grew drunk on kisses, and trembled with need.

She drew one leg up, her heel digging into his haunches, her silky wet heat open and rotating against his raging hard-on. *Aww hell.* He lifted his hips, positioned the head of his cock at her entry, ready to stab into paradise. And stopped. Teeth gritted and body taut, he willed himself not to move.

Daniel stared down into her eyes, running a litany over and over in his mind: *Getoffgetoffgetoff.* But for the life of him he couldn't go forward, couldn't go back. Her slick sucking heat held him in place.

Then she wiggled beneath him and he sank infinitesimally closer to nirvana.

"Don't. Move." Pressing his forehead to hers, he bit out each word before taking several controlling breaths. He rolled away and reached into the bedside table. Must have broken some kind of record as he turned back, condom on, and pulled her onto her side. Sliding one slim leg over his hip, he grabbed her ass.

"Now move."

Daniel stroked into her hard, capturing her gasp in a rough kiss as he kept thrusting, fast and deep. He kept pounding until the sharp edge of his need dulled and his desperation melted away. Then he slowed, savoring the sensation of being in her body again.

"Look at us, at how your body accepts mine," he whispered hoarsely, gazing down to where they were joined, where the ruddy flesh of his erection slid back and forth, disappearing within the sweet confines of her tight heat.

Each time his shaft appeared, it glistened with her juices and he felt her clenching grip, sucking him back in.

And with each return stroke he was rewarded with another of her intoxicating moans.

Daniel moved his hand between them and touched the exposed pink nub of nerves where she was most sensitive.

"*Noooo.*" It tore from her guttural and fierce, even as her body moved in contradiction.

"Yes." His finger was slick with her cream and he felt her clit swell and firm beneath his touch. Daniel pulled out, leaving just the tip of his cock inside her. He made the barest motions with his hips, building the heat that would consume them both as she dug her nails into his upper arms.

When they were together like this, it was as if nothing existed beside what they could taste and kiss and hold. Nothing except her heart beating against his.

He caught Felicity's mouth in another kiss as he started pumping again, and felt the rhythmic grip deep inside her squeeze his cock. He joined the race, hammering faster and harder, till she cried out his name, coming in sweet convulsions that milked coiling steams of ecstasy from his own body.

He rolled her onto her back, his mouth still sealed to hers, drinking from her passion, feeding her his love.

Daniel felt his heart grow with each desperate pounding stroke he made; then it threatened to burst with the words he held back as he came.

I love you.

Chapter Nineteen

Daniel was busy for most of the next day, but he cleared the hours around lunchtime to spend with Felicity and they headed up to Queen Street. Not the trendy part, but farther west, where local galleries, secondhand shops and tiny exotic eateries still dominated. They hit the stores there, then doubled back to King Street East and visited several high-end showrooms. Three hours later he dropped her back at his place with an impressive amount of booty.

Before Daniel left, he warned her he'd be home late, then planted a very long, very deep kiss on her, just to tide them both over.

At first Felicity amused herself arranging and rearranging the new accessories, but eventually grew bored as she wandered from room to room. Disquiet nagged at her until she realized what she was doing. *Memorizing.*

The way the sunlight streamed through the windows and how those same rays would warm Daniel's hair to a brilliant gold. And the exact spot where he'd propped his feet up on the coffee table when he sat on the couch. Then she stared at the sheets still rumpled from their tickle fight this morning—

She turned away, angry. *Not yet!* She wasn't ready for the pain of being...*not here.* Without him. They still had four days left to collect memories.

She lived like a crazed woman for the next two days, at times desperately soaking up every nuance of sound, taste, touch, then at others, holding herself distant, only aware of the jabbing ache in her heart.

When Saturday came, Daniel's birthday, she surprised him with a framed reprint of a vintage advertising poster she'd spotted on one of their recent shopping trips.

"It's your favorite winery," she pointed out anxiously, aware that he was used to getting much more expensive gifts.

"You remembered." There was an odd note in his voice.

"I wanted to get you something special." Felicity slipped from his arms. "Something you'd remember me by when I'm gone."

It went so quiet, you could hear the proverbial angelic chorus line, tap-dancing on the head of the infamously dropped pin.

He cleared his throat. "Felicity, we have to talk."

"How about later?" She blew him off with a little smile. There was no way in hell she was going to have that "we need to talk" talk right this minute. "I have to shower and get ready for work."

Daniel tipped her chin up, holding her gaze. Somehow she kept the tears deep, deep inside. "Later," he agreed.

She nodded and escaped.

Except, she didn't escape. Because he insisted on driving her into work. For the entire ride she was quiet, the drag of returning to Tony's muted under a heavy numbness that invaded her body and smothered her pain.

The only part of her functioning was her brain. And it was fueled purely by fear. There was no way she could let Daniel see where she worked.

Luckily, when it came time for specifics, she was able to choose a bistro several blocks away from The Uptown for him to drop her off.

As he pulled up to the curb she reached for the lock.

"Felicity." He stopped her. "I know you probably don't want to hear what I have to say—"

"I really gotta go. We'll talk later, okay?" Her voice was almost pleading as she climbed out of the truck. She slammed the door shut on any further discussion and walked hurriedly to the restaurant, did a quick spin around to wave him off, then disappeared inside.

Daniel pulled out into traffic, driving on automatic. He slowed at the yellow lights, braked at all the red. Stayed in his lane and well within the speed limit. In no hurry to get back to his big, white condo.

Once upon a time his privacy had been sacred, now it meant loneliness without Felicity's presence. Stifling silence without the crystal tinkle of her laughter. Boredom without the mysteries held in her gaze. Nights without her in his arms didn't bear contemplating.

He swore and flashed a glance at the rearview. A right was coming up fast and he swerved to take it, then cruised down the side street as he left the blare of car horns behind.

Forget about *later.*

The return trip uptown took twice as long, and, of course, it took another ten minutes to find a damn parking spot; but he finally made it back to the restaurant.

Daniel looked around the dining room for Felicity, he just wanted to know when she had her break, he'd come back then and say his piece.

A waiter approached him. "For one?"

"Actually I'm looking for someone. Felicity."

The guy stared at him blankly.

"A waitress. She works here."

A negative headshake met his statement.

"I just dropped her off. Reddish brown hair, wavy, down to her shoulders?" Daniel went on to describe what she'd been wearing.

Comprehension lit the server's face. "Oh, you mean the dancer. She was only in here five minutes tops. Looked over a menu then changed her mind and left."

"Dancer?" A buzzing filled Daniel's ears.

"Stripper." The guy was trying for sympathetic, but Daniel detected a hint of a smirk.

"I don't know what she told you, but this isn't where she works. I've seen her around, though. After awhile, you get to know who lives or works in the area." He shrugged. "Check at The Uptown—it's two lights north. Maybe someone there can help you out."

Daniel unclenched his jaw enough to mutter, "Thanks."

Once he hit the pavement, he spied the flashing marquee up the street. With every step he took, the buzzing in his head got louder. He entered the club, squinting against the smoke and flashing lights, wincing at the painful throbbing at his temples that increased with the blaring music.

His gaze skimmed over the too-round breasts of the dancer on stage, his gut untwisting in relief that it wasn't Felicity. *Wasn't her.* The waiter had to be wrong. Yet Daniel didn't leave, he move further into the room, scanning the other inhabitants.

There was a guy, running to fat, behind the bar and a couple of guys nursing brews in front of it. Daniel made out several personal performances taking place in the back and froze. His eyes were burning, straining to see. His heart hammering so loud the music faded. At some point he realized Felicity wasn't there. At the same time he realized, he didn't want to know. He felt like he was falling apart, his head like it was about to go spinning off his body. Daniel turned to leave when the DJ announced the next dancer...

Vanessa Jaye

Felicity had managed to evade Cheryl's gentle probing. And thankfully the other girls seemed to sense her wish to be left alone. For her set, she asked the DJ to play the music loud— hard rock and gangster rap. She wanted to give vent to her pain and anger.

Why bring Daniel into her life, and give her a taste of such complete happiness, when it couldn't last?

And where would she find the strength to continue working with him on design projects, when it was officially over between them?

That was a stupid thing she did with the poster today. She should've gotten him a card or tie or some other impersonal gift. Something that didn't signal so clearly she was getting sappy.

She stormed onto the stage and for the first two songs never stopped with high kicks and sneers, hair flips and air punches.

Then the last song came on.

Time to face the music.

Time to take it all off.

Oh goody, here came an appreciative audience member from the back, probably turned on by the suppressed violence in her act. She dismissed him, but in the next second her gaze jerked back to his distinctive silhouette.

Felicity's movements became mechanical and broken as she squinted then blinked several times. She told herself it was a trick of the bright lights. It wasn't. In a few steps, his harsh features telescoped into recognizable detail.

Daniel.

He walked right up to the stage, squeezing between tables and Felicity came to a standstill. The music faded, leaving only the raw thud of her heart punching against her ribs. Each punch left a bruise that was pummeled again and again.

Her hands flew to her mouth, her bra fell away, and his gaze raked over her bared breasts. When he raised his eyes

232

again, Felicity not only saw his revulsion, but that she deserved it. Blinded by scalding tears, she crossed her arms over her nakedness and scuttled backwards till her spine pressed against the cold mirrored wall. He jumped on stage, following her, and each breath she took became a gasping broken moan.

Daniel grabbed her arms. He didn't know whether to drag her against him, hide and protect her. Or shake her so hard it would rattle every goddamn tooth in her deceitful little head.

Felicity stared up at him with eyes that were two dark pools of tarnished silver, and Daniel's control cracked; so did his voice. "Why?"

Her lips parted but no sound escaped them.

"Is this the only thing you do here?" He tightened his grip. "Answer me."

She shook her head.

For a brief moment pain flitted over Daniel's face, then his eyes filled with loathing as he released her, practically flung her away from him. She stumbled as he called her a name that made her gasp, a quick intake of air that hit the back of her throat with enough pain to choke on.

But not more pain than what he'd called her, dirtying every single kiss, every touch they'd ever shared. She crumpled, sliding to the ground.

The music stopped abruptly; there was a sudden blur of movement just before a muscular arm swung around Daniel's neck.

"No!" Felicity screamed and tried to crawl to him, but Cheryl was there, blocking her way.

"Come on, sugar, let's get you out of here," Cheryl urged, her voice barely discernable over the sounds of breaking glass and overturned furniture.

Enraged male voices rose on a volley of curses, punctuated by panicky screams. Felicity cringed into a tight ball, rocking back and forth.

Cheryl slipped an arm around her waist, softly crooning in her ear. "Fil sweetie, get up. You can do it."

No she couldn't.

"He's gone now, honey. Come on now, get up."

She knew he was gone. Why else this black, crushing emptiness inside of her? The music was back on again, the DJ Keith joking over the mike. None of it penetrated her nightmare. Felicity made herself stand up and with Cheryl's help, walked, rather than crawled, like she wanted to, off stage.

"I don't want no trouble," a deep rumble grated in Daniel's ear as his arm was twisted further behind his back. "I can't have this kinda shit happening here. It's no good for business."

Daniel found himself shoved forward. He caught his footing before he fell.

"If you come in here again, I will make it the business of my fist to interfere with your face. *Capisce?*" The bartender used a thick beefy finger to stab the air. "Now beat it."

Daniel took one last look at the stage. She was gone.

The outer door banged open against the wall and ricocheted back from the force of his push. He started down the block, kicked at a pile of garbage bags and then slammed his fist into a sapling. The slight pain was welcomed. He could focus on *this* pain. It was defined and contained. Not like the miasma of pain, anger and confusion writhing inside him.

Driving by rote, Daniel somehow made it home without totaling his truck. A couple hours and beers later, and the bleeding edge of *going-out-of-his-fucking-mind* had been dulled. That's what really hurt, understanding the true extent to which she shut him out. He wondered what else he didn't know about her.

With his feet braced up on the coffee table, he opened and closed his fist experimentally, studying the bruised knuckles.

Had he even known the woman he'd fallen in love with?

He could kick himself for being such an idiot, then in the next minute he was thanking his lucky stars that he'd kept his yap shut and not spilled his guts to her about how he felt.

Man, she'd played him.

Every fiber of his being recoiled from the memory of other men looking at Felicity. The lust that had been virtually palpable in the air. Daniel relived again the long minutes it had taken him to walk up to the stage, the pain and shame evident in Felicity's expression when she'd recognized him. All he'd wanted to do was take her away, hide her from the leers—

He expelled a humorless laugh. Yeah, like she hadn't been loving every minute of her performance, taunting every man in the room with her body.

And that taunting had included him. Despite his shock, he'd responded as if she'd been dancing for his eyes only. Even now he was semi-hard at the memory of those lush curves spilling from that outrageous outfit and the sweep of her hair tangled about her face as if she'd just been made love to. He scrubbed at his eyes, but the image on stage superimposed itself over the vision that had writhed in his arms last night.

Is that the way she saw him? Just another guy, another Stuart, another fuck, another buck? Pain surged in his chest, but he knew what he'd seen.

Yet every night she'd lain in his bed and made love to him— he laughed mirthlessly. *Love*. What the hell was that? Certainly not this feeling of being shredded alive from the inside out.

The elevator doors opened.

"Daniel?"

He looked up at her, with her red, puffy eyes and lying mouth.

"Can I explain?" she asked, slowly walking towards him.

He answered with stony silence.

She dropped her bag on the floor beside the nearest chair and sat. Nothing in his demeanor welcomed her to come closer.

"I couldn't tell you about working at The Uptown, because I knew how you'd react." Her voice got lower and lower with every word she forced out.

"Oh, you knew that, did you? You don't know shit."

"No, you don't know shit," she spat out hoarsely. "You don't know how I've lived, scraping and scrounging for every cent to pay the bills since I was sixteen." Felicity fought for control, but she couldn't stop. The words tumbled out, an eruption of all her pain, her years of being alone, and the stark hopelessness that faced her now.

"It's about survival, Daniel. I've worked every shit job you can think of just to have something to eat and to keep a roof over my head." She saw him wince.

"I didn't always succeed. Tony's is one of the best paying jobs I've ever had."

His mouth twisted into something ugly and the expression in his gaze made her skin shrink. "I don't want to hear this," he rasped.

"Of course you don't. You want to be justified in thinking I'm not good enough for you," she said bitterly. "That's why I never met your family till your mother walked in on us."

He sat up straighter. "That's bull—"

"I'm speaking. My turn. You don't get to be the only one throwing around accusations."

"Not accusations. The truth, Felicity," he yelled, his face flushed dark. "Do you even fucking know what that is?"

"Look who's talking. How can you point a finger at me when I didn't even know you lived like this until the fire—"

"Ah, yes, now we get to the point." Daniel's eyes were little chips of ice. "Regretting that you didn't know how rich I was earlier so you could've gotten more money out of me?"

She sprang up, trembling. "That's not fair!"

He spread his legs and shifted in his seat insultingly. "You can always give me a lap dance. Hell, I've been getting the goods for free, might as well start paying."

A heavy crushing weight squeezed all the air out of her lungs. That he of all people would reduce her to that.

"St-stop." She couldn't speak, she was hiccupping instead of breathing, her nose clogged and eyes blurry with tears. "I did what I had to, don't you see? I was only a waitress at Tony's right up until you evicted me. The rent was so good there, I couldn't afford to live by myself anywhere else unless I made more money.

"But I'm not fit to do anything else, Daniel." The painful admission was a raw whisper. She cleared her throat. "Nothing that pays as well. I had to dance."

He'd gone pale by the time she'd finish speaking. They stared at each other in silence. There was more to say, but where to start? And was he even interested? She silently begged him to understand but his face remained a mask. She'd lost. Him. It *had* been too good to be true.

Finally she said, "This is my life, Daniel. This is me."

Another long silence stretched out.

"Yeah, I see that. Now." He sounded weary and his gaze held a wealth of sadness. "Remember when I said that I'd never lie to you?"

"Yes," she whispered. Her throat felt like a pincushion for pain.

"And I asked the same from you?"

Her nod was a series of staccato jerks.

"You had another choice, Felicity. You could have told me truth. We could've worked—" He broke off and looked away, a muscle pulsing in his jaw. "All you've done is lie our entire time together. I can't accept that. I can't accept your life."

He stood and faced her. "I can't accept you."

Her capacity for pain had just been surpassed for the day.

You hear that? Whichever little troll of fucked-upedness who was in charge of her life. *Surpassed.*

Daniel grabbed the empty beer bottles on the table. "I'm going to hit the shower. We have about an hour to get out of here and meet my parents."

"You still expect me to go to dinner?" she asked, shocked.

"What I expect doesn't matter. My mother expects you there," he said, walking over to the kitchen. "I think we can survive together for a few more hours."

She pinched the bridge of her nose. What she really wanted to do was scream in frustration. She didn't want to go. Did. Not. But Lise had been nothing but good to her. Supportive. A friend, and she was counting on Felicity for the pass-key. She had to go. *Damn.*

"Felicity?" Daniel's voice was much softer, her heart stuttered with faint hope.

She looked up.

"I'm sorry. For everything." He left the room.

He'd just said goodbye.

Daniel's hand rested lightly against her back as they went through the doors of the restaurant. The first time he'd touched her since he'd left The Uptown. She glanced at his profile, but he gave no indication he'd noticed her flinch.

"Daniel!" An elegant man swept forward to greet them. The men exchanged quick pleasantries, before the maître'd led them into the dining room.

"And now the celebrations can begin," their host announced as he brought them up to the table.

"Marcel, thank you." Lise held out her hand, which he gallantly kissed.

"Madam, the pleasure is all mine." Then he turned to Felicity and captured her hand also, pressing his lips briefly to the back. "*Enchanté, mademoiselle.* Enjoy your visit with us."

Not a chance.

Daniel pulled out a chair for her. He could give the Grim Reaper tips on decorum—that's how warm his demeanor was.

And like father, like son, Michael Mackenzie's delight was also nonexistent. This was going to be some party. *Whoo-hoo.*

"I bring you some more wine? Yes?" When Lise agreed, Marcel left them.

"Happy birthday, son." She beamed across the table.

"Yes, happy birthday, Daniel." Mr. Mackenzie gave the briefest of nods in his son's direction. When his gaze slid to Felicity his mouth curved into a rictus of distaste.

"Felicity, is it? You look eye-catching, white suits you."

"Thank you," she mumbled and nervously fingered the neckline of the wrap-around dress. It was one of Daniel's purchases, or his payment according to his earlier accusations. If she'd had anything else to wear she would have.

"Is it part of an ensemble? A matching coat, perhaps or some other pieces?"

"No." She shook her head, bewildered by the questions and his cold tone.

"Michael, since when have you been so interested in fashion? Stop giving Felicity such a hard time," Lise scolded. "Don't let my husband frighten you, dear. His bark is worse than his bite."

As far as Felicity was concerned his bark was a breath of biological warfare.

"I was just admiring her choice of clothing."

"Admire something else," Daniel advised.

"I saw someone in a similar outfit just recently—"

"Either you find another game to play tonight, or I'm leaving." Daniel glared at his father.

"Can't you two behave? Just for one damn hour." Lise pushed away from the table and stood.

"Elle."

"Mother—"

"Excuse me; I need to freshen up." She turned and walked quickly towards the back of the restaurant.

"I'll—I'll just go and see how she's doing." Felicity escaped after her.

In the ladies' room she found Lise at the mirror studying her tight reflection. The other woman let out a deep sigh when she caught sight of Felicity.

"Those two men are going to be the death of me." Lise smiled wryly.

"They seem to have issues," Felicity offered.

"Issues! You can say that again. Those two need the U.N. to mediate. I don't know why I think I can."

"Because you love them, you can't give up." The words tumbled from her before she could stop them.

Lise held her gaze through the mirror. "Yes, I do love them. And I won't give up." She turned to face Felicity. "And you shouldn't either."

Felicity's heart stopped. "What do you mean?"

"I mean you love Daniel— *Ah-ah*, don't try to deny it. I have eyes, I can see." She took Felicity's cold hands in hers, and gave her a little reassuring squeeze. "It's obvious you two had some sort of tiff today. Trust a Mackenzie male to pick a day of celebration for a fight." Her smile turned wry.

"I can tell you one thing, Mackenzie men don't take to falling in love easily, and they're not the easiest to love either."

"You're mistaken. Daniel doesn't love me." She bit her lip to stop from saying more.

"You're wrong you know. But I won't pry any further." Lise tucked a lock of Felicity's hair behind her ear. "You two kids will eventual find the key—" Lise's expression froze.

"The key!" they said in unison.

Felicity dug the pass card out of her purse. At least the evening wouldn't be a total waste.

Lise clapped her hands together, laughing as she took the small rectangle of plastic. "Not that I forgot, mind you. I'd actually planned for us to make a trip to the ladies' room. Men are always complaining how we can't seem to go to the bathroom by ourselves. Poor dears wouldn't have suspected a thing."

Lise pulled a cell phone from her elegant little clutch and punched in a few numbers. "Marcel, please. It's Lise Mackenzie."

Felicity frowned. *Wasn't Marcel—?*

"Marcel! Yes, dear. I have that little package we spoke about earlier. Could you send one of the waitresses to the ladies' room to pick it up?" Lise was silent for a moment as she listened, then she *tut-tutted.*

"You're such a naughty boy. What would your guests think, seeing the owner skulking about outside the ladies' room?" She laughed and hung up, the twinkle firmly back in her eyes.

"Now if we can just keep Daniel and Michael from using the cutlery on each other for the next hour or so, we'll go back to the condo and the party should take care of itself!"

Dinner was the longest sixty minutes of Felicity's life. Michael Mackenzie remained chilly throughout the meal. And Daniel seemed more interested in what was in his wineglass than what was on his plate, or the company at the table.

Lise tried to keep up a non-stop stream of chatter with her, but Felicity could barely make the effort. Sitting beside Daniel while her heart crumbled to a slow death had her jaw locked tightly to stop the tears from coming.

Finally, dinner was over, the check taken care of, and they were out on the sidewalk.

"I think the perfect end to this evening would be nightcaps," Lise exclaimed brightly.

This statement was met by silence. A truly perfect ending to their evening would be a rousing game of Russian roulette. All chambers full.

"Well, Michael? Don't you think so?" Lise asked tightly.

"Daniel, your mother would like a final nightcap."

"Then why didn't we have drinks inside? The waitress asked, and you demanded the check right away."

"Because I don't want drinks here, dear. Let's go to your place."

"My place?"

"Yes, your place. Where we're going to have one last toast to celebrate the anniversary of the day that God, in His infinite wisdom, blessed me with you—my one and only son. Is there a problem?"

Well, since she put it that way.

Chapter Twenty

"*Surprise!*"

"*Happy Birthday!*"

A mass of bodies surged forward, hands reaching for Daniel to pull him out of the elevator.

"Your mother, guy! She set the whole thing up." Rob's voice rose over the din. "Hey, where is she?"

The crowd parted to let Lise through and, to Felicity's consternation, Lise latched onto her wrist and dragged her along.

"No, please," she whispered fiercely.

People were looking at her with open curiosity. Some of them were familiar, men from Daniel's construction crew, or guests from the barbeque at Lise's house. At least they were smiling. But one person was downright hostile. VD. Already clinging to Daniel's arm like glaze on a donut.

"I should have known you had something like this planned," he said darkly, but he kissed his mother and gave her a big hug.

"This was a really fabulous idea." VD exchanged air kisses with Lise. "But it must have taken so much work. I wish you had asked for my help," she cooed.

"I knew how busy you were at the firm, dear, I just couldn't ask you to take on more. Besides, Felicity helped me."

"Oh." Deirdra's mouth imitated an anus.

"Honey?" Lise looked up at her son. "Aren't you going to thank Felicity?"

"Really, I didn't do anything," Felicity protested, but Lise practically pushed her into Daniel's arms.

Daniel's head dipped towards hers, and she allowed herself...*to dream*. Her lids slid down, lips parting as she felt the warmth of his breath sweep closer.

The kiss was brief, cool and impersonal. His mouth barely touched her cheek. But as Daniel pulled back, she saw that his pupils were enlarged and irises darkened. He still felt the attraction. It was a small, but empty triumph.

"Thanks."

"No problem," she choked out. Felicity looked around wildly and met Deirdra's malicious gaze.

"Hey, this is a party! Why aren't you people drinking?" Rob slapped Daniel on the back, then draped a casual arm around Felicity's shoulder and steered her away, over to the kitchen where the bar was set up.

"Okay?" he asked in an undertone.

She nodded.

"So, what's your poison?" he asked in a more hearty voice, rubbing his hands together.

"Anything." She didn't care.

"Now, you're my type of date." He winked and snagged three flutes of champagne from a tray for her, Lise and Deirdra.

"What are you having, good buddy?"

"Beer."

"That's my boy." Rob gave Daniel another enthusiastic slap on the back. "Two beers—Labatt's Blue," he ordered from the server manning the makeshift bar.

"Now, Daniel, you can't stay mad at me. This is a nice party. All your friends are here, not just business associates. And no clowns." Lise sipped her champagne.

"I see at least one clown," Daniel said dryly, eyeing Rob.

"Better a clown than a fool," Rob answered cryptically.

Lise gave a delicate ladylike snort. "And on that note, I think I'll go find my husband." She laid a hand on Felicity's arm, her gaze questioning.

"I'm fine."

"Good. I'll catch up with you kids later."

As Lise glided off, more well-wishers came forward. After awhile it was barbeque déjà vu all over again, with Felicity pushed to the group's edge, while VD stayed by Daniel's side.

From then on Felicity took care to stay on the opposite side of the room from Daniel and Deirdra, but she had the constant sensation of being watched. When she finally gave in to temptation to look, Daniel's expression lumped the breath in her throat before he wiped the brooding anger from his face.

Someone in the group surrounding him said something that they all found amusing, particularly VD, who tossed her long dark hair back and forth like she was orgasming.

I have to get out of here. Felicity turned towards the elevator, but saw Lise holding court in the foyer with a small knot of people. There was no way she could get past Daniel's mother without being stopped and questioned.

Felicity headed for the terrace and quickly slipped outside; skirting several intimate groups, she made for the private space just outside of Daniel's bedroom. She turned the corner. *Empty.* Thank God.

As soon as her butt hit the cushions on the lounger, the trembling began. Felicity impatiently wiped at the tears that streamed down her face. It wasn't as if she hadn't been through heartbreak before, or gone through really rough times. She'd make it through this one. *She had to.*

"Got to keep circulating. Thanks for coming." Daniel smiled and moved away. He'd been moving all night. On the run from his thoughts. Reaching out to shake another hand, receive another slap on the back, stopping for a minute to exchange some good-natured ribbing. He hated this shit.

When he came to the bank of French doors, he peered out at the terrace, tapping his beer bottle against the glass. He didn't see Felicity, but he knew she was out there somewhere. He'd watched her slip out of the party twenty minutes ago, just as he'd watched her keep a careful distance from him all night.

Daniel's leg twitched, ready to take the first step over the threshold. But could he take the next steps that would lead him to face her? And then to do what—beg? That was all that was left for him to do at this point. When he'd said he couldn't accept her, he'd lied. A reaction to the absolute epiphany of that moment, of just how deeply he'd fallen for her. And just how much further he could go.

He swore, and took a slug of the warm beer he was nursing.

"Thirty-one ain't so old you know, pup."

Lost in his thoughts, he hadn't seen Rob's approach. "Pup? You're only one year older than me."

"Chronologically yes. But in maturity, sophistication and sheer good looks, I'm light years ahead of you, man."

"I guess that makes me younger and smarter."

"Touché." Rob tapped his beer bottle against Daniel's, drank deeply, wiped his mouth and burped.

"Sophisticated?"

"Eh. Two out of three." Rob shrugged. "So if you're so smart, what are you doing in here when Felicity is out there?" He jerked his head towards the terrace.

"You're not going to hold on to those good looks much longer, pal, if you keep sticking your nose in my business."

"Quitting?" Rob prodded further.

He held his friend's gaze for the length of another swallow

of beer, then walked away from Rob's smirking face.

Daniel cut a path through his guests until he reached the sanctuary of his study and shut himself up in the darkness. For long minutes he just leaned against the door and stared across the room.

It called to him like a siren's song.

Aided by the weak stream of moonlight through the windows, Daniel went to his desk where he turned on the lamp, bathing the room in a deep sweet glow. He shoved aside some files to make room for his beer, then opened the middle drawer.

The small box was still there, perfectly centered on a sheaf of papers. He lifted the lid, removed the ring and held it up to eye level. The diamond held an inner fire that shone with false promise and sparkled with ridicule. So much for lovers' journeys. Emotion lumped in his throat and he sighed, the final death rattle of this whole screwed up mess.

The door leading to the hall opened, followed by a soft gasp. "Daniel?"

"What are you doing in here?" He clenched his fist around the ring as Deirdra came closer. She stopped inches away.

"I was looking for you." Her stunned gaze veered from his face to his hand and back again. "So you do...really love her?"

It was that little hitch, a faint pleading note in her voice, that fully revealed what she'd been hiding from him.

"I'm sorry," he said, knowing it was inadequate. The sting of unrequited love was too fresh for him not to understand. He plucked some tissues from a box and handed them to her.

"Thank you." She dabbed at her eyes. Then she touched his closed fist, sliding her fingers under his until he opened up and let the ring drop into her palm.

"It's beautiful. So when's the lucky day?"

"There won't be one." His throat threatened to close. "She doesn't love me."

"It hurts doesn't it? And it hurts even more because you don't want to believe it. Don't want to accept it...

"...until you hear the words."

"Deirdra, don't do this."

"Say it. Give me that at least."

The muffled happy noises from the party sounded grotesque and taunting in comparison to the somber atmosphere that swaddled them in here.

"Say it!"

"I- I don't love you."

"See?" Her head tilted to an awkward angle. "Closure. You should get some for yourself. It's the wondering, the hope that festers and never lets you heal. I should know. It's been six long years."

"Deirdra—"

"You should find Felicity, Daniel. Tell her. Ask her. Know for sure." She closed her eyes, shutting him out.

Daniel stared at her, torn in two. He felt like a piece of shit, but his body was already angled towards the door.

"Are you going to be all right?" He ran his hand down her arm and she nodded, acknowledging the goodbye.

"I just need to be alone."

He hesitated a moment longer then headed for the door, uncertainty shifting in his belly like an indigestible meal.

"Felicity?"

She stiffened at the voice. What did he want? She refused to turn around and sensed, rather than heard, his continued approach. Finally he came into view and Felicity looked up into the achingly familiar masculine beauty of his face.

Daniel may have his mother's coloring, but everything else came from the man who stood before her. Michael Mackenzie.

"I'm not one to beat around the bush, Miss Cameron." He slid a hand into his suit pocket. "Obviously, you and Daniel have developed an attachment. I'm disappointed, but it's understandable. Daniel reacted as any man would to the showcasing of your attributes."

"Showcasing my attributes?" The neckline of her dress was low, but not indecent. She adjusted the edges of it now.

"Please. Such attempts at modesty won't fly with me." His eyes narrowed. "Or perhaps my son doesn't know?"

Darkness started crowding her vision. "Kn-know wh-what?"

He made an impatient sound. "That you're a damn stripper. Don't try to deny it."

"Daniel told you?" she asked faintly, sick to her stomach.

"So, he does know." Michael looked out over the lake with a pained expression. "Idiot."

He pinned her again under his scathing gaze. "No, he didn't tell me anything, I saw you with my own eyes. I have a client with the unfortunate habit of frequenting questionable establishments.

"It was the night of your inaugural performance as Miss Candee Kane," he said the name with acid derision, "that I had the misfortune to be in attendance.

"I couldn't quite place where I'd seen you before at the barbeque. The dress was the final tip off tonight. It reminded me of the trench coat you wore, so very briefly, that night."

The moon shone too bright. The stars were too plentiful. They should all disappear. Make the night dark enough to hide her shame.

"Do you have some kind of agreement with my son, Miss Cameron? I think I know Daniel well enough to know he would want to be your only—" He hesitated, his mouth curled, as if he were taste-testing several distasteful word choices.

"Client?" She stood to face him on unsteady legs. "Are you calling me some sort of prostitute?"

"Calm yourself, please." He rebuked her as if speaking to a child. "I implied no such thing."

"Bullshit. That's all you've been implying. For your information, I love your son!"

Oh the words felt soo good to finally say out loud. She said them again, slowly, wishing she'd been brave enough to say them earlier. "I...love...Daniel. And I would never be with him for money. *Never.*"

Michael Mackenzie laughed in disbelief. "Oh no? Who bought that dress you're wearing? My wife has enough over-priced designer scraps hanging in her closet, that I can tell quality." His gaze raked down to her toes, making clear that she was not what he called quality.

"Or do you make that kind of money taking your clothes off for strangers?"

"That's none of your business—"

"Wrong. Anything that has to do with my son's future is my business."

They stood staring at each other in the quiet darkness—mere feet apart but worlds away.

Felicity drew a shaky breath and raised her chin. "And you want to make sure that I'm not a part of that future."

"I see you like plain speaking. That's good. Let's get to the point. I'm sure you're a nice girl. My wife seems to have taken a liking to you and she's usually a good judge of character." He reached out as if to touch her, but when she flinched he shoved the hand back into his pocket. When he spoke again his voice was gentled, and his expression softened a bit.

"I'm sorry, but you must see that you and Daniel don't belong together."

Felicity's head made several abbreviated jerks as she tried to swallow her bitterness. He meant she wasn't good enough for his precious son.

"I'd always hoped that he and..."

"Deirdra?"

"Well yes. For awhile there I thought…" He shrugged. "They practically grew up together, and her father and I sit on several boards together." He shrugged again. Michael was the one now who seemed uncomfortable. His hostility gone now that he was sure she wouldn't be a problem.

Instead what she read in expression was worse than hostility. It was pity. Pity for the slut who actually thought she could have his son.

"You know what I think, Mr. Mackenzie?" she asked softly.

He cocked a brow.

"I think you should go fuck yourself." Felicity turned before he could witness the first tear fall, and walked rapidly to the bank of doors off the master bedroom.

She slid the glass open, stepped into the room, and slid the door shut again. Michael was where she left him, staring back at her. Felicity gave birth to her pain in a low guttural moan, before rushing across the room to the closed study door. She would lock herself away in there, safe from the dream-killing gaze of Michael Mackenzie.

She shoved the door open blindly then turned to close it, pressing her forehead against the smooth solid panel. How could she bear this unbearable pain?

At the sound of the breathy giggle, Felicity spun around, then cursed under her breath. She closed her eyes and gritted her teeth, striving for control. But she couldn't stop the trickle of tears. Or the mortification that this person should see her like this.

Deirdra was perched on the edge of Daniel's desk, draining the last of her champagne. There was a beer bottle on the desk beside her, the brand Daniel had been drinking all night. Felicity's gaze swerved around the room in panic.

"Daniel's not here right now, sweetie. He went to find something." Deirdra gestured with her empty glass. "But he'll be back soon; why don't you hang around? He has something to tell you." Deirdra's baby talking voice would have caused Felicity to suspect she was drunk, if it weren't for the hard glitter in VD's eyes.

"Oh what the hell, I'm sure he won't mind if I start things off."

A sense of inevitability caused Felicity's heartbeat to slow. The intense emotions on the other girl's face pinning her to the spot when every instinct told her to *run*.

Deirdra giggled again, rolling the champagne flute back and forth across her collarbone. "Poor Felicity. You haven't got a clue, do you?" she singsonged, then pouted.

Her expression slowly cemented into a mask of hate. "After all those weeks of getting fucked by Daniel you still don't realize how he really feels about you, do you?" She stood, weaving slightly.

"Poor fucking clueless Felicity," she sneered as she advanced. "Well, here's a clue for you." Deirdra pulled out the hand that she'd kept hidden behind her back, and held it up to Felicity's face.

A brilliant white stone, flashing fire in the low light, was on Deirdra's finger. *Two souls intertwined, soaring in love and joy.*

It was the ring. *Her ring.*

The one she'd admired in the mall with Daniel.

A taunting whisper penetrated her stunned senses, "Look what I got."

Felicity pushed VD aside and fled. Chased out of the room by Deirdra's vicious giggles. Hands sliding against walls, she stumbled down the hall in a daze, barely able to see through her tears. She mumbled apologies as she stepped on toes and jostled arms holding drinks, but her only thoughts were of escape.

When she came to the great room, disoriented in her grief, she looked around aware of the odd whispers and attention she drew. A shift in the crowd gave her a glimpse of Daniel's wide back stepping out onto the terrace and she went in the opposite direction.

Holding her head down, she quickly wove through the maze of bodies. She was almost at the elevators, her outstretched arm wedging open a path, reaching for that small button, when her hand hit something that would not be moved. A hard male body.

"Let me pass." She tried to go around Rob, but he wrapped her in a big bear hug and held her close.

"I will in a second, if you tell me what your hurry is." He loosened his hold enough so he could look down into her face.

"Please, Rob. Let me go."

"Nothing to see here, folks. Just something she ate." Rob waved away the curious. "I'd avoid the shrimp if I were you," he advised in a stage whisper as he turned and, with one arm still around her hunched shoulders, guided her to the elevator.

She kept hitting the button, glancing over her shoulder repeatedly as she wiped at her eyes and nose. With a discreet bell the doors slid open and she tripped inside the cab.

Felicity jabbed at the ground floor button, as Rob followed her in. "What are you doing?"

"Maybe I can help—"

"*Rob!*"

At Daniel's yell, they both looked back into the condo. She met Daniel's gaze across the short distance, saw his frown go blank as he came to a halt.

"Felicity? Rob? What's going on?"

"I'm leaving," she said simply as the doors closed.

She didn't release her breath until the declining numbers on the panel told her she was safe. Then she started to laugh.

"He thinks I'm leaving with you."

"Somehow, with you laughing and crying at the same time,

I'm not too flattered."

This time her laughter was more genuine. "As you once told me, you're no consolation prize." Now the tears came in earnest. Nothing could make up for losing Daniel.

Rob made a move to comfort her, but she raised a hand to hold him off as they came to the ground floor. "I'm okay."

"No you're not."

"But I will be." She stepped out into the lobby and made a beeline for the double doors that led outside. Rob's long legs easily kept pace with her.

"Where are you going? I'll drop you off."

Felicity stopped in her tracks. Where was she going? She clutched her purse to her chest. A short list cropped up in her head. Her parents? Forget it. She'd had enough insults about her morals for one day. And Cheryl probably wouldn't be home for several more hours. That left Stuart, he had a second bedroom. But was he home?

"Do you have a cell?" She turned to Rob, hoping.

He handed her the phone, and she punched in Stuart's number as she continued across the marble floor towards the exit.

"Yo-yo." For once Stuart's stupid greeting was music to her ears.

"Thank God you're home!"

"Felicity? What's up, babes?"

"I need a place to stay tonight."

"What happened to your psycho boyfriend?" A hint of petulance came through in Stuart's voice.

"He is not my boyfriend. Listen, can you help me or not?" Rob held the door open for her and she headed for a taxi parked at the curb.

"Sure, sure, I always got room for you, baby, you know that." He reverted back to his smooth seductive tones. "Do you want me to pick you up?"

"No, but I'll need the cab fare."

"Okay, just get here. I'll take care of it."

Felicity rang off, handing the phone back to Rob. They'd reached the cab, but Rob grabbed the handle first.

"You don't have to take a taxi; I can drive you wherever you're going."

"I think it's better if you went back upstairs. I just want to be alone." Once she got into the cab, Felicity rolled down the window. "Thanks, Rob."

"Don't thank me yet." He glanced behind him. "You better get going."

Felicity gave the cabbie the nearest intersection to Stuart's apartment as the car drove off.

The last thing she saw was Daniel racing out of the building.

"What the hell was that all about?" Daniel made a gesture with both hands, tempted to wrap them around Rob's neck. "Why did you let her get in that cab? How could you let her get away?"

"I think you've got it backwards, pal." Rob folded his arms, supremely unruffled. "The real question is, why did *you* let her get away?"

All the anger drained out of Daniel. Why had he let her get away?

But he would go after her. After what his father had told him on the terrace, Daniel was willing to do whatever it took.

"Then after I confronted her with the truth, she actually claimed she loved you."

"Wh-what?" Daniel's heart had stilled at the words. Even now, just remembering them, strangled the breath from him.

"She claimed to be in love with you. A blatantly pathetic bid

for sympathy, of course."

Daniel had spun on his heel and left his old man, afraid of what he might have done if he'd stayed one second longer.

He'd gone through the master bedroom, but there was no sign of her. As he strode back to the main room, several guests said, yes, they'd seen her pass by and she'd been visibly upset. If it hadn't been so important for Daniel to find Felicity, he would've returned to the terrace, and God knows what he would have said to Michael Mackenzie.

When he found her in the elevator with Rob and she'd looked straight through him with those dead, red-rimmed eyes and said, *"I'm leaving"*—the words had ripped out what was left of Daniel's heart.

But he would find her. He'd get her back.

"Did she say anything? Tell you where she was going?"

"Nope." Rob shrugged. "But it sounded like she was going to stay with a friend for the night."

"A friend? Did she say who?"

"That's all I heard of the conversation, buddy. Sorry."

"What conversation?" Daniel ran both hands through his hair to keep them occupied, otherwise they'd be twisted in Rob's shirt, shaking some answers out of his unusually reticent buddy.

Rob waved his cell phone in Daniel's face.

Daniel snatched it out of his hands, studying the buttons.

"Hey, careful."

He elbowed Rob back and pushed redial.

The phone picked up almost immediately. "Hey, babes, I got the pillows all fluffed on your side of the bed, waiting for your pretty little head. Everything okay? Felicity?"

Daniel snarled and flung the phone away.

"Aw, no! No, no, no!" Rob went lumbering after the cell. "I said 'be careful', as in 'have care'."

Daniel ignored Rob, ignored his party, and started walking down the street, headed for nowhere, with his father's mocking voice in his head. *"What else was she going to say?"*

But why the hell did she have to say that?

Chapter Twenty-one

By the time Daniel got back home, only three guests were left. His mother buzzed around the catering staff, helping with the clean-up. Rob was sprawled on the sofa, throwing grapes up in the air and catching them in his mouth. The last one bounced off his chest when he saw Daniel step off the elevator.

"Hey, bud. You okay?"

He nodded, throwing his jacket over the back of a bar-stool at the kitchen island. He raked both hands through his hair. The walk had done him some good. Cleared his mind a bit.

For the last few months his life had gotten out of control with working at the law firm, putting hours in with Rob, fighting his father, and then there was Felicity...

But first things first. He worked his loosened tie completely undone with a couple of yanks, staring across the room at the solitary figure out on the terrace.

"Honey, we've been worried." His mother came up to him, her face heavy with concern. "Did you—did you speak to her?" she asked in a hushed voice.

"Speak to *her*?" Daniel's mouth twisted and he shook his head. *Her* was with *Him*. "No. She's currently reconciling with her ex, I doubt she'd welcome the interruption."

His mother frowned. "What nonsense. Felicity wouldn't go back to that schmuck." Then her expression softened and she placed a hand over his heart. "It's you she loves, Daniel."

"She told you that?"

"Well, no. But it's obvious."

"Then I must be the densest poor bastard for not seeing it all along." There was no irony in his voice. Hindsight had that effect. Now Felicity's every word, every touch, every glance came back to haunt him. That's what desperation could do to a man, make him blind to the *possibilities* right under his nose.

Daniel rubbed his jaw, the bristly rasp of new growth rough against his palm. Once again his gaze drifted outside. "Besides, I think Dad trumped us both on this one."

His mother shot a quizzical glance at her distant husband.

"She told him she loves me."

Her mouth made an "O" as her face lit up and she grabbed Daniel's arm. "Why, darling, that's wonderful!" Then her eyes narrowed. "Although how Michael managed to get that information— Oh, never mind, this is—"

He pressed his fingers against her lips.

"Felicity left me. She left because I all but told her to go earlier, because I thought we'd come to an impasse. And because I was full of shit."

"Oh, Daniel."

He swallowed and said the hardest part. "But most likely she wanted to leave, was going to, anyway." He gave his mom a little nudge on the chin. The kind she used to give him, along with a pep talk or two, when he was a kid.

"She might have cared for me. But it wasn't love. If it had been she'd never have left. She would have fought a little harder." Daniel sucked in a deep painful breath that couldn't even begin to fill the emptiness inside him.

"One thing we can both agree on is that Felicity is a fighter. She does whatever's necessary to get what she wants," he said bitterly. "She just didn't want me."

His mother's gaze filled with compassion, she covered his

fingers, pulling his hand from her jaw.

"Uh-uh," he said when she started to argue. "Give me a few minutes with Dad, okay?" He pressed a kiss to her forehead and she held onto his shirt.

"Daniel?"

"I'll behave. Promise. Now go have a last drink, put your feet up, and stop Rob from scratching and sniffing all the magazines."

It couldn't be that bad, he reasoned, if he could joke about the things Felicity had left behind. Just too goddamn bad he was one of those things.

As he passed Rob on the sofa, they did a high-five hand clasp. "Sorry about the phone, guy."

"No worries. I jacked-off on your laptop a few minutes ago."

Daniel burst out laughing and cuffed Rob in the head. This was his good bud, they didn't get any better. "I love you, man."

Rob held up both hands. "Whoa. The seminal emission was revenge, not a love letter."

"Not that there's anything wrong with that," they both said at the same time. Daniel moved on, his smile fading the closer he got to the terrace.

He stepped outside and paused to taste the summer air. It tasted different. It lacked something. He approached his father. Standing beside him, Daniel leaned on the cold metal railing and stared out to where the dark waters and fathomless sky merged into a seamless inky mass.

"To think you would choose a cheap—"

"Shut up, Dad." Daniel looked at the man whose name he shared, and felt something hot and ugly growing and coiling inside him. He'd wanted to make peace, not go down the same road again. He took a deep breath. "Just listen for a sec."

"I knew there was something about her. I told your mother. No class—"

"*Shut up,* Dad. Don't say another word. Not another *fucking* word*.*" Daniel had never felt closer to violence where his old man was concerned. He paced away a couple of steps and tried to get his emotions under control.

The view was magnificent. The neighboring condos and office towers checkerboards of light and below, the diamond trail of the Don Valley highway continually glittered with moving traffic. But Daniel's gaze was drawn to the absolute inky solitude of the lake.

"Tell me again, what she said," he asked softly.

"What? That she l—"

"No. Don't say it like that. Say it like she said it." He held his father's gaze. "Say it like you mean it."

There was still anger deep inside of him at his father's part in running off Felicity, and he wasn't sure he'd be able to forgive him for that. He wasn't sure he could forgive himself, either. Ever.

But he could make a new start. Take the chance to make things right. A chance he never had with Felicity. He wanted to gather the people he cared for closer now that he'd lost the woman he loved, all due to careless words, suspicion, intractability. All the things that marked the situation between him and his dad.

His eyes were burning now and he watched the muscles work in his father's throat. The old man's face slowly went slack. "She said, 'I love Daniel'. Then she said it again, more slowly 'I love yo-your son'."

Daniel hung his head, squeezing his eyes shut. He couldn't swallow the emotions that bubbled up inside him fast enough and the tears leaked out. But he savored the words, imagined them coming from her sweet mouth. He scrubbed the heels of his palms over his eyes.

"I'm sorry, son. I didn't think she was right for you." His father touched his shoulder. Eventually Daniel covered the hand with his own.

Daniel took a moment to collect his thoughts, and when he spoke, his voice was calm. "You know, Dad, you have to stop thinking *for* me." He looked at him. "You raised me to think for myself. To have goals, go for them and never quit. To be a man both you and Mom can be proud of. A man like you." He gripped his father's hand harder.

"You did your job. Now let me do mine. Let me be that man. I have my *own* goals I want to achieve. Rob and I more than doubled our business in the last year. And next year's forecast is looking even better."

An edge crept into his voice. "I may have quit the law firm, but I didn't quit on you. I gave it an honest try, and I always did my best. You *know* that."

He saw the admission was hard in coming, but finally his old man got it out. "I know."

"I tried to please you, Dad. Make you happy. Now you have to accept what makes *me* happy."

The silence stretched between them. He let his father think about what not accepting would mean, while he recalled his own fatal mistake, uttered earlier. *"I can't accept you."*

He ground his teeth together. Non-acceptance was the reason she'd left her parents' house, but he'd been too stupid, caught up in his own shock, to really hear what she'd been saying.

Now he was drawing his own line in the sand.

"This won't be easy."

Daniel released the breath he'd been holding. "No."

"You're asking me to give up a dream."

He shook his head slowly. "I'm asking you to share one."

His father stared into Daniel's eyes for an eternity. The old man's mouth tightened, he swallowed and blinked rapidly as he squeezed Daniel's shoulder. Then he left.

Daniel sighed, and looked back over the lake. Not the hug he was looking for, but no more angry words either.

It was a start.

ʚ

"Oh, I just love this story." Lise chuckled.

Felicity glared at her from the corner of her eye before refocusing, sort of, on the fairytale. Personally, she was rooting for the evil witch.

Lise seemed to be in extra high spirits today, and it was getting on Felicity's nerves. She couldn't help wondering if Lise's *perk!perk!*perkiness had to do with her son's engagement. But she wouldn't ask.

She'd made it plain a week ago that the topic of Daniel, and why she'd left the condo, was off limits. Surprisingly, neither Daniel nor his father had told Lise about her stripping. Felicity wasn't sure how she felt about their silence, but she'd take her small blessings where she could.

"You're drifting, sweetheart, and we're getting to the best part. The happily-ever-after," Lise chided. Perkily.

Like the type Daniel was going to have with VD?

She concentrated really, really hard on not letting one single tear fall, clearing her throat before she continued to read.

"The end," she said triumphantly many minutes later and sat back.

Lise, however, wasn't paying her any attention, instead she craned her neck to look over her shoulder. "Oh—what? You finished? Great!" She jumped up. "Looks like the ladies' room is free now. Start the next story, read silently until I get back."

As Lise slipped away, Felicity stared at the book without an ounce of enthusiasm. One thing for sure, these sessions had become sheer torture. She could barely concentrate past the constant ache that massaged her heart, and how many times did she bite back a question about Daniel, hungry for any morsel of information?

She could stop the tutoring with Lise— Felicity instantly rebelled at the thought. She may have given up her heart to Daniel, but she wouldn't give up her goals because of him.

The week with him, visiting the stores and showrooms, and his talks on how the business worked, had been a small taste of a dream. Now she was taking things a step further.

Just days ago, she'd lowered her pride—*hah!* Like she had a big honking supply of that left—to ask Cheryl's help with her new job search. Retail sales in a store was her best option to get a foot into the industry, Felicity had decided, but places like that wanted a resume.

On the other hand, asking for help meant confessing about her dyslexia. Briefly she'd thought about asking Lise, but she didn't want any more Mackenzie involvement in her life. So she'd practiced how to phrase her request, then braced herself for the pity, or shock, or reassessing look from Cheryl.

But Cheryl just paused in filing her nails, shrugged and said, "Okay." No big deal. She'd been more concerned that they'd lose touch once Felicity left The Uptown.

She was still a little stunned by her friend's reaction, or lack of one. But maybe that was it—Cheryl was a friend. The people from her past, who'd made cruel jokes at her expense, weren't.

A lump formed in her throat. It was good to have real friends like Cheryl. Even Stuart had pulled through Saturday night with plenty of sweet, hot, milky tea and a shoulder to cry on. Then he'd tucked her into the pullout futon bed. Without trying to climb in with her.

And Lise was her friend too. That's what made it doubly hard for Felicity, knowing she had to end the friendship if she had any hopes of holding on to her sanity. The constant reminder of Daniel—his eyes, his smile, his hair—in his mother, was too much for her to deal with.

She sniffled. Wiped at a tear. Then another and another. She had to pull herself together before Lise came back. She started using her sleeve, gulping back the waves of pain, but her chest felt cleaved wide open with the need for Daniel, his arms, his kisses. *His love.*

Oh God. She was losing her mind. She could actually smell him. The warm, citrusy scent teased at her and a chill raced down her spine.

"Baby, don't cry. Please." Calloused fingers joined hers, wiping at the wetness on her cheeks.

Felicity's heart stopped beating, then raced to catch up. "Daniel?" Was it really him hunched down beside her chair, his gaze so sad, and his smile so tender? There were dark circles under his eyes, and he seemed pale as if he'd been sick.

"Yeah, it's me." He thumbed away another tear.

"W-what are you doing here?"

"I came for you."

Not looking for you. *Came for you.*

"I miss you, Felicity," he said softly.

She dragged his hand away from her face, but held on to it, just as she was holding on to the glimmer of hope that spurted to life in her.

"What about Deirdra? She showed me the ring." Felicity's self-control crumpled and her voice dropped to a rasping whisper. "Why that ring, Daniel? That was mine."

She cringed in mortification. No, that wasn't her ring. Then her eyes widened at Daniel's string of vicious curses.

"Felicity, I swear on a stack of Bibles that I did not give Deirdra that ring." His fingers tightened on hers. "I went into my office to get away from the party. I couldn't stand the fact that there were all those people in my home when the one

Vanessa Jaye

person, the only person, I wanted to be with was leaving me."

He stared into her eyes. His were burning with an emotion that made her dizzy, and she hardly dared to breathe.

"I had the stupid idea that that ring could bring me, I don't know, good luck with you." He laughed as splotches of color flagged his cheeks. "Like a talisman."

"Deirdra saw me with the ring, and—" Daniel grabbed the nearest chair and sat, facing her. He took both her hands in his.

"And?" Felicity prodded.

"I told her how I felt about you. Then we had a talk we should have had years ago. I told her I didn't love her." He looked down at their clasped hands, twining her fingers around his. "She was hurt. So when she asked to be left alone, I didn't think twice about leaving the ring with her." Daniel looked up again. "It meant nothing to me at that point if I couldn't give it to you."

He pressed a dozen tiny kisses to the back of her hands. "I know I messed up, and you still have feelings for Stuart."

"No, no, no." She shook her head. "Stuart's just a friend."

"Then why did you go to him?"

"Because he *is* my friend. He makes a play for me like he scratches an itch." She laughed softly. "He can't help himself. That's why we never lasted. He couldn't stop helping himself to other women, too," she ended on a wry note.

"He's an ass. I would never do that to you. Never cheat. Never lie." Daniel reached out and stroked the hair away from her face. "Can I have a second chance, Felicity?"

Her throat seized with emotion. Her tongue swollen with confessions of a love so big and so deep and so strong, she knew the words would come out pure gibberish. Overwhelmed, Felicity dropped her gaze, ready to say the only three words that were adequate, and froze. Sunlight shone bright on the pages of the book that still lay open on the table, and beyond it a

266

cardboard placard, clearly printed with: *Reserved for Learning Partnership*, stood tented.

"Felicity?"

She reached for the book to close it. Then she thought of how secrets had almost ruined things for them before, and she pulled the book of fairytales towards her.

"Let me read you something," she said huskily. At Daniel's expression, she added, "It's important."

Felicity cleared her throat and started to read. Slowly at first, just by sight. But she began to stumble and then to backtrack. And the loud thudding of her heart almost drowned out her dwindling voice as she fell into the old habit of guessing words from the sentence's context. Then she tried to use her finger as a guide, but her damn hand was trembling so damn bad, and her vision started blurring, and—

"Stop." Daniel laid his hand over hers. His voice choked. "Why didn't you tell me?"

"I-I couldn't bear for anyone to know. People don't understand dyslexia. When you get called 'stupid' and 'retard' enough times, you start believing it."

She shrugged, still not meeting his eyes. "Dropping out of high-school seemed like a smart thing to do. But things just got worse. I couldn't get a decent job, and ended up working at places like—"

"The Uptown."

Felicity nodded, and finally looked at him when he forced her chin up. The lines of his face had softened.

"Don't feel sorry for me."

"I don't. I think you're one of the bravest women I know," he smiled, "besides my mother."

That made her giggle.

His smile slowly died. "About The Uptown...."

"I did what I had to do, Daniel. I can't apologize for that.

But I've been looking for another job in the decorating field."

He let out a huge sigh. "I am so glad you said that. I don't want you stripping."

Felicity raised an eyebrow. "Oh really? I haven't even said I'd get back with you, and already you're trying to lay down the law."

Daniel froze. "You don't want to come back?"

She stared at him. There wasn't an eyelash or laugh-line on him that she didn't love. His passion, his stubbornness, his thoughtfulness, his smarts, his humor, she could be here all day listing it all. "I do."

A huge grin split his face, then he wrapped his hand around her nape and pulled her to him, ravishing her mouth until somehow she was on his lap and ravishing him back.

"Excuse me!" A frigid voice doused the heat of their passion. "You can't do that in here!"

Felicity broke away from Daniel and stared at the tight-faced librarian bemusedly. "Sorry." Not really.

But it *was* kind of embarrassing. She slid back to her seat. Daniel slid the open book over his lap. The librarian's lips disappeared into a thin white line of disapproval.

They started giggling as soon as she turned her back.

"Well, I'm glad to see you kiddies behaving yourselves." Lise returned. Her smile was nothing if not gloating.

"You told him!" The pieces suddenly fell into place.

"I did not!" Lise looked offended. "You asked me not to say anything."

Felicity turned to Daniel.

"She didn't say a word."

"Then how did you know to find me here?"

"I followed her," he said, without a hint of shame. "I remembered you two had some sort of book club." He glanced at the fairytale and reached for her hand. "So this morning when she mentioned she was going to drop by the library today, I decided to tail her."

"And a very poor job you did of it, too. I almost lost you twice."

They both stared at Lise, shocked.

Her eyes sparkled with enjoyment. "Honestly, I was tempted to throw a trail of breadcrumbs out the window. I just couldn't stand to see the two of you moping around. It was severely depressing."

Lise bent down and kissed them both on the cheek in turn, then she wrapped them in her embrace. "Be happy, my darlings," she whispered fiercely.

"We will," Felicity said.

"I am," she heard Daniel reply.

Lise straightened up. "Well, I expect you both over to dinner soon. We'll make plans later, call me. Now I—"

"—really must run. I've got so much to do," Daniel and Felicity said in unison and started laughing.

Lise wagged her finger at them, blew kisses in their direction and she was off.

They watched her go.

"Your mother is scary."

"Absolutely." He reached over and pulled her back onto his lap. "But enough about my mother. Let's talk about us. And how much I missed you." He kissed the tip of her nose. "And how much I need you," he added hoarsely.

Felicity felt her heart tip. *Just so.* She traced his lips. Then tenderly sealed her touch with soft kisses.

"That's it. I'm afraid I'm going to have to ask you two to leave." It was the boot-faced librarian.

They left, giggling like a couple of teenagers, but not saying much else. Each of them aware of how fragile this thing between them was. When they got into his truck, though, Felicity had to ask, "Where're we going?"

"Home. The condo." He reached over and twined his fingers in hers. "I want to make love to you."

She felt awkward suddenly. "Are you sure?" Felicity turned her face away to look out the window. "You said some pretty ugly things before, Daniel."

"And I'm sorry. For every stupid, hurtful thing I said." His voice was rough and dark and hoarse. "I was crazy with jealousy. And pissed-off, and hurt that you were keeping secrets. Not that that excuses me, but I thought we were growing closer, then to find out...and in that way." He shook his head.

She turned back to him and he saw the question in her eyes. "I was angry and talking out my ass. I know I hurt you and I'm more sorry than you'll ever know for that. But that's not how I think of you, Felicity. And I will never say anything like that to you again, ever. Promise."

She remained silent and he swallowed. He was scared of losing her again, but they had to do this thing right.

"We have to let this go. We both have to get past this thing with your stripping, or we haven't got a chance of making it."

The path to her love lay in her trust. He would earn that trust and he'd give it back, unquestioned from now on.

Felicity nodded, her fingers tightening around his. That's all he needed. Another chance.

They made the condo in record time and rode up in the elevator, only holding hands and avoiding eye contact. The tension between them was palpable.

Once they were in the foyer, Daniel let go of her. Felicity bit her lip, practically vibrating with need. By the intensity in his gaze she thought he'd jump on her right away, but he surprised her instead with gentleness. And his words were unexpected, also.

"You know, for the longest while, I wanted to be Stuart. I wanted to be the guy you could never leave." He trailed fingertips lightly along her neck, then fanned his hands out to bury them in the heavy curtain of her hair.

"You don't want to be Stuart," she whispered, reaching up to caress his face.

Delicate fingers traced his mouth and he parted his lips in a kiss, his tongue remembering the salty taste of her skin. The heady taste of her. He wanted to taste her again, make love, but on a new level, sharing totally this time—mind, body and soul.

"I only wish..." He stopped, the words jumbled on his tongue, each declaration fighting to be the first.

"You only wish what?" she prodded.

He made a frustrated sound and dug his hands further into her hair, cradling her head. "God help me. I love you, Felicity."

"Oh." She was robbed of speech; all she could do was act. Felicity poured every ounce of the wild emotions brimming inside her into a kiss, telling Daniel her own truth.

With a guttural sound he ended it. "I need you now."

Her hand firmly clasped in his, Felicity practically had to skip to keep up with him as he strode towards the bedroom. But she would have skipped anyways with happiness.

When they got to his room, Daniel stopped, pulling her back into his arms, kissing her like there would be no more kisses after these, and he was saving up for forever.

She was on tippy-toes and still his hand on her ass pressed her higher and closer. Felicity wrapped one leg around his hip and he moved his hand to support her weight. Then he urged her other leg up, until her limbs were scissored around his waist and the thick hot length of his arousal pressed against her dampness. Moans mingled with sighs. Gyration met thrust, then Felicity was falling back onto the bed with the solid satisfying mass of Daniel covering her.

The soft landing also softened the edge of their passion.

This was home, the two of them together in this bed. Slowly they undressed each other, kissing, tasting, rediscovering.

"Closer," Daniel whispered as he moved against her warmth. His fingers delved into her, stroking in and out. Then spreading her wider, he softly fingered the hidden swollen nub of flesh. Felicity's moans sent an answering shiver of satisfaction winding down his spine. This could be enough, bringing her pleasure, watching the mix of emotions race across her face.

Felicity buried her hands in Daniel's thick hair, urging him on. She wanted more and he complied, suckling, nipping, tasting. Each hot wet kiss entering her bloodstream like molten honey. Every other thought or feeling not tied to this moment, squeezed out of existence.

Heart pounding, gasping for air, she was going to explode, or expire or...*Oh my God.*

He entered her.

Slow and deep.

Daniel groaned, his face twisted with sweet gratification. Then he drew out just as slowly until only the swollen head of his cock was left to pulse at her entrance before he thrust back into her, again and again with pounding measured strokes.

"You have been and will always be my fantasy," he whispered with hoarse intensity, his gaze holding hers. "Always."

This felt so right. It *was* so right. Her happiness was complete.

"What are you smiling about?"

"This." Felicity stretched beneath him, her arms raised to grasp the headboard behind her. Rocking her hips, she tensed her muscles and was rewarded with the flash of deep pleasure that crossed his face. Pure womanly satisfaction rippled through her and she chuckled.

Daniel loosened her grip, intertwining his fingers with hers as he pressed her hands into the pillow on either side of her head. Then he changed his rhythm, moving in short shallow strokes, which caused Felicity to wrap her legs around him, using her heels to press down and urge him deeper. He resisted, delivering a kiss on her mouth that he quickly pulled back from when she tried to nip at him.

"You're not playing fair."

It was Daniel's turn to laugh. "Why should I play fair, when playing dirty is so much better?"

Felicity stared up at him, sobered. "I like playing with you," she said softly. He stopped moving.

"I like playing with you too." The admission came out dark and raspy.

He delivered a power thrust, slamming her into the bedding. The force of him against her, the rotation of his groin against her clit, pushed her higher into an ever tightening coil of pleasure.

Then Daniel stopped again, buried deep inside her. Sweat dripped from him, trailing along Felicity's neck to mingle with her own sweat. His face showed his strain in holding back.

"I want this, you...forever. Not just this moment, but mornings waking up with you in my arms, every morning. I want forever. *Marry me.*"

Before she could answer, Daniel's mouth took hers in a bruising kiss as his hands swept down to lift her legs over his arms. He angled his hips, almost pulling out entirely, then swiftly drove his cock back into her.

"Marry me, Felicity." His guttural command accompanied another hard stroke that sent her over the edge.

"Yes!" She spiraled into a vortex of ecstasy. And Daniel was right there with her.

Afterwards, Daniel rose from the bed. He didn't say a word as he took her hand and led her into the bathroom. They went into the shower, where he soaped her up, placing feather light kisses on her face and neck. She wanted to speak but he shushed her with one finger pressed against her mouth.

When they were done he drew her from the stall and Felicity found herself enveloped by a plush towel as Daniel focused on rubbing her dry. He grabbed a bottle of body lotion and led her back to the bedroom.

"Sit."

"Daniel?"

He shook his head, but his eyes didn't meet hers, instead he kneeled beside the bed and proceeded to apply lotion onto her skin, his touch lingering here and there until his gaze grew heated and he dipped his head to capture an erect nipple into his hot mouth and suckled deeply. It was brief, and sweet. Yet rising desire couldn't loosen the delicate tentacles of fear that were tightening around her heart.

He tore his mouth from her body with a muttered curse. "I can't think straight with you looking like this." He rose to his feet and strode over to the chair where his robe was carelessly thrown. Daniel handed it to her, then took the damp discarded towel and wrapped it around his hips.

"Get dressed; let's go into the kitchen, we need to talk."

We need to talk. She watched his back disappear through the door and slowly got to her feet. What a fool she was. It was said in the heat of passion. Of course he didn't mean it. It was too soon.

Felicity found him sitting at the kitchen island, two glasses of wine poured out. When she went to take the stool next to his, Daniel pulled her to him, his hard thighs bracing her hips and he ravished her mouth.

Finally he eased back, his eyes glittering with wild fire. He took a deep breath then another. "Okay, I just want there to be no doubts or confusion about what just happened—in either of our minds."

Her stomach plummeted. So she was right.

"While we were making love, when I looked into your face, into your eyes," he traced a finger down the bridge of her nose, then swept it across her jaw up to her temple, "I couldn't help myself, the words just burst out."

Daniel took her hands and cradled them in the warmth of his palm. There was a tightness around his mouth when he spoke again, his voice so low that Felicity had to lean forward to catch his words.

"I don't want you to feel obligated to keeping what you said in the heat of passion." He looked up then.

Felicity blinked. There was real fear in his eyes. There was also unmistakable tenderness.

"But if you haven't changed your mind, I won't pressure you any further; we can take this nice and slow. You can have as long an engagement as you'd like."

"Would twenty-four hours be long enough?"

Daniel started, then wrapped his arms around her as they both started laughing.

"Well I think my mother would have something to say about that. She has this thing about throwing big parties."

"Your mother?" Felicity's spirits sank just a bit. "Daniel, your father—"

"Is not the man you're going to marry. I wasted a lot of years trying to please that man, and fulfill *his* dreams. Now I please myself. And my dream is you."

Felicity found her smile.

"I take it that was a resounding yes?"

"You can take it anyway you like it, baby. I'm yours."

He kissed her, she kissed him back, then things got blurry.

"Say it," Daniel demanded, his lips trailing along her jaw.

"Say what?" Felicity could barely get the words out, much less think about forming a cohesive sentence.

He grasped her shoulders, tearing their bodies apart. "Say

it." The expression in his eyes was one she recognized from looking in the mirror every day since she realized that she loved him.

A slow sweet smile curving her mouth, Felicity looked him dead in the eye, said the words:

"I love you, Daniel Mackenzie."

He threaded his fingers through her hair. "Say it again."

"I love you."

"Again." This plea was softer still.

"I love you, I love you, I love you."

Daniel crushed her to him, rubbing his face into her hair. "Every day. I need you to say it every day for the rest of my life," he whispered fiercely.

"I'll say it as much as you need me to." Felicity wrapped her arms around him and squeezed. "And I can assure you that statement was not influenced in the least bit by mind-melting passion," she teased, her voice partially muffled in his chest.

Daniel eased back, a grin on his face. "Mind-melting passion?"

"Yes, mind-melting passion—shall I refresh your memory?"

And she did.

The *freakin'* End

About the Author

To learn more about Vanessa Jaye, please visit http://vanessajaye.blogspot.com. Send an email to vanessajaye@hotmail.com.

Together they find a special love—
can it survive the threat stalking her?

Giving Chase
© 2006 Lauren Dane

Some small towns grow really good-looking men! This is the case with the four Chase brothers. The home grown hotties are on the wishlist of every single woman in town and Maggie Wright is no exception.

Maggie has finally had it with the men she's been dating but a spilled plate of chili cheese fries drops Shane Chase right into her lap. The sheriff is hot stuff but was burned by a former fiancée and is quite happy to play the field.

After Shane's skittishness sends him out the door, Maggie realizes that Kyle Chase has had his eye on her from the start. Now that Shane has messed up, Kyle has no intention of letting anything stop him from wooing her right into his bed.

Despite Maggie's happiness and growing love with Kyle, a dark shadow threatens everything—she's got a stalker and he's not happy at all. In the end, Maggie will need her wits, strength and the love of her man to get her out alive.

Available now in ebook and print from Samhain Publishing.

A romantic game of chicken—
and they're both too stubborn to flinch.

Dare to Love
© 2008 Jaci Burton

Lucy Fairchild, lawyer and heiress to the Fairchild fortune, has just had the worst day of her life. Her father has found the perfect man for her to marry. Yes, she's thirty and single, but that doesn't give her father the right to run her life. She'll choose her own husband—someday.

Jake Dalton is struggling to make his fledgling construction company a success. Ever mindful of his father's derogatory comments that he'd never amount to anything, he's spent his entire life trying to prove he's not a failure.

From their first meeting on a construction site, verbal sparks fly. Their argument escalates into a dare for a date—and the game is on. Lucy thinks Jake is the perfect fake boyfriend to parade around in the hopes of getting her father off her back. Jake is amused by the chance to annoy both Lucy and her dad—he doesn't intend to take the dating thing seriously.

But the heart is a fickle thing, and not above playing dirty. In their quest to prove something—to each other, or maybe to themselves—they find themselves building a case...for love.

And suddenly all the rules have changed.

Available now in ebook and print from Samhain Publishing.

GREAT cheap fun

Discover eBooks!

THE FASTEST WAY TO GET THE HOTTEST NAMES

Get your favorite authors on your favorite reader, long before they're out in print! Ebooks from Samhain go wherever you go, and work with whatever you carry—Palm, PDF, Mobi, and more.

Printed in the United States
149757LV00011B/1/P